DEMOCRACY
SOCIETY

John Christmas

DEMOCRACY SOCIETY

AUTHOR'S NOTE

Layout provided by **Everything Indie**
http://www.everything-indie.com

[T]he once happy and peaceful plains of America are either to be drenched with blood or inhabited by slaves. Sad alternative! But can a virtuous man hesitate in his choice?—George Washington

CONTENTS

PROLOGUE 1
Friday, December 19, 1788 1
(1) Mid afternoon at Mount Vernon, Virginia 1

Thursday, January 27, 1789 10
(2) Mid afternoon at Mount Vernon 10

DEMOCRACY SOCIETY 13
Friday, October 31, 2014 13
(3) Morning in Greenwich, Connecticut 13
(4) A moment later at Bradley Air National Guard Base, Connecticut 25
(5) A moment later in Greenwich 37
(6) Evening in Hyde Park, Chicago, Illinois 48
(7) Evening flying over San Francisco Bay 65

Saturday, November 1, 2014 71
(8) Morning at the Sea Hotel and Spa, Arabia 71
(9) Afternoon at the Red Sea coast by the Sea Hotel and Spa 86
(10) Morning in Hyde Park, New York 98
(11) Daytime flying from White Plains Airport to Dulles Airport 106
(12) Daytime driving to Midway Airport, Chicago 113
(13) Morning at Yosemite National Park, California 120
(14) Evening at the Sea Hotel and Spa 126

Sunday, November 2, 2014 135
(15) Daytime flying over the Pacific Ocean 135
(16) Late afternoon at an industrial port in Korea 141
(17) Afternoon at Mount Elbrus, Russia 145
(18) Late morning at Washington National Cathedral, Washington, D.C. 157
(19) Daytime at Everglades National Park, Florida 164
(20) Evening at Mount Elbrus, reception 172
(21) Evening at Mount Elbrus, tower 180

Monday, November 3, 2014 191
(22) Before dawn on the Red Sea, between Eritrea and Arabia 191
(23) Evening at Mount Vernon—The Presidential Election Debate 202

Tuesday, November 4, 2014: Election Day 218
(24) Before dawn on the Red Sea 218
(25) After dawn on the Red Sea 234
(26) Evening at Mount Vernon 238

EPILOGUE 242
Wednesday, November 19, 2014 242
(27) Afternoon at Mount Vernon 242

About the Author 249
Thanks for Reading *Democracy Society* Drafts 251

PROLOGUE

Friday, December 19, 1788
(1) Mid afternoon at Mount Vernon, Virginia

James Madison was exhausted as he navigated the final turn on his eight-mile horse ride from Alexandria to Mount Vernon. The four-beat gait of the Spanish Mustang below him had done little to provide comfort on this cold and tense day.

Madison's heavy wool coat, the same black color as the mare, protected his slight body from the wind as he rode along the snow-covered path. The thirty-seven-year-old statesman let go of the reins with one gloved hand to adjust his tri-cornered hat. His blue eyes, a contrast to the all-black clothing, peered forward. The mansion house came into view at the far end of a snowy field bordered by a careful arrangement of trees.

The serpentine path wound for half a mile from the gate toward the mansion. The tulip poplars, white ash, and elm trees were leafless and icy.

Madison's journey through the cold and snow had been arduous, but he felt confident that his work today would be met with reward—a better future for the republic.

Inside his great coat, he could feel the scroll tube fastened across his chest. It held the document drafted by the Constitutional Convention on September 11, 1787, the only day which Madison knew he must omit from his notes on the convention when he someday made the notes available to the public.

All of the participants in the Constitutional Convention had been in agreement with Madison that the newly created republic would quickly revert back to tyranny unless democracy was limited. That was why they composed and approved the document.

Madison looked up to see the inspirational dove-of-peace weather vane atop the cupola on the white mansion house and smiled even as a chilly wind blew against his face. He knew that his friend, the General, was a proponent of peace.

For example, the General's reaction to Shays' Rebellion had been wise and appropriate.

A mob of levelers in Massachusetts threatened to reverse the liberty that had been earned in the Revolutionary War and bring the nation right back to tyranny by redistributing private property.

Madison had been frightened when he learned how Shays convinced his followers that occupying property owned by others and printing paper money to make themselves rich was an exercise in natural rights and equality. The common folks were led to believe that they were not thieves for repudiating debts to merchants, but rather merchants were thieves for insisting on payment!

How could anyone expect that commerce could function in a society without property rights protection? How could commerce function in a society where transactions were involuntary exercises of force rather than voluntary exercises of contract?

Madison recalled that the General had been presented with two options. He could reward the violent thieves by giving in to their demands. The result would have been another decade of poverty and violence.

Or, he could punish the thieves by ordering the troops to open fire on them with cannons. He choose this second option and peace was promptly restored. Prosperity soon followed since the people of Massachusetts started working to provide goods and services to each other instead of working to rob each other.

Madison neared the mansion house and pulled back on the reins. The mare came to a halt. He dismounted and was immediately approached by a footman who helped to control the horse. The young black man in the red uniform called out toward the mansion house as he led the horse toward the stable. Nobody else was outdoors on this cold day.

Madison removed his hat and shook out his long queue of braided black hair. He stood in his black top boots on the frozen pathway gazing across the ellipse at the familiar mansion house. At the time of his last visit, in July, the ellipse was green and grassy. Now in December, it was blanketed with snow.

As he stepped carefully on the ice to the mansion house doorway, a beautifully plumed wild turkey burst from the willow trees and ran right in front of him, across the snowy ellipse.

The heavy wooden door swung open. Madison removed his gloves as he climbed the steps to the threshold.

A tall, commanding man stood in the doorway. He had gray hair, also tied in a queue, and an unmistakable hawk-like profile. Madison noticed that the General looked stately and proper even in his working clothes: a plain blue coat, white cashmere waistcoat, and black breeches.

"Welcome to Mount Vernon, Jemmy!" said General George Washington. "It is nice to have you here in time for Christmas celebrations and I hope you will stay for the entire holiday. You must be chilled from your journey. I am in the same condition, having ridden twenty miles this morning to inspect the farms." He broke into a grin. "And I am twenty years your senior!"

Madison, standing only five-feet-five-inches tall, stepped forward and shook hands with the General.

Washington, who stood a towering six-feet-three-inches,

gave a firm handshake in his characteristic manner of confidence and leadership. "Please tell me that the next step in the critically important follow-up work has been completed."

Madison opened his black wool coat, displaying the scroll tube strapped across his torso.

"Let's go into the parlor and warm up while we prosecute our follow-up work to protect the democratic republic," said Washington as he guided Madison into the house.

*

James Madison and George Washington sat on wooden-backed chairs with cushioned seats near a cozy fireplace. Their feet, clad in thick wool stockings, warmed up by the fire. The men were not wearing coats anymore, but Madison still had the scroll tube strapped across his body.

Washington called out, "Linda! Please bring a bottle of madeira to the parlor!"

Madison looked around the room. The Prussian-blue walls were the same as he remembered, except they were decorated with a trim of fresh green pine boughs for the upcoming holiday.

An attractive black woman dressed in a fetching purple frock stepped into the room carrying a silver tray with a crystal decanter of madeira wine and two glasses.

Madison stood briefly and greeted the familiar house servant, "Hello Linda, it is a pleasure to see you."

Linda's eyes sparkled as she bowed slightly. "Good day, Mr. Madison. It's a pleasure to see you back at Mount Vernon. The General mentioned several times that you'd visit us on your return home to Virginia from New York. I hope your time serving in the Congress of the Confederation was productive. The whole household is happy to have you as our guest once again."

Linda set the tray on the mahogany table between the two men and poured generous amounts of the heavy Portuguese wine into the glasses. She exited the room empty handed and closed the door.

After watching her depart, Washington turned to Madison. "Linda is a wonderful woman and extremely intelligent. She taught herself to read and has finished all of the English-language books in my library. Linda and I spend many evenings together talking about government since Martha is usually ill with colic attacks and bilious fevers."

Madison, always a good listener, let the General continue.

"I grew up being bombarded with prejudiced opinions from nearly everyone I met," said Washington as he unbuttoned his waistcoat. "Getting to know Linda has been a mind-opening experience for me. I am working on documentation to grant freedom to the slaves at Mount Vernon, with the hope that they and their descendants will succeed in gaining education, rewarding employment, and happy family life in America in the future."

"Yes," agreed Madison as he opened the scroll tube, "I hope our republic lasts for a long time, providing future generations of Americans with the freedom to pursue happiness. And with that goal in mind, let me show you the document you have been so eagerly waiting for."

Madison removed a parchment from the scroll tube. "I present the signed Charter of the Democracy Society." He unrolled the parchment and handed it to Washington.

Washington put on his reading glasses before taking the parchment. "You will permit me to put on my spectacles, for I have grown almost blind in the service of my country."

"As you remember," explained Madison, "the Charter was drafted on September 11, 1787 at the Constitutional Convention and signed by all conventioneers. Now, it also has the signatures of all of the Congress of the Confederation delegates present at the final quorum of that body on

October 10, 1788. Support was unanimous and enthusiastic. Of course all delegates were well educated in matters of government and were aware, based on the writings of scholars from Ancient Greece and Rome, that republican government faced great danger of reversion to tyrannical government. Nobody desired this result.

"There were no witnesses to the Charter except for the signers and no written record exists except for the Charter itself.

"The Charter is law. The only secret law of the new republic. In the future, nobody will know about the Charter except for the director and thirteen hereditary members, one from each original state. Future presidents and congressmen will not know about the Charter and membership of the Democracy Society. The Democracy Society members have the authority to exert covert interference in government operations, including presidential elections, to prevent erosion of property rights."

A smile grew across Washington's face as he read the Charter. "This is perfect, Jemmy. It is clearly in the best long-term interest of all of the American people, rich and poor. Protection of property rights is and will always be the core function of government and the Democracy Society will ensure continued protection thus ensuring survival of the government."

Madison agreed. "Government exists to protect property and a government that fails to protect property will collapse. This reality was at the core of the Declaration of Independence, as written by Thomas Jefferson who based it upon the observations of John Locke."

"The protection of property rights must be reinforced again and again," said Washington. "It is in the Bible. Thou shalt not steal. It is the core of English Common Law, a system of law that evolved from common sense. It is the essence of the Golden Rule. Do unto others as you would have them do unto you.

"We must be certain the republican government protects property rights even if the rabble that comprises the majority of Americans objects. We must protect property in a Bill of Rights. And, we must have the Democracy Society as a back up. Otherwise the republic will collapse into tyranny and our experiment with democratic government, which has already won us the ridicule of European monarchists, will only serve to prove that they were right and we were wrong."

"Remember, sir, the Charter names you as the original director. However, it does not name the thirteen members, leaving the original membership to your discretion. Have you thought through how you will do this?"

Washington rose from his seat and stepped toward the wall. "As you know, Jemmy, I am the President General of the Society of the Cincinnati."

Washington reached up and unhooked a frame hanging on the wall over the fireplace.

"I did not create that society, and I did not ask to run it. In fact, I would have an easier life if that hereditary society was never formed since it is so controversial in the eyes of hard-line anti-monarchists. Here is the badge for that office." Washington handed the frame to Madison.

Madison studied the badge in the frame. The famous, some would say infamous, gold and silver badge was the likeness of a bald eagle studded with numerous diamonds, emeralds, and rubies.

"The badge was designed by Pierre L'Enfant," said Washington. "He was the Captain of Engineers in my staff during the War of Independence."

Madison knew about this diamond eagle badge, and the similar golden eagle badges without diamonds worn by the former officers of the Continental Army who were now members of the Society of the Cincinnati.

Washington gently took the frame from Madison, flipped

it upside down, and handed it back.

"What is this?" asked a surprised Madison.

"L'Enfant designed the badges in France in 1783," explained Washington, "when Benjamin Franklin was our ambassador there. Franklin told L'Enfant that the eagle was not the best symbol for the new American republic.

"Franklin argued that the eagle has poor moral character. The eagle does not fish for himself but rather sits and watches while the other birds fish. Then, the eagle swoops down and redistributes the fish to himself. The eagle is the leveler of the bird community."

Madison was staring at thirteen badges mounted in the back of the frame, each the profile of a different bird with a diamond eye.

Madison held the frame up, displaying the thirteen golden profiles of striking wild turkeys. "I remember now. Franklin argued that turkeys were more respectable than eagles."

"The Democracy Society will be a secret inner circle of the Society of the Cincinnati," said Washington. "I will select the most enlightened member from each state. Those thirteen original members will be invited to the headquarters of the Democracy Society, here at Mount Vernon, to receive badges.

"The members will have a life-long, self-interested duty to protect their democratic republic by covertly defending against demagogic levelers. And, they will have a duty to raise their sons to be educated in regards to history, government, and commerce and also trained in combat. Therefore, when the sons eventually become members, they will be prepared to assume their duty.

"I promise you a confidential letter in January naming the original membership. Since I am changing my testament at this time, I am considering leaving Mount Vernon to the Democracy Society. Therefore the Democracy Society will be publicly known only as a property management entity. The powers within the Charter and the identities of the hereditary

8

members will be secret. Funding for the Democracy Society will be the income from the Mount Vernon property. I will also explain a personal issue regarding Linda that will tie into this.

"My worst nightmare is a demagogue getting elected to the presidency. Imagine a charismatic candidate promising a constituency of fools that they can have anything they want for free, and winning majority support. Hopefully the Democracy Society will be able to prevent America from having such a disastrous future."

Madison peered directly into the General's clear blue eyes in an uncharacteristically bold manner. "Yes, I also fear the future emergence of a demagogic leveler. The election of such a man would cause a violent end to the republic. The demagogue could be a well-intentioned leveler who does not understand that commerce will cease and people will suffer if property rights protection ceases. Or, the demagogue could know that leveling will cause suffering and he could pursue that course anyway because of a perverse goal. If any such man gets elected, the republic will revert to tyranny. And, the ironic result could be a new leader worse than the British monarch. The new leader would be selected through struggle to be the most cruel and dishonest person in society, whereas a hereditary monarch would not necessarily have those qualities. I also hope the Democracy Society will be able to protect us."

Madison held up his glass of madeira wine and Washington did likewise.

"To the Democracy Society!" toasted Madison. "Long live the republic!"

"To justice, rights, equality, and liberty!" toasted Washington. "Long live the republic!"

Clink! Both men enjoyed hearty sips.

Thursday, January 27, 1789
(2) Mid afternoon at Mount Vernon

George Washington reviewed his long list of tabulations for the final time. He had accomplished quite a bit of paperwork on this winter day when he chose to remain in his study for the entire morning and into the afternoon.

His final plan for 1789 included planting certain acreages of wheat, peas, corn, potatoes, carrots, turnips, pumpkins, and cabbage. He based his decisions on financial *pro formas* using best guesses of future costs of inputs and market prices of outputs. Noticing a recent increase in the market value for corn, indicating increased demand for corn, he decided to increase corn cultivation. Noticing a recent decrease in the market value for wheat, indicating decreased demand for wheat, he decided to decrease wheat cultivation. This strategy would yield two results: he would maximize his profits and consumers would get what they demanded.

Washington's plans also considered cash flows for future years. He no longer planted tobacco, having seen too much evidence of soil depletion caused by that demanding crop. And, he planted clover in every field on a rotating basis as a replenishment measure even though the clover itself did not have a market value.

He gathered the papers into a leather binder, keeping only one item out. It was a clipping from the *Virginia Journal and Alexandria Advertiser* about the benefits of clover. He had found the article informative and thought that his friend James Madison would also benefit from reading it. Washington's Mount Vernon in eastern Virginia and

Madison's Montpelier in western Virginia had different characteristics in terms of climate and distance to market. The comparative advantages of each property led to variances in optimal strategy. But anyway, Washington knew that Madison wanted to learn about soil replenishment options.

Washington folded the clover article and slipped it into an envelope.

Next, he placed a letter with information about the directorship and original membership of the Democracy Society into the envelope. This information was highly confidential, of national and personal importance, and therefore he did not keep a transcript of this letter as he customarily did with other letters. He expected that Madison would not keep a record of this letter either, and would return it when traveling back through Mount Vernon to New York in February.

Washington addressed the envelope to Montpelier and then replaced his goose quill in the holder next to the ink well. He affixed a wax seal to the envelope. A horseman would bring the letter to the post office in Fredericksburg that very afternoon.

Washington removed his spectacles, placing them on a wooden stand on the desk. He rose from the desk chair.

He approached the handsome, pine-paneled wall where the fireplace was located and warmed his hands.

He reflected on his dual role as a businessman and a civil servant with a function of preserving the republic so that he and others could operate their businesses in tranquility. Would his work to protect the republic ever end? Would he ever be able to enjoy the domestic ease that he so craved?

It seemed unlikely that his responsibilities as a civil servant would end anytime soon. Knowledgeable men had told him that the Electoral College would probably vote unanimously to make him the first President of the United States under the Constitution, even though he was not campaigning.

As always, he would look at the available options and make decisions in accordance with reason.

He returned to the desk chair, put the spectacles back on, and opened his fascinating new book *The Wealth of Nations* by Adam Smith.

Washington wanted to re-read a section that he had been discussing with Linda. The section eloquently explained a concept that was brilliant in its simplicity and truth: the baker bakes bread for his own self-interest and not because of altruistic love of community.

DEMOCRACY SOCIETY

Friday, October 31, 2014
(3) Morning in Greenwich, Connecticut

As the wind blew on this chilly but sunny October morning, Roberto Rojo ran his fingers through his rippling dark hair and looked down from the rooftop vantage point at thousands of screaming supporters.

The handsome 48-year-old had a look of satisfaction and confidence. His widely set, oaken-brown eyes framed by dignified crow's feet projected an image of strength and protection.

His toned musculature was clearly accented by his well-tailored charcoal-gray suit, while his tanned face stood out against the crisp white shirt and American-flag tie. He reached a powerful arm forward and adjusted the microphone upward since he was much taller than the man who had arranged the podium.

Rojo was pleased with the venue here in Greenwich, Connecticut. He stood atop the Easy Cheap discount superstore on the western shore of Cos Cob Harbor. His podium and the ten-meter-tall video monitors and speaker stacks on either side looked over a parking lot crammed with cheering fans.

He yelled into the microphone, "Justice! Rights! Equality! Liberty!"

The crowd roared with approval. Rojo studied the colorful, but not properly fitted, new clothing of the men, women, and children below him. The garments were no doubt liberated from the closets of Greenwich homes as the crowd made their way from New York State to Cos Cob Harbor.

As the television camera zoomed in on Rojo's face, he broke into a broad smile. His perfect teeth gleamed pure white as the smile engaged the strong dimples in his cheeks and accentuated his handsome cleft chin. The roar of the crowd grew.

Rojo could have been a movie star. But as it turned out, he had a different job. He was the 45th President of the United States, and he was campaigning to win a second two-year term with every expectation that the vote would go in his favor by a landslide even larger than in his first election.

The President looked across the crowd to the right and saw twisted metal structures poking out of the water from a demolished railway line that used to cross the harbor. To the left, he saw the elevated concrete bridge that carried Interstate Highway 95 deeper into Connecticut.

There was no traffic on the bridge this week. On the far side of the bridge he saw armored shields for the machine guns of the Connecticut National Guard. Worse, a line of howitzer cannons stood ready to blast any redistributionists who attempted to cross.

Rojo sighed. The redistribution of Connecticut was not going as smoothly as his Great Deal Party had hoped. When the New York National Guard and a million socialists from New York City rushed into Connecticut a week ago, they had planned to seize the entire state in a day or two. However, the Connecticut National Guard had managed to block the mob here at Cos Cob Harbor.

Fortunately, the New York National Guard, with its huge numerical advantage, was able to negotiate a surrender agreement with the Connecticut National Guard. Rojo was happy to know that the screaming mob of socialists would rush across the bridge, redistributing the rest of Connecticut to themselves, when the Connecticut National Guard retreated at midnight in accordance with the agreement. The victory would come just on time for the Tuesday election.

He addressed the crowd, "The Great Deal Party gave you a new human right. Free cash!

"These hundred-dollar bills have a picture of me instead of Benjamin Franklin since you don't know who he was anyway!"

Rojo paused and made a mental note to ask an aide to figure out who Benjamin Franklin was, just in case the question ever came up.

Suddenly, a deafening blast sounded as twenty truck-sized containers secured to towering metal scaffolds spanning the parking lot tipped millions of dollars onto the audience. Clouds of freshly printed bills fluttered in the air like confetti. The crowd went wild as people pushed and shoved to grab the falling cash.

Rojo remembered when an adviser told him that showering cash onto voters might be perceived as corruption or "buying votes." But this didn't make any sense! Obviously, the government was supposed to give free stuff to the voters. What other possible purpose could the government have? Corruption was the opposite. Corruption was when right-wing politicians promised not to confiscate wealth from the rich in order to get votes from the rich. That was "buying votes."

Rojo reflected back to 2012 and the unprecedented rapidity with which the Democracy Amendment to the United States Constitution was ratified.

The Amendment was the result of unanimous bipartisan action connected with the disintegration of the Democratic Party and Republican Party.

The Amendment was intended as a final apology to the American people. It was a complete overhaul of voting and residence laws which overpowered all state laws.

15

Constitutional amendments require ratification by 38 states and the process can take years. But this amendment was ratified unanimously by all 50 states in just two weeks since both major political parties choose to cooperate.

All elected offices (federal, state, local) were put on matching two-year terms. The Electoral College was eliminated to allow direct election of the president by the people.

Because of the chaotic situation with citizenship and residence, where many people had questionable citizenship and resided in districts other than where they were supposed to be resident, and the desire of the outgoing Congress to give every living human a vote, voting rights were greatly expanded.

The right to vote and the right to be a candidate were guaranteed for some groups that were previously denied the franchise: people under the age of 18, non-citizens, and convicted felons. Registration requirements were eliminated. Everyone who was in a particular district on election day was entitled to vote in that district.

Voting was scheduled bi-annually on the first Tuesday in November using a split video screen at each polling station where the voter just pressed his or her fingers on the selection. Computers entered the fingerprints into a database. If the computers found that the same person had voted more than once, only the first vote counted. The system worked so well that election results could be calculated immediately. The winners were sworn in the next morning. There was no need to wait for two months as was done historically.

Rojo's smile grew into an expression of triumph. The Democracy Amendment had paved the way for his Great Deal Party to gain power.

In the election of 2012, Rojo's newly created Great Deal Party had captured not only the presidency, but also over two-thirds of the seats in the Senate and the House of

Representatives. They also captured governorships and state legislatures in 37 of the 50 states.

Rojo looked over his shoulder at a huge platform where the popular band 'The Founding Fathers' pounded and strummed away on drums and guitars. He glanced to his right and left at the huge stacks of loudspeakers. Thumping music with a captivating drum beat blared toward the crowd, reverberating along the harbor.

Bang bang bangabanga bang bang clang!

The chorus kicked in and the hyper-energized crowd joined in the rhythmic command, "TAKE-WHAT'S-YOURS!"

New Yorkers in the crowd below banged weapons ranging from clubs to assault rifles as they yelled encouragement at their elected leader.

They chanted loudly and wildly along with the chorus of the song.

Bang bang bangabanga bang bang clang! "TAKE-WHAT'S-YOURS!"

Several crazed fans, young women with long dreadlocks crying with tears of passion, threw grappling hooks onto the retail center and climbed upward toward Rojo. Uniformed soldiers from the New York National Guard, strategically positioned on the roof, ran forward and cut the ropes from the hooks.

Rojo caught the signal from the sound technician as the noise of the band faded from the loudspeakers. Time for the speech.

Rojo yelled into the microphone, "The Great Deal Party gave the American people more rights and equality with the Great Deal Act!

"American employees outnumbered American employers, so the Great Deal Act gave you the unlimited right to strike! You keep getting paid when you're on strike and replacing you is illegal!"

"Hurray!" the crowd replied.

"American renters outnumbered American landlords, so the Great Deal Act suspended all rent payments!"

"Hurray!"

"American debtors outnumbered American creditors, so the Great Deal Act suspended all debt payments!"

"Hurray!"

Rojo thought about his enthusiastic supporters from New York State and in particular New York City. These people not only embraced the letter of the Great Deal Act, they also embraced the spirit.

He decided to speak briefly about economics. "The store that I am standing on used to oppress you. The store that I am standing on used to exploit you. Now the products and the employees from this store have been liberated!

"The retail chain Easy Cheap oppressed you in three ways.

"First, the products were too expensive. Customers were getting ripped off because they needed to buy things and had no choice but to pay the sticker price. This was oppression and exploitation. This was evil!

"Second, the products were too cheap. The store sold foreign goods at dumping prices. This was oppression and exploitation. This was evil! Foreign criminals were stealing jobs from honest American labor unionists and hurting the American consumer by selling goods that were better and cheaper than domestic goods.

"Third, Easy Cheap oppressed workers by offering jobs at salaries which resulted in profits for shareholders. This was oppression and exploitation. This was evil! Whenever an American voluntarily accepted a job offer at market salary, he was enslaved.

"Now, these problems are solved. The employees are on strike with $100,000 annual compensation paid bi-weekly in fresh bills distributed from government offices, just like all striking workers and unemployed people in the Great Deal States. And, imports are illegal."

Rojo stomped symbolically on the roof of the empty retail center which had been fully stocked and operational until just a week earlier when the New York redistributionists smashed out the windows and grabbed all the goods off the shelves.

Intelligence sources had informed him that the rest of the Easy Cheap stores in Connecticut, not yet liberated by the New York redistributionists, were being emptied out now by Easy Cheap management in clearance sales to fleeing Connecticut families. The concept disgusted Rojo since he firmly believed that the more numerous New Yorkers had human rights to take these goods for free.

He assumed, pessimistically and cynically, that history would repeat itself in Connecticut. When enforcement of the Great Deal Act commenced in New York State in 2013 and all of the New York Easy Cheap stores were emptied out by redistributionists, the greedy store managers refused to re-stock and therefore the redistributionists were unable to empty out the stores again. Probably the same would happen now in 2014 with the Connecticut Easy Cheap stores.

He reflected on the tough battle of bringing socialism to America. It would be easier to help the American majority if it weren't for the blood-sucking, profit-mongering, parasitic capitalists who were always trying to sabotage progress.

When the Great Deal Party congressmen passed the Great Deal Act and Rojo signed it into law in June 2013, the Supreme Court justices unanimously said that it violated the property rights protection in the Bill of Rights. They vowed to rule it unconstitutional at the earliest opportunity.

Rojo had responded by ordering the arrest of the Supreme Court justices. He said they were corrupt because they owned property that would be redistributed by the Great Deal Act and therefore they wanted to strike it down to protect their own narrow self-interest against the interest of the majority.

The justices responded by fleeing from Washington, D.C. to Alaska at the invitation of the Governor of Alaska, a member of the rival Property Rights Party. Once in Alaska, the Supreme Court set up operations in the United States Federal Building in Anchorage and held a session in which they ruled the Great Deal Act unconstitutional.

Rojo remembered his sadness when he heard from his advisers that the Great Deal Party was unable to end the dispute by repealing the Bill of Rights because they only controlled 37 states and they needed 38 states to amend the Constitution.

The Great Deal Act was implemented in the 37 states where the Great Deal Party controlled state government. The Great Deal Act was not implemented in the 13 states where the Property Rights Party controlled state government. The Property Rights governors did not recognize Rojo as having any authority since he was enforcing an act that was ruled unconstitutional and was therefore in violation of his oath to defend the Constitution.

The Great Deal States included New York. The Property Rights States included Connecticut.

Rojo looked at the thousands of New York socialists now standing in Connecticut and was overjoyed they would vote in Connecticut on Tuesday. He needed a 38th state. It would be Connecticut.

He spoke confidently into the microphone, "The Property Rights States refuse to implement the Great Deal Act! They are denying your rights! They are denying your equality!

"The Founding Fathers of America promised rights and equality, and the Great Deal Act gives rights and equality!

"The Founding Fathers of America promised democracy, and the Great Deal Act is the result of democracy!

"The corrupt Supreme Court ruled the Great Deal Act

unconstitutional. The greedy misers on the Supreme Court did this because they hate the majority of Americans. These misers talk about protecting property rights when I talk about protecting human rights!

"If we put ordinary people with huge debts and no property on the Supreme Court, their ideas would be different!

"The cold-hearted Supreme Court justices and Property Rights politicians say the Bill of Rights guarantees that private property will not be taken for public use without fair compensation. But the happy feeling of surrendering property to the government for redistribution is fair compensation!"

Rojo paused and thought about the ingrates in Connecticut. He had implemented the Great Deal policies with the rich in mind also. He knew the rich had problems since the poor were jealous of the rich and therefore often tried to rob them. Rojo believed he was helping the rich by using assets taken from them to fund a government the primary function of which was, through violent coercion, preemptive redistribution of those assets to the poor.

"The Great Deal Party must win in Connecticut! We must repeal the Bill of Rights!

"We can achieve the full rights and equality that the Founding Fathers of America envisioned!"

Rojo felt confident with his logic. Didn't the Founding Fathers, George Washington and James Madison, write in the Declaration of Independence that everyone was equal? Didn't this mean poor people should take things from rich people? In a democracy, shouldn't the majority do anything it wanted to the minority? Why then, would the Founding Fathers protect private property in the Bill of Rights? It must have been a mistake. By repealing the Bill of Rights, Rojo would bring the country closer to what the Founding Fathers intended.

"The Great Deal Party has a strategy for victory,"

continued Rojo. "Democracy was expanded in 2012, and the result was greater freedom for the American people. Democracy will be further expanded on Tuesday, and the details will be released at a press conference tomorrow. We are giving America absolute democracy so that America can have absolute equality."

He waved his arm in the direction of the distant shore. "Look over there at the people of Connecticut: they've been exploiting New Yorkers for generations by investing in New York companies and hiring New York employees and collecting the profits from your work. You're fighting to redistribute the property of Connecticut to yourselves and this makes you heroes! And the people of Connecticut are resisting. This resistance makes them criminals! Everyone knows that in democracy, the majority has the human right to redistribute wealth to itself from the minority. The majority people of New York outnumber the elite misers of Connecticut. Soon the Connecticut misers will be gone and you can cross this bridge!"

The crowd cheered. The band got louder.

Bang bang bangabanga bang bang clang! "TAKE-WHAT'S-YOURS!"

Rojo scanned the other side of the harbor and the defenses set up by the Connecticut National Guard: long stretches of bullet-proof shielding, pill boxes hiding machine guns, and the howitzers. All of this would be disassembled in a matter of hours. The Connecticut National Guard had agreed to withdraw east on Interstate 95 and north on Interstate 91 to New Hampshire—the last state in the East to remain under the control of the Property Rights Party. Most of the Connecticut civilians who were supporters of the Property Rights Party had already evacuated that way, allowed to pass through the states of Massachusetts and Vermont provided the evacuation was orderly—with all capital and infrastructure in Connecticut surrendered in good condition and ready for redistribution.

Rojo turned his attention back to the crowd in front of him and correctly assumed they were on the edge of boredom since he'd discussed economics for a full four minutes. It was time to use buzzwords to restore enthusiasm.

"Justice! Rights! Equality! Liberty!"

The crowd went wild.

"Vote for the Great Deal Party on Tuesday!

"And remember, the big majority victory party for Connecticut will be in Bridgeport. Everyone who deserves a free surprise from the government should come there on Wednesday!"

The pictures on the huge video monitors changed from the live image of President Rojo to a countdown of numbers.

"Everybody please clear out of the parking lot in twenty minutes. This evil store that used to oppress you is being pumped full of gas and turned into a giant bomb. When the bomb goes off, you'll want to be at least a block away!"

Rojo watched as the crowd went into a panic. People began to push and shove and run in all directions with more than a few people trampled underneath. Rojo felt confident that this was okay because, obviously, individual people had to suffer and make sacrifices to implement socialism for the collective good. The same thing happened at all of his political rallies.

Again the music blared with the familiar chorus and the catchy drum beat.

Bang bang banga banga bang bang clang! "TAKE-WHAT'S-YOURS!"

Rojo felt optimistic as he left the podium. Good could win over evil!

He thought of his opponent, David Goldstein, the leader of the Property Rights Party. True, Goldstein was not the one commanding the rogue national guards, since that was being done by rogue governors. But anyway, as the presidential candidate for the Property Rights Party, he must be held responsible for the delay in full redistribution.

Rojo planned to defeat Goldstein and the Property Rights Party in 38 states on Tuesday. And, the paperwork was already prepared for Wednesday morning for Congress and the state governments to hold votes to amend the Constitution by repealing the Bill of Rights. Once that happened, resistance by the remaining 12 Property Rights States would disappear. Their contention that the Great Deal Act was unconstitutional would no longer be valid.

Rojo knew he was unstoppable. He momentarily considered, but quickly dismissed, the possibility that there might be a self-interested, elitist, evil, minority person in Connecticut who could jeopardize this triumph of the majority.

Rojo abandoned the podium. New York National Guard troops ushered him across the Easy Cheap roof to the stairway that led to his waiting motorcade.

(4) A moment later at Bradley Air National Guard Base, Connecticut

Captain Jack Cannon cried as he sat by the medic's gurney clutching the hand of his dead father. It had been impossible for the medic to save him. After all, the grass was drenched with blood where Jack had knelt beside his father, who was still clutching an assault rifle, just two hours earlier at the family farm in Litchfield.

The family farm, which was actually a well-managed maple forest with a sugar shack for processing maple syrup, had long been vulnerable to looting even though it was in Connecticut since it was near the border with New York State.

Jack was proud of his father for making the enlightened choice of fighting the socialists instead of submitting to slavery.

Jack had been there at the family farm in the morning when a gang of New York looters, some armed with handguns, ran through the forest to steal or destroy everything in sight. He had seen his father in the field near the sugar shack firing the assault rifle at the redistributionists. They were apparently coming for the farm's valuable maple syrup inventory.

Jack still shook with emotion as he recalled his father heroically killing at least a dozen of the left-wingers before the last one accidentally ignited himself with a giant Molotov cocktail.

Tragically, the final looter shot his gun wildly while he burned to death and hit Jack's father in the chest.

As Jack cried next to the gurney, he remembered the

25

curious final conversation with his dying father as they awaited Connecticut National Guard assistance.

Jack's thoughts raced. Democracy Society? What could Dad have been talking about? Could it be something connected with the Society of the Cincinnati? Jack remembered Dad sometimes talked about a time of great challenge as a university student when Grandfather died and Dad was organizer of a California business roundtable that had a huge impact on state, and eventually national, politics. Could that have been a project for the Democracy Society?

Jack knew that the management organization at the Mount Vernon estate in Virginia was called the Democracy Society. They organized tours of the historical home and they probably made good money from ticket sales and the gift shop, until Virginia voted for the Great Deal Party and all businesses were shut down. Could that be the same organization his father was talking about?

A man in a baggy camouflage jumpsuit stepped forward for what must have been the tenth time. "Captain Cannon, your slot for takeoff is fast approaching. The ground crew is waiting by the jet fighter."

Finally, Jack staggered to his feet.

Standing six-feet-one-inch tall, he was the same height as the man from the ground crew. Both men had patches on their shoulders depicting the state flag of Connecticut: a white shield with three grapevines and the motto *"Qui Transtulit Sustinet."*

Jack's jumpsuit was different, however. He wore a flight suit of a shiny synthetic material, light-green color and cut with a close fit over his muscular frame. The sporty suit had tubes and wires cleverly worked into the fabric, including life support and electronics.

He had the high-tech suit because he was a jet fighter pilot. And, an accomplished one at that. He had flown many overseas and domestic combat missions and received several decorations.

Jack thought the government decision back in November 2012 to eliminate the United States Armed Forces by withdrawing from Europe and Asia and dividing the troops amongst the state national guards was crazy. But, mainstream Americans were no longer interested in paying a non-compulsory, professional military to fight foreign, psychopathic tyrants to promote global peace.

He was also disturbed by the decision of the old Congress to unilaterally dismantle all nuclear weapons. But at least the North American Missile Shield, completed in 2012, was still operational. And, it was safely under the control of the Property Rights Party because it was located in Alaska.

All of the military personnel, including Jack's old United States Marines unit, had been in the process of splitting up between the fifty national guards when Roberto Rojo became president, and therefore Commander-in-Chief, in November 2012. That was how Jack came to be flying in Connecticut after several years flying abroad.

He turned to the medic who was sitting in the corner of the room. "Please see that my father is buried in Connecticut soil because he died fighting to defend his Connecticut home."

Jack followed the crewman out of the medical building directly onto the airfield. They were at Bradley Air National Guard Base and this was the day that the Connecticut Air National Guard was retreating from the base in accordance with the surrender agreement signed with the New York National Guard a few days earlier. Every hanger was open and crews prepared every aircraft for takeoff.

Although Jack was able to stifle his emotions as he crossed the airfield, he still had intense thoughts racing through his head. America always had thieves. But nothing like what society was facing now ...

The country was being overrun by mobs that had been

brainwashed to believe God himself had given them the human right to take anything they wanted from their neighbors.

This attitude was incompatible with the continuance of the United States as a peaceful and prosperous republic. Jack swore to fight this destructive degeneration in American outlook. If someone was purposefully inflicting this damage on America, then Jack was going to find him and stop him. It was an urgent matter of self-defense.

As Jack approached his assigned jet fighter, the *Flying Yankee*, he noted the large fuel pods that had been installed under the swept gray wings of the radar-absorbent aircraft.

The short flight from the Bradley Air National Guard Base in Connecticut to the Pease Air National Guard Base in New Hampshire would not require any extra fuel. But he knew the Connecticut Air National Guard had a goal of bringing as many supplies as possible to New Hampshire before the looters took complete control of Connecticut. There was no point destroying fixed capital such as hangars and control towers because the looters would predictably destroy the fixed capital themselves. That was what always happened with communally owned assets.

A man from the ground crew stood at the boarding ladder and handed Jack a light-green helmet matching the flight suit. The decal on the side of the helmet was, again, the grapevine shield of Connecticut.

Jack pulled the helmet over his short blond hair. He immediately slammed down the tinted visor to protect his watery, glacier-blue eyes from the sunlight.

As he climbed up the boarding ladder into the pilot's section of the two-man tandem cockpit, he noticed the back seat was filled with equipment: a bundle of extra flight suits and helmets.

When he was seated, he buckled the harness and connected his air hose as the tinted cockpit canopy lowered automatically. The sun-sensitive helmet visor went from tinted to clear.

The onboard computers booted up and the instrument panel displays came alight. Jack initiated the start sequence.

He had always been proud of his home state of Connecticut and his pride had never been in doubt, until this past week.

True, Connecticut was in the most difficult position of the thirteen Property Rights States since it was surrounded by Great Deal States.

New Hampshire, the only other Property Rights State in the East, bordered on Canada and therefore still had a functioning economy. Likewise, Idaho, Montana, Nevada, Utah, Wyoming, North Dakota, South Dakota, Kansas, Nebraska, and Iowa were able to trade with and through Canada. Even better, Alaska had an unimpeded coastline. Cargo ships were travelling between Alaska and Asia.

The banks still functioned in the other Property Rights States, having repudiated their deposits from clients in Great Deal States since the Great Deal States suspended payments on loans. People in the Property Rights States, other than Connecticut, could still conduct commerce using bank transfers and Canadian currency.

Connecticut was at a disadvantage. But anyway, Jack thought, the decision of the Connecticut National Guard and Connecticut State Police to surrender the state to the numerically superior New York looter mob, the New York National Guard, and the New York State Police was nothing to be proud about.

He shivered with disgust as he thought about more than a million socialists rushing into Connecticut with the intention of stealing everything in sight and, worse still, voting in Connecticut on Tuesday.

The *Flying Yankee* accelerated along the airstrip and lifted off at a ground speed of two hundred kilometers per hour.

Upon reaching cruising altitude for the short flight to New Hampshire, Jack engaged the autopilot.

He reached a gloved hand into his chest pocket and removed a golden badge. This was his first opportunity to study the gift received just a few hours earlier from his dying father. The badge had a beautiful design. It was the profile of a striking wild turkey with a glittering diamond as its eye.

Jack flipped the antique badge over and saw a small brand-new electronic device welded onto the back, including a USB connection. He plugged it into the jet fighter's instrument panel and a video display showed an image.

He peered into a futuristic laboratory with computers, video screens, and several swivel chairs. He was immediately struck by the repeating pattern on the metallic walls of the laboratory—the same wild turkey from the badge.

He saw a black man dressed in a well-tailored dark suit standing erect in the center of the room.

Based on his graying hair, Jack guessed the man was in his late 50's, but still he looked fit and powerful. The man appeared to be about six-foot-three and stood with the bearing of a general.

This leader was barking out orders to a team of a dozen white-smocked scientists who were running around the laboratory and typing on various keyboards that appeared linked to a central supercomputer. One wall had a large video screen showing the image of a brain. Two empty metal beds were arranged in the center of the room.

The man suddenly noticed a beeping red light on his wristband and came to the corner of the room, approaching the camera that fed into Jack's video display.

The man stared into the camera with alert and intelligent black eyes, apparently seeing a monitor for himself at the other side of the communication link.

Tears appeared in the corners of his eyes as he spoke in a tone of authority. "You must be John Cannon's son. The fact that you have the badge indicates that John Cannon is no longer with us. Your father made a great contribution to his country and he will be dearly missed. I have read your biography and I know your father prepared you well. I know you earned the rank of Captain in the Marine Corps and the Connecticut Air National Guard, so I will address you as Captain in the Democracy Society. I am to be addressed as Director."

Jack resumed crying as he thought of his father, even as the *Flying Yankee* screeched through the air. "Director? Who are you? How did you know my father? My father said something about the Democracy Society when he gave me the badge."

The Director continued, "Captain Cannon, you are heir to a membership in the Democracy Society. Your father was a member. All of the male-line descendants of Colonel John Cannon of the Continental Army have been members."

"Continental Army? Do you mean General George Washington's army? The Revolutionary War? Is this about the Society of the Cincinnati? I know all about that. I have attended Cincinnati events with my father. I also know you are not the President General of the Society of the Cincinnati." Jack turned up the volume on the headset in his helmet to be certain to catch every word of the reply.

"The Society of the Cincinnati is a social organization with chapters in thirteen states," explained the Director. "The Democracy Society is a governmental organization. The members of the Democracy Society are a secret and elite team of thirteen soldiers responsible for preventing the collapse of our republic back into tyranny."

Jack was skeptical, "How am I supposed to believe that?"

The Director pushed a button on his wristband and a drawer extended from the turkey-pattern wall with a shielded document inside. He held the shielded document up to the video.

31

Jack had seen important historical documents in climate-controlled shielding before, for example the Constitution and the Declaration of Independence.

But what was this?

Jack pushed the zoom button on the instrument panel to enlarge the video image.

The parchment was titled 'Charter of the Democracy Society' and the script was difficult to read. Jack guessed it had been handwritten centuries before.

He could make out a block of text beginning with "We hereby authorize General George Washington to be first director of the society charged with defending our liberties …"

Then, Jack's eyes scanned to the bottom of the parchment, where he saw signatures. The first block of signatures was identified as 'Philadelphia, September 11, 1787' and the second block 'New York, October 10, 1788.'

He recognized the names of most of the signers since he was well-educated on the subject of American history. These people were the Founding Fathers of the United States of America.

He pushed another button on the instrument panel to go back to the original video image of the whole laboratory.

The Director continued staring into the video screen. "This is the Charter of the Democracy Society. It holds the signatures of all of the delegates at the Constitutional Convention and at the final quorum of the Congress of the Confederation. The Charter preceded the United States Constitution and supercedes all federal and state law. The Charter gives us legal authority to undertake covert actions to prevent the erosion of property rights. If we fail at our duty, the democratic republic will revert to tyranny."

The Director, still standing, closed the secret drawer, hiding the Charter.

The Director turned back toward the video screen.

"Throughout most of our history, we have been inactive. Most Democracy Society members never had any mission, and remained on standby. There have only been a few cases where we took action to protect the republic.

"I am offering you an opportunity to fight for American democracy and you can exercise your free choice about whether to accept my authority. Our current mission is this: stop the Great Deal Party from repealing the Bill of Rights on Wednesday."

Jack sighed as he looked through his clear visor at the instrument panel display. "To be honest, I don't want to be in any military organization and I don't want to fight anyone. My dream is to stay at home running the maple syrup farm. I made some new plans for maximizing the farm's long-term profitablity."

He paused and a contemplative look spread across his face.

"However, I cannot run the maple syrup farm when the farm and the country are being attacked by socialists. I must win a battle of self-defense against the socialists first before returning to the farm. Obviously, there is no point in efficiently managing the farm if there is no Bill of Rights to prevent the majority from confiscating my family's property.

"I am thinking back now to some things that my father told me when I was younger. What you are telling me about the Democracy Society is consistent with what he said. Therefore, I feel convinced that you are telling the truth.

"I accept my membership in the Democracy Society. I will be honored to participate in your lawful efforts to save the Bill of Rights. How can I be of service?"

"What are you doing now?" asked the Director. "Are you flying? I see that you are wearing a helmet."

"I am a pilot in the Connecticut Air National Guard. I am in the process of bringing a jet fighter from Connecticut to New Hampshire as part of the evacuation of Connecticut."

"Jet fighter? That is very interesting."

The Director turned and waved at someone out of sight in the background.

Jack watched on his video screen as a slim man dressed in white coveralls with a pocket protector appeared. This new man had an academic look with glasses and a gray beard. Despite the geeky appearance, the man stood tall and seemed strong and fit. He spoke English with a Russian accent. "What is going on?"

The Director explained. "Doctor Zaicev, regarding our need for immediate backup for your daughter in Arabia, I found a possible helper."

The Director resumed talking to Jack. "The Democracy Society has a project underway to save the republic. Some of the work is being performed here in our secret bunker under Mount Vernon. But the project also has an international aspect."

The doctor turned toward the screen and elaborated. "I am Doctor Zaicev, formerly of Moscow University. The international work will be done in cooperation with my daughter, Valentina. We are Russians, however our objective—saving democracy and preventing reversion to tyranny—puts us in alliance because the defective democratic governments of the United States and Russia are linked."

"In fact the link between the United States and Russia is not the only international aspect of the situation," interrupted the Director. "We are also working with the King of Arabia. I have a close relationship with the King because we served together in the United States Army, obviously before he became King, in the Gulf Wars. Arabia is a victim of the United States decision to purchase oil only from Russia.

"Doctor Zaicev was recruited to the team because he is the world's foremost expert in a niche scientific field and therefore he is uniquely qualified to help with the mission."

The doctor resumed speaking. "My daughter's

contribution is in her professional field: investigative journalism. She performed a research task in Russia. She has a top secret research file that is the compilation of her investigation. She brought the file to Arabia to give it to the King of Arabia and also to a representative of the Democracy Society. The file is critically important for the ongoing mission at the Democracy Society."

"Captain Cannon," said the Director, "we have a serious problem that just came to our attention a few hours ago.

"The Democracy Society member from Georgia was lost this morning. He was in the process of flying an aircraft from a defunct private parcel delivery company in Atlanta to meet with Valentina in Arabia and collect the file. In his last radio contact, he indicated he was losing control of the aircraft over the ocean because parts had been stripped from the engine and wings, probably by a looter.

"We need an immediate replacement to meet with Valentina. Your assignment is to commandeer the jet fighter and fly across the ocean to Arabia. Valentina is already there. You are to attend the grand opening event at the Sea Hotel and Spa and meet the King of Arabia. I will inform the King and Valentina that you are replacing the Georgia agent.

"And, the assignment doesn't stop in Arabia. The very next night you will attend the grand opening event at the Peak Hotel and Casino in Russia. American Vice President Clark and Russian President Ivanov will be there."

"I see how this ties together," observed Jack. "This must be something to do with the Trans Pacific Trading Company and the obviously corrupt oil trade between the USA and Russia."

"You will learn the details when you meet Valentina," said the Director. "Just know this now: the King of Arabia is our friend and Clark and Ivanov are our enemies. Valentina will provide a file to you and the King. Then, you must fly with Valentina to Russia to spy on Clark and Ivanov.

"Valentina received invitations to both hotel grand openings as a journalist. I am able to send you to the Sea Hotel and Spa event because the King is our ally. You can attend the Peak Hotel and Casino event as Valentina's guest.

"The Democracy Society is lawfully chartered and completely dedicated to promoting sustainable democracy. Do you accept your first assignment?"

Jack had a good feeling about these people and this organization. He felt happy that the Democracy Society continued to fight the socialists even while the Connecticut National Guard retreated. "I accept. I am ready to go immediately. Please give me the flight coordinates for the Sea Hotel and Spa. Also, you should know I have a highly sophisticated communications and encryption system here on the jet fighter and therefore, when I have the file from Valentina, I will be able to send it to you without any fear of interception."

The Director typed on a tiny keyboard on his wristband. "That is good news, Captain. Now realize that we are on a tight schedule. We must save America before Wednesday. If we do not succeed before then, all will be lost and our democratic republic will be replaced by tyranny. I am uploading your new flight plan and a photo of Valentina so you will know who to look for."

Jack had one final thought before switching to battle mode: as soon as he was finished saving the republic, he would return to the syrup farm.

He saw the new flight coordinates appear on the video screen. He tapped away on the keyboard to override his Connecticut Air National Guard instructions.

He felt the G-forces as the jet turned hard and began its new course—across the Atlantic Ocean to the other side of the world.

(5) A moment later in Greenwich

President Roberto Rojo heard a massive explosion and felt satisfied the Easy Cheap store had been destroyed. He considered it likely that some of his socialist supporters got blown up as well, and he silently thanked them for having martyred themselves for the common good.

He sat in his armored limousine as it drove back toward New York State on a side street, escorted by jeeps from the New York National Guard. The Connecticut natives had already fled from this occupied part of Greenwich. Rojo watched through bullet-proofed windows as mobs of New Yorkers redistributed armloads of goods from abandoned Connecticut homes.

His trademark smile of determination, confidence, and power now faded and was replaced by a worried expression.

He switched his attention to the man sitting next to him on the wide back seat in the limousine, the founder of the Great Deal Party and incumbent candidate for vice president, Clarence Clark. Clark, the youngest vice president in American history since he was only 28 and would not have qualified to be vice president prior to the Democracy Amendment, sat in his usual pose, short and plump arms folded across his round belly.

Rojo was aware that Clark was not handsome. The Vice President looked absolutely goofy with puffy cheeks, baby-blue eyes, and pepper-brown hair in a nerdy part. He wore his usual schoolboy-smile expression since he was not having one of his "episodes" at the moment. Rojo was not surprised the Great Deal Party usually kept Clark out of sight during publicity events.

However, Rojo knew Clark had a good heart. Clark had amassed his fortune without stealing it from society. In other words, he never obtained money from interest, rent, or profit. And, he was dedicated to the principles of socialism. Therefore Rojo was happy to be teamed with Clark.

"What did you think of the speech, Clarence?"

Clark responded in his usual high and squeaky voice. "Roberto, you're a star. The crowd loved you. In fact, the crowd did not even notice when you made a logical error by arguing that Easy Cheap prices were both too expensive and too cheap!"

"What logical error?" asked Rojo, observing an instant and disturbing change in Clark's demeanor.

Clark's body began to shake. And, his schoolboy smile disappeared as he pressed his lips together hard in what appeared to be an effort to suppress a scream. He whipped open the door of the refrigerator in the back of the limousine, grabbed a small whiskey bottle and glass, and quickly poured and drank a big gulp. He stopped shaking.

Clark, now seemingly relaxed, spoke. "It is my favorite Scotch whiskey, from the Scottish Lowland. Most experts prefer whiskey from the Scottish Highland and they pay a premium for it. I, however, prefer the dry finish of Scottish Lowland whiskey, resulting from the use of unpeated malt in the production process."

Clark then calmly removed a bottle of apple juice from the fridge. He handed the apple juice to Rojo. "Your English apple juice, 100% natural of course, and my Scotch whiskey, both continue to come to me from the same British smuggler, purchased with British pounds. Both are high-quality products. They remind me of the apple juice and whiskey that used to be produced in my home state, Tennessee."

"Thanks, Clarence, for bringing my favorite drink— natural apple juice. Of course I feel slightly guilty about this."

Clark tilted his head, "Why? Is it because all apple juice

and whiskey production in the Great Deal States ceased after you signed the Great Deal Act? You should not feel guilty about that. As you said many times yourself, the reason why the orchards and production facilities were burned down was not because of a fault in the Great Deal Act, but rather a fault in human nature. Owners did not come out-of-pocket to fund the operating losses."

Rojo tilted his head now. "What? You misunderstood me. I don't feel guilty about the destruction of the apple juice and whiskey companies. I feel proud that I liberated the slaves who worked at those companies at market salaries under voluntary employment agreements. I only wish I could help to free the slaves in Great Britain also."

Clark slouched as he poured the rest of the whiskey into his glass. "Yes, that statement is consistent with what you have said in the past. But anyway, our responsibility is for America. Maybe someday the British will elect a demagogue like you and all their companies will also shut down. They must do that themselves."

"What's a demagogue?" Rojo asked.

Clark sat up straighter. "Oh, did I use that word? Errr … It means a great leader who does everything for the majority."

Rojo relaxed and replied, "Thanks for the compliment!" He then decided to launch into a monologue on economic theory, because he wanted both to impress and get advice from his running mate.

"I know the economy is a big pizza pie. A certain amount of money appears each year like it came from the pizza delivery man. It is called GDP. The money gets split up between the people and if one person gets a larger slice, then a different person must get a smaller slice. The key to bringing peace and prosperity is for government to split up this pizza pie equally. I didn't have to go to University of Chicago, like David Goldstein, to learn that."

Clark sat silently for a minute, nodding his head, before

replying. "Don't you think it is possible that events could occur that would cause the size of the pizza pie to change?"

Rojo often got a funny feeling he was being tested when he talked with Clark. "Well yes, Clarence. Obviously it is possible for the pie to get smaller. For example, if a company spends $100 to produce a product with a market value of $110, then the economy will get smaller by $10 because that is the amount of profit that is being stolen from society by the company owner. Conversely, if a company spends $100 to produce a product with a market value of $90, then the economy will get larger by $10 because that is the amount of the altruistic gift to society from the company owner."

Clark began shaking again, but this time more severely. His whole body twitched in spasms. He swallowed all of the whiskey and closed his eyes. The spasms subsided.

Rojo was disturbed, but tried hard to act as if he didn't notice anything. He continued speaking. "I always dreamed of creating a democratic, self-managed, bottom-up, participatory socialism. I'm completely against the elitist, top-down, central-planning, police-state communism that used to exist in the Soviet Union.

"When we implemented the Great Deal Act and all of the employees went on strike and all of the companies were put in the control of worker councils, I expected employees to receive huge raises and do less work. I expected society to become more prosperous.

"But it didn't happen like that. Owners did not come out of pocket to pay the strikers. The result was completely unpredictable.

"Now, we need the Temporary Police State Act to back up the Great Deal Act. The entire population is on the government payroll. We have many thousands of pencil-pushers staffing a Central Planning Bureau and Fair Price Agency. All wages and prices are set by government edict.

"And, by unlucky random coincidence, there was an

explosion of black market corruption at the exact instant when all of this was implemented.

"We have armed soldiers rounding up millions of people in the Great Deal States and marching them to prison camps or exile. In short, we wound up creating a new Soviet Union. I hate using a huge military to enforce our edicts since our intention was reducing government and giving freedom and power to the people. However, we must stamp out the black market in order to create universal prosperity."

Clark opened his eyes and rested his hand on his running mate's shoulder, "Roberto, be patient. Think of your, I mean our, idol: Franklin Delano Roosevelt. When FDR implemented his New Deal policies, the economy got worse before it got better, obviously because of the actions of greedy profit-mongers and not because of any faults with the New Deal. It took FDR four elections and thirteen years of persistence. Americans suffered through the Great Depression and World War II hoping his reforms would begin to work. Throughout all that time the people were impoverished, miserable, and getting slaughtered, but they had faith and kept voting for FDR. It took so long for the New Deal to work that FDR died and much of the New Deal was repealed before the economy turned around. We have only been working for two years on our reforms. And, since our reforms are less compromising than FDR's reforms, I expect things will turn around in less than thirteen years."

Rojo still felt saddened. "I hope things will turn around in less than thirteen years. Then, we can repeal the Temporary Police State Act. I just wish we could find a natural way, without police coercion, to allocate labor and capital efficiently to produce goods and services that people need. And, this natural way must avoid any reliance on self-interested behavior because, as everyone knows, it's evil for people to be self-interested."

Clark nodded and removed his hand from Rojo's

shoulder. "I agree and everyone else also agrees. Of course, the subject is non-controversial. All self-interest is wrong and all self-interested people know their behavior is unethical."

Rojo sighed, "I hope people stop being self-interested soon so that our socialist policies begin to work. I love the majority of the American people and the whole reason I am implementing my economic reforms is to help them!"

Rojo had a tear in his eye as he looked out the window. As the limousine passed a 'Welcome to New York' sign, all he could see were smoldering remains of burned out homes and garbage blowing along the street.

Clark changed the subject. "I have asked the driver to drop me at White Plains Airport before bringing you back to headquarters. I have a difficult schedule now with mandatory appearances over the next three days in California, Korea, and Russia."

Rojo shivered, "Good luck dealing with the Russians. It disgusts me that we have to transact with that cruel Adam Smith-style capitalist President Ivan Ivanov. He is exactly the same as David Goldstein of the Property Rights Party.

"Please explain to me again why our government is buying imported oil from Russia? All imports are prohibited by the Great Deal Act for the benefit of the American people. The Great Deal Act only allows exceptions by presidential order. Why did you pressure me to sign an exception for Russian oil? And, why are we purchasing the oil through a specific offshore company?"

Clark tried to speak reassuringly with his mouse-like voice, "I don't like imports either. I understand that they hurt American consumers. We only made an exception in this case because we need the oil to keep the military running, and we need the military to enforce the Great Deal Act and the Temporary Police State Act.

"Roberto, cheer up. You are doing great work for the American majority and they will thank you when they vote on

Tuesday.

"Since I won't see you before the debate with Goldstein, here is some quick advice. You don't have to talk about details of economic theory. Just stick to the buzzwords: justice, rights, equality, liberty, la, la, la, la, la.

"And don't forget to label Goldstein with the word 'greedy' at every opportunity.

"Goldstein will make the same mistake he always does. He will talk about things that most people cannot understand. If you interrupt him by yelling out something like 'equality!' then you will win and he will lose.

"Also, remember to continue promoting the majority victory parties. All people who believe they deserve free surprises from the government should come to the parties on Wednesday. I am making the arrangements myself for the gifts that will be delivered. In our 38 states, the party will be in the largest city in each state with a couple exceptions. The party for Vermont and Maine will be in Boston, Massachusetts. The party for Florida will be in Orlando. And, California will have parties in both San Francisco and Los Angeles. Obviously Washington, D.C. will also have a party."

"Thank you, Clarence, you are a very generous man," said Rojo.

"And finally," Clark concluded, "here is the most important advice for successful performance in the presidential election debate: use the tanning bed that I had delivered to your office. When you use the spray-on stuff, your skin looks a bit orange and voters don't like that."

*

The limousine brought President Roberto Rojo to headquarters. It had already delivered Vice President Clarence Clark to White Plains Airport, leaving Rojo alone in the back of the huge black car.

As the limousine drove past farm fields where the crops had been burned, Rojo had time to think about the odd career path that had led him to the presidency.

He had been a populist hero before Clark approached him with the offer to be presidential candidate for the Great Deal Party.

Rojo had received a lot of press attention as a labor union activist, a role which made him into a hero in the left-wing press read by the majority, and a villain in the right-wing press read by the minority.

From 2003 until 2006, he had been an employee in the shipping department at a company called Bedford Glassware Corporation in his hometown of Pershing, Illinois. The company was non-unionized when he accepted a voluntary employment offer.

Initially, he had low-level functions in the shipping department.

As the years rolled by, he gained more responsibility and developed his ethical beliefs—specifically that earning money was sinful and the duty of an employee of a for-profit corporation was to sabotage the corporation to lessen its ability to exploit society. This concept of ethics had been drilled into him since childhood by television, movies, parents, grandparents, teachers, friends, politicians, priests, and co-workers. Nobody ever gave a reason for this ethical concept, nor could they since there is no reason, however Rojo accepted the socialist ethic as an indisputable truth. He assumed all people who did not accept the socialist ethic must be evil.

He began creating false documentation to help factory employees embezzle the glassware shipments. He never stole anything himself, since he was motivated by altruism. And, he didn't think of it as 'stealing' when an employee took something from an employer because he believed all employees had human rights to take everything from their employers and anything not taken was effectively 'stolen'—by the employer.

He had a warm feeling in his heart from assisting in embezzlement. But, he kept hoping he could do something more to hurt Bedford Glassware Corporation since it continued to make profit for the evil owner, Mr. Bedford.

Rojo's big opportunity came on a Tuesday afternoon in 2006, when Bedford caught an employee with a truckload of embezzled glassware. Bedford fired the employee immediately.

Rojo sprang into action. He could not tolerate Bedford's greed for another moment. It was Rojo's day to choose whether to courageously take action or shamefully submit.

He climbed up on the factory roof and yelled to the other employees about how they must immediately organize into a union and punish the corporation as harshly as possible for exploiting them.

The speech delivery was incredible. The workers went into a frenzy and built barricades around the factory.

Half the employees stood out front guarding the barricades and waving signs in the air with slogans such as "Bedford is a cheapskate!"

The other half threw the glassware inventory, crate by crate, off the factory roof so that it smashed to pieces on the asphalt truck apron. While the workers destroyed the inventory, they screamed in unison, led by Rojo, "Give us cash! Give us cash! Give us cash!"

So far, so good. But where was Bedford with the free cash? As it was later revealed, he had left the factory because he had a second job as a volunteer administrator for a children's charity that he financed.

Rojo had been in the factory gathering more inventory to destroy when he saw the gas balloon. The 1,000-cubic-meter balloon was used to fuel the multitude of torches that shaped the glassware. He knew that by loosening the valves at the end of the gas balloon and sealing the doors and windows to the factory, he could make the entire building into a giant bomb. So that was what he did.

And his creation worked perfectly. As he strolled away from the building toward the gathered television cameras, there was a loud KABOOOMMM!!!

Rojo was propelled forward toward the television cameras with a scream of triumph coming from his mouth and flames leaping from his jacket and pants. The image was broadcast around the world.

It was a great moment for socialism. One thousand employees survived the explosion and therefore became liberated. In other words, they became unemployed and eligible for government handouts.

Rojo later read that when Bedford heard the news about the factory, he decided to collect the insurance money, move to the Caribbean, and never return to the United States again. Good riddance!

Rojo shifted in the limousine seat and finished his apple juice.

A tragic tale that he did not want to think about right then was the death of his father Hugo and his wife Lolita in the aftermath of the strike.

But one detail always remained in the forefront of Rojo's mind: David Goldstein was responsible. He was a murderer! What was his sick motivation? Extreme conspicuous consumption?

Rojo could not understand the twisted concept of prioritizing private property above human beings. He imagined the overwhelming feeling of guilt that Goldstein must suffer because of making profitable investments. How could Goldstein sleep at night? How could his conscience take it?

Now Rojo was able to take control of his emotions and relax. Goldstein always spoke about negative things. He said the government must balance its budget. He said the government must reduce handouts. He said people must pay something for education and healthcare. He said people must pay their rent and their debts. He said people should save something for their own retirements. These were not things that voters wanted to hear.

Rojo grew happier as he remembered Goldstein did not present any real obstacle to making America fair and equal. After all, America was a democracy. Rojo represented 80% of the population trying to justly redistribute the wealth from the other 20%. Rojo felt quite certain that Goldstein represented only the greedy 20% who were set on oppressing and exploiting the 80%. In the 'one person—one vote' American democracy, Rojo knew he would win.

(6) Evening in Hyde Park, Chicago, Illinois

The wide-screen television was tuned in to the prime-time program on the 'Greed Free Network' or 'GFN,' just like most of the televisions in the Great Deal States.

Early in the program, scenes of American wealth and poverty from the 1930s and 1960s flashed across the screen.

Then came footage of the current year.

A caption read 'Great Deal New York' and the program showed scenes of wealth. A family danced on the lawn of a beautiful suburban home, celebrating with a big feast and washing their fancy new car.

A caption read 'Property Rights Connecticut' and the program showed scenes of poverty. A family wallowed in the garbage outside a burned-out home, crying in hunger.

The commentator appeared on the screen to deliver a conclusion. He lifted a bushy eyebrow and smiled wide, his teeth shining like piano keys. He summarized, "All Americans would be dirt poor without the restrictions on self-interested competition provided by the New Deal, the Great Society, and the Great Deal.

"Greedy competitive capitalist company owners would have reduced worker salaries to lower and lower levels until compensation was zero.

"At the same time, the greedy competitive capitalist company owners would have made working hours longer and longer until people worked 24 hours a day 365 days a year.

"And if that didn't leave any time to go shopping, it wouldn't matter a bit. The same greedy competitive capitalist company owners would have made prices of all goods so high that it would be impossible for anybody to buy anything.

"All apartments would be vacant and we would all live on the streets because greedy competitive landlords would make rent so expensive that no one could pay it.

"So we should thank the few presidents who believed in self-sacrifice for the purpose of building an equal society. Of course this includes the Founding Fathers George Washington and James Madison who had the original dream. And the more recent presidents who took action to make this dream come true: Franklin Roosevelt with the New Deal, Lyndon Johnson with the Great Society, and Roberto Rojo with the Great Deal.

"And we should fight the evil people who only care about themselves and want America to be a poor, dog-eat-dog, competitive prison instead of a rich, peaceful, egalitarian paradise: the people from the Property Rights Party and their heartless leader—DAVID GOLDSTEIN!"

This was the moment when David Goldstein jumped up from his chair and pushed the 'off' button on the television.

He stood next to the television and stared into the large sunken fireplace. He held back a scream as his face turned the same red color as his hair and his wide-collared shirt.

"This television propaganda campaign hurts me very deeply," he said in a rage. "I dedicated my entire career to the study of theoretical and applied economics so that I could live in a peaceful and prosperous world. I have developed an economic program that will bring maximum wealth to all of society. My program was not implemented, and the result is poverty. And now the GFN is blaming the poverty on me! These lies are absolutely disgusting. How can you stand working for the GFN?"

The only other person in the room, Maria Diaz, jumped up behind Goldstein and massaged his shoulders. The attractive Hispanic woman was significantly taller than he was. She was a brunette with olive skin that contrasted with his pasty complexion. The two friends were in their mid-forties and extremely accomplished in their fields. They had developed a close friendship over a decade in which their careers and therefore their lives intersected in Chicago and Washington, D.C. and elsewhere. But, their relationship had never grown into anything more than just a friendship.

Maria spoke softly into Goldstein's ear, "David, don't the voters receive some benefit from Rojo? In particular, the poor people? Rojo is promising to give everyone free cash and you're not. Your platform of open trade and enforcement of voluntary private contracts and government operating with a balanced budget might sound nice for rich people, but how can it help poor people?"

Goldstein began to relax from the massage. Although he was a small man, he did his best to stay fit and his shoulder muscles were feeling very good now. "Surely you are smart enough, Maria, to understand people must engage in productive work to create wealth. I want the American government to provide a framework of law and enforcement that will channel people's energy toward productive work. Do you really believe printing a trillion dollars in fresh cash and dumping it on the population can make us richer? Obviously, printing more cash without a corresponding increase in production can only result in inflation. And, since the Great Deal Party has actually stopped all production and set prices by edict at below-market levels, the result we are observing now is that no goods are available at all except through black-market barter."

"Of course it is not logical that we can become wealthier just by printing cash," replied Maria. "But is such extreme polarization necessary? Some people believe in redistributing everything and some people believe in redistributing nothing. How about redistributing half? Wouldn't that make everyone satisfied and bring peace?"

Calmed by the massage, Goldstein turned to face Maria. He noticed that the colors of her beautiful chestnut eyes and the neatly tailored suit that flattered her sensual figure were further enhanced by the natural hues of the room, including the carved wooden panels above her and moldings along the walls.

"Maria, think about what you are saying. If you go out on the street and a man points a gun at you and demands all your money, and you give him half of your money, is anyone going to be satisfied? Will you be satisfied? Will he be satisfied? Having gained money as a reward for his actions, won't the gunman be out doing the same thing the next day?"

"But David, what about socialist Sweden in the 1970's? The Swedish socialists weren't as poor as the Russian socialists."

"I agree that the Swedish socialists weren't as poor as the Russian socialists. But it is also good to remember that Swedish socialists were poor compared to Americans of Swedish descent."

"I see your point," conceded Maria. "I understand wealth must be created by people doing productive work. Printing cash and changing salaries and prices by edict cannot make people wealthy if people aren't producing goods and services anymore. But it must be possible to find a compromise …"

Goldstein turned away again and began pacing across the carpeting, noticing the attractive linear design. "This television program about how wealth is created by government and not by productive work is deceiving and you know it."

"David, don't worry so much about the GFN. There is no media censorship in America today. The only problem is that all the private media companies in the Great Deal States failed economically when the Great Deal Act became law. Relax and remember that viewers in the Great Deal States are able to receive programming flattering to you from private media companies in the Property Rights States, Canada, and Mexico.

"And you have to admit the footage aired tonight is worthy of voter discussion. We saw real households in Great Deal New York and Property Rights Connecticut. Sure, there must have been selection bias. But anyway, the voters are entitled to see this sort of information."

Goldstein was surprised to hear this. "Selection bias? The GFN must have found the luckiest family in New York and the unluckiest family in Connecticut to make that video. I have been in both states recently and I can say for certain that the people in New York are suffering terribly with the Great Deal Party and the people of Connecticut have been doing much better with the Property Rights Party. It is a shame the people of Connecticut are being forced to evacuate their state now …"

"Remember, I've been a professional television news anchor since long before the political shift occurred in America and the GFN is the only network still operating in my home city," said Maria. "I realize I could flee to the Property Rights States, or flee from the country entirely, and work for a private station. However, all my family and friends are in Washington and I refuse to leave no matter how bad things get. Plus, the $200,000 salary for GFN employees since we were merged with the Virginia National Guard is important to me. You know I must support my parents."

Goldstein stopped beside an elegant geometric wall lamp and again turned to face his friend. "Ha, ha, ha. The $200,000 premium salary that goes to all national guard employees, introduced by the Temporary Police State Act when Rojo realized that it was impossible for everyone to be on strike and that people who were not on strike had to receive double salaries in order to be motivated. This salary policy is an admission of the stupidity of the entire Great Deal Act. Rojo realized when his water faucet went dry and television turned off that some people actually had to work!

"And, even more ridiculous is the way the payout is

conducted for the $200,000 premium salaries for national guard employees and $100,000 standard salaries to everyone else. Since all the banks in the Great Deal States have shut, you must go to a government office to pick up the money— paid in worthless freshly printed hundreds with Rojo's picture on the front!"

"Okay, I will admit something," said Maria. "The fact that my salary, as a national guard employee, is double the regular salary received by the striking people and unemployed people, is not the main attraction to having a national guard job. Rather, the main attraction is the privilege of shopping in the special government stores that are the only stores stocked with goods these days.

"You should know I have always respected you for your integrity. The most important thing to me is truth. People have different opinions and that does not bother me. But a person who is deliberately dishonest will always be my enemy. I did not respect the capitalist candidates of the past who hid their plans for free trade and flexible hiring behind issues such as forcing prayer in schools and banning gay marriage. I remember that some supporters encouraged you to call your party the 'Christian Family Values Party' instead of the 'Property Rights Party' and you refused. I admire your insistence on having an honest campaign platform, even though you would be more popular with a false platform."

"My idea was to name the party the Property Rights Party because preservation of property is the purpose of government," said Goldstein. "This is a truism not because some theoreticians said so, but rather because human nature dictates so. If there is no preservation of property, then people are living in a state of nature. Civilization can only exist when property is protected. A government that does not protect property rights will collapse because it will not serve any purpose. The Founding Fathers of the United States based the whole government, including the Declaration of

Independence and the Constitution and the Bill of Rights, on this truism. Since production stopped and civil war broke out when the Great Deal Party abolished property rights, we have seen that the Founding Fathers were correct."

"Do you recall my idea for your campaign two years ago?" Maria said. "I suggested getting a male model to be the presidential candidate for the Property Rights Party. That is effectively what the Great Deal Party did and it worked for them."

Goldstein now stood in the center of the room with arms folded across his chest as he looked straight at Maria. "My running mate Professor Pradeesh Gupta is no male model," Goldstein said, smiling. "And yet the Property Rights Party carried Iowa in the last election in no small part because Pradeesh ran the Economics Department at University of Iowa!"

"Is that why you won in Iowa?" asked Maria as she moved closer. "Remember that your gubernatorial candidate in Iowa was absolutely gorgeous."

"We did not run Governor Paceman in Iowa because of his good looks! He happens to be a very capable executive and clear-headed on economic issues."

"Yeah but executive experience and understanding of economics are not what got 'Faceman' Paceman elected," said Maria. "I know this isn't perfect democracy as George Washington and James Madison had hoped, but it is practical reality with universal suffrage and television."

Goldstein turned toward a row of windows. He stared through the stained glass and across the street at the modernistic concrete construction with smashed out windows that used to house the University of Chicago business school. He noticed a lone looter dragging what must have been the last bit of furniture out of the building.

"I have had one of the most successful careers in America," explained Goldstein. "I rose to the pinnacle of university academics. I am the most accomplished economics professor in the country. I have earned millions of dollars through productive work and value-creating investment. I am the presidential candidate for one of the two major political parties.

"I achieved my success by following the path of integrity and honesty. Sure, there were times when I faced a temporary setback because a dishonest person cheated to get ahead of me. But in the long run, I have always prevailed. Since integrity and honesty have always served me well, I will continue to follow this path.

"Sure, it was disappointing to see the American people choose the wrong party in the last election thus devastating their own economy. However, I firmly believe in universal-suffrage democracy because I firmly believe that human beings have the capacity to learn from mistakes. The voters will not make the same mistake in this election that they made two years ago."

Maria put her hands back on his shoulders. "You will get clobbered on Tuesday. I don't think you deserve to get clobbered. But, anyway you will get clobbered. Rojo is an incredibly handsome man promising free cash for everyone. Mainstream voters love that. Also, a lot of capitalists have fled or been marched out of the country into Canada, Mexico, and the Caribbean. They can't vote on Tuesday. Also, Rojo will win in Connecticut. He will have 38 states and he will have the Bill of Rights repealed on Wednesday."

"It is too early to give up on democracy," insisted Goldstein. "Rojo will be voted out of office. I have seen reports indicating that mass starvation will begin within months. Almost all food production in the Great Deal States has been halted. Our military is blockading our own ports. And, people are using up their stashes of canned food. If it weren't for black marketeers smuggling looted white goods out of the Great Deal States to exchange for food from the

Property Rights States, everyone in the Great Deal States would be starving already.

"Voters must see that they will die unless they go back to capitalist government. It is impossible they could be so dumb not to understand that, no matter what the television programs are saying. The majority will vote for my Property Rights Party and begin a period of rule of law and widespread prosperity."

Maria stepped back toward the center of the room. "I hope you are right, David, but I doubt it. Anyway, I must jump in the van and get out to Midway Airport so that I can fly to White Plains Airport and take another van to the Great Deal Party headquarters. They offered to provide accommodation on-site which will make it much easier for me to prepare for the television spot tomorrow."

"In case I haven't told you already, I am impressed by your incredible assignment," mused Goldstein. "I can see how every television personality in America would love to be the commentator covering Roberto Rojo's final days before the election. Of course you deserve the honor since you were the person who broke the story about the bribe network in the Republican and Democratic Parties. Am I correct that you will be with Rojo in New York, Florida, and Virginia?"

Maria blushed. "You are correct. I will be the television commentator for all three events. I won't have the same level of celebrity enjoyed by the stars of 'Pirate Heroes' but I suppose this is the next best thing. And, I will do what I can to limit any bias in the format of the presidential election debate. I am very excited it will be at Mount Vernon."

Goldstein turned toward his friend, "See you on Monday at Mount Vernon. I will fly to Virginia already tomorrow. The historical home of George Washington should be an advantageous setting for the debate since my beliefs are exactly in line with the beliefs of Washington and Rojo's beliefs are exactly opposite."

Maria replied with a wink, "That is not what Rojo thinks!"

*

When Maria Diaz departed, David Goldstein sat down again on the straight-back wooden chair. He thought about how fortunate he was that the Frank Lloyd Wright Preservation Trust invited him to use the historic Robie House as the campaign headquarters of the Property Rights Party again for this second attempt to win the presidency. He loved the stylish look of the house and furniture, although he experienced difficulty sitting for long periods of time in the angular chairs, particularly on days like today when his small but strong body was sore from judo practice.

Two years ago, the location of Robie House had been convenient because of its proximity to the University of Chicago where he had been a professor. But, sadly, the university was gone.

There had been a mass exodus of educated professionals from Chicago when the Great Deal Act became law and the looting began. Many large institutions, such as the Chicago Mercantile Exchange, Chicago Board of Trade, and University of Chicago, shut down in Chicago and reopened in the Caribbean with reduced staff. However, the bulk of Illinois capitalists were now in Iowa, since that was the nearest state governed by the Property Rights Party. In fact most of the Property Rights Party staff was now in Iowa, leaving only a skeletal staff here at the official party headquarters.

The University of Chicago was now located in the British Virgin Islands and Goldstein was aware that some of his former colleagues were working on the new campus and would be enjoying tropical sunshine all winter. He found it more than a little ironic that talented people were fleeing from the United States, with an elected head of state, to the

British Virgin Islands, with a Crown-appointed governor. What was the point of having the Revolutionary War two centuries ago?

Two Chicago buildings, Robie House and Goldstein's own house, were spared from looting only because the Great Deal Party supported the concept of democracy and did not want properties associated with the Property Rights Party to be attacked. For the same reason, people like Goldstein who had formal positions within the Property Rights Party were excluded when the Illinois National Guard rounded up the capitalists who had not already fled into Iowa and marched them to Iowa by force. The Illinois National Guard put rings of soldiers around Robie House and Goldstein's house back in 2013 and the soldiers were still there.

Goldstein felt disturbed that the Great Deal States had changed from capitalist societies of peace and prosperity to socialist societies of violence and poverty.

He reflected on the election two years ago. How had things gone so wrong?

It was the first election for the new political parties after the blow-up of the Democratic and Republican Parties. Goldstein had not been surprised when Maria broke the story. Her program showed clear video evidence that an organized network of bribe funneling existed within both of those old political parties. Finally the special-interest-group spending and legislation of the past several decades became understandable.

Just after the blow-up, Goldstein had been approached by an influential business roundtable to form a new party for national politics. They selected him because of his unassailable record of honesty, his tremendous success as a banking consultant, and his status as the most brilliant academic economist in the United States. In summary, he was the most qualified American for the presidency. The roundtable was not concerned about his geeky appearance, short stature, and bachelorhood. He was then, and again now, the presidential candidate for his Property Rights Party.

Goldstein sighed. There was so much hope in that first election! America finally had a well-funded political party with a platform finely tuned to maximize the efficiency of the market economy.

Government spending would be slashed. Laws would be simplified. Tax rates would be reduced, although government revenue would increase as the economy grew. Protective tariffs would be eliminated.

Exports would grow for the good of producers. Imports would grow for the good of consumers. Obviously, there is no point selling goods to foreigners if you cannot use the earnings to buy goods from foreigners. If you always export and never import, then you are just giving goods away without getting anything back.

'Right to work' laws where employment contracts were voluntary and thus mutually beneficial would replace 'right to strike' laws where employers were prohibited from firing employees who refused to work. Productivity would soar as employees were allocated between companies in the optimal way to serve the marketplace.

It was clearly obvious, thought Goldstein, that the capitalist policies of the Property Rights Party would make the United States richer.

He thought of some historical examples where capitalist economies succeeded and socialist economies failed. The best examples kept an important variable constant—by comparing the same ethnic group under two systems.

He had studied the Cold War economies of West Germany and East Germany extensively. Capitalist-leaning West Germany was rich. Socialist-leaning East Germany was poor.

He had studied the economies of South Korea and North Korea extensively. Capitalist-leaning South Korea was rich.

Socialist-leaning North Korea was poor.

The examples of West Germany and South Korea were not the best, however, since those countries allowed labor unionists to extort money from consumers. If those countries had been more free, specifically if they gave the freedom to employers to fire unionized employees, they would have been richer.

This brought to mind the most stark example of all: the economic shift in Chile. Until 1973, Chile was ruled by socialist Salvador Allende and was the poorest country in South America with a population on the brink of starvation. Beginning in 1973, Chile was ruled by capitalist Augusto Pinochet and became the richest country in South America immediately after redistribution and price-control policies ceased and labor unions were shut down.

Goldstein knew that if his market-oriented policies could be implemented, the result would be increased prosperity for everyone in America and everyone in the world! But this was not what happened in 2012.

He remembered every detail of the grim saga. Rojo created class warfare by convincing the least wealthy 80% of the American population that they were extremely poor, despite the fact that even the poorest Americans were much richer than most people elsewhere in the world. Then, he said their 'poverty' was caused by the wealthiest 20% of the population, despite the fact that actually workers benefit tremendously from living in close proximity to rich people.

Rojo convinced the 80% that they had human rights to take everything from the 20%. He won the election.

Goldstein found the percentages interesting, because the 20% that was to be dispossessed was the same 20% that supported the Property Rights Party in the election. And, this 20% had paid 80% of taxes in the previous year. The election outcome would have been reversed if voting rights had been proportionate to taxes paid. But alas, this was not the case.

America in the Twenty-first Century suffered from the same "taxation without representation" issue that caused the Revolution in the Eighteenth Century.

He could see disaster all around: the economy shut down completely in the Great Deal States and the population on the brink of starvation. If Rojo won the upcoming election, it was impossible to imagine a pleasant future for America. Increased suffering would be the result.

But now, America had a chance to recover from the disaster. Surely, the voters must have learned from their mistake! Surely, the voters would not make the same mistake twice!

Goldstein stood up and grabbed his well-worn briefcase. It had sentimental value to him because he bought it with his first paycheck from University of Chicago many years earlier.

He walked down the stairs and said goodnight to the soldiers at the doorway. The walk home was two blocks. In the weeks following the signing of the Great Deal Act, the walk was dangerous with violent looters running everywhere. But nowadays the streets were mostly empty with little left to steal.

He marched along the sidewalk past burned-out homes toward his home, an ivy-covered, three-level, century-old mansion. It had been ordinary for the neighborhood when he started renting ten years earlier. But now, the home stood out since the neighboring homes had been reduced to piles of bricks and ashes.

He greeted the soldiers at his front gate. He walked through the garden that had not been kept up since the gardener went on strike a year earlier.

Goldstein stepped into his home and walked up the dusty stairs to the second level. Since his maid went on strike a year earlier, he had not been able to keep the entire house clean and therefore he only cleaned the library and master bedroom on the second level and the judo studio on the third level.

His hobby since childhood was judo and he had earned a black belt. He greatly enjoyed the physical fitness aspect of judo. And, another thing he liked about it was the police or military aspect. When he was growing up, his ambition was to become a City of Chicago police officer or a United States Marine. He had a strong sense of duty to punish thieves so that society could enjoy peace and prosperity. Obviously, if everyone who tried to steal something received immediate punishment, then people would not try to steal from the community in a destructive process but rather would try to earn from the community in a productive process.

As it turned out, Goldstein's body type was better suited to academics than combat. But he still enjoyed judo as a hobby.

Coming up to the second level, he stepped into the library and seated himself on his favorite cushioned reading chair. All around him he could see his collection. Thousands of books. Many were first editions of classic books in the areas of business management and economics. The library was his main indulgence: a reward for the productive work and profitable investing that he had done in his career. The judo studio upstairs was also an indulgence, although exercising up there had become less fulfilling since the trainer went on strike.

Relaxing in the soft chair, Goldstein thought back on his career. He had made a lot of money as a university professor and banking consultant. Since he had always been an honest and efficient worker, his employers had raised his salary repeatedly with the fear that otherwise he might get bid away by different employers. And, he had multiplied his salary earnings through wise investing. His stock portfolio was worth approximately $30 million two years ago.

His secret to successful investing was looking for companies with huge profit margins. The higher the profit margin, the better. No amount of profit was too much since more profit always indicated more benefit for himself and all of society provided the company was engaged in the efficient production of goods and services for consumers, rather than fraud or corruption.

Alas, the portfolio had been hit badly. When the Great Deal Act became law, employees gained the so-called 'right to strike' and every private company in the Great Deal States ceased to function immediately. Employees who refused to work and seized control of assets owned by other people were still entitled to full salaries while 'scab' employees who continued working were denied their salaries and arrested.

Goldstein's stock portfolio was not completely worthless. In fact, he was still wealthy, but much less so. The New York Stock Exchange, now operating from the British Virgin Islands near the University of Chicago, recognized his ownership of many shares. The value of these shares had plummeted because all corporate property within the thirty-seven Great Deal States had been nationalized. However, the remaining parts of the companies were not bankrupt because debts owed to residents of the Great Deal States were canceled and production and sales in the Property Rights States and in foreign countries continued.

One of Goldstein's favorite investments was Easy Cheap. Easy Cheap was the most profitable retailer in North America because of the wide selection of products available at low prices and the friendly, customer-oriented service. He had studied the backgrounds of senior managers and found that all had histories of high integrity. Also, he had studied the sophisticated logistics system of Easy Cheap which enabled efficient distribution throughout the chain.

The majority of Easy Cheap stores were in the Great Deal States and were now gutted junk heaps, stripped of goods and abandoned by staff. Only the stores in the Property Rights States and Canada still functioned. The stock had lost most, but not all, of its value.

Goldstein rose from the chair. He slid open a concealed panel in the wall and saw the stash of food cans he had hidden when the Great Deal Party won the election, correctly anticipating that the implementation of redistribution policy would cause civil war.

He moved aside some food cans to reveal stacks of hundred-dollar bills. He had the wisdom to withdraw some of his bank savings prior to the shut down of all of the banks in the Great Deal States. He counted out fifty bills and put them in his briefcase. The old bills pictured Franklin rather than Rojo and therefore had value.

Although the Great Deal Act suspended all rent payments, Goldstein considered it to be in his self-interest to continue paying the agreed rent to his landlord each month so that he could maintain his reputation for credibility. Remarkably, the elderly woman still resided nearby. He would seek her out in the morning before heading to his next campaign function.

He closed the wall panel and retired to the bedroom. Alone. Sadly, there had never been much romance in his life and he never found a wife. He wasn't the most handsome guy around, and his career dedication didn't leave time for singles bars. He thought it was a shame he never connected with the right woman because he knew he would make an excellent father based on his success mentoring many adoring university students. Perhaps the future would bring new opportunity.

He undressed and tucked himself into bed. He slept soundly and peacefully with a wonderful feeling in his soul because of the benefits he had caused himself and society through profitable investing.

(7) Evening flying over San Francisco Bay

Vice President Clarence Clark sat in his executive chair at the head of the ovular, walnut table in the main cabin on *Air Force Two*, hardly noticing the mild turbulence as he enjoyed a sip of wine.

It wasn't California wine, of course, since all California vineyards ceased production when the Great Deal Act was implemented and all wine inventories were looted.

Therefore, he was drinking Swiss wine purchased from a Swiss smuggler in exchange for Swiss francs. It wasn't the most expensive Swiss wine, but it was Clark's personal favorite. He much preferred the Amigne grape variety to the more-popular Chasselas grape variety.

Since he had some time alone, he reflected back on the painful experience of his original career being destroyed by socialists.

After graduating from college with a degree in mathematics, he worked as an actuary for an insurance company in his home state, Tennessee. He was extremely proud of this job. He often reminded himself that the insurance company had given a mathematics test to over one hundred applicants from his college, and he got the job because he got the highest score on the test.

He had a quick and logical mind and therefore he was talented as an actuary. He worked all day every day creating actuarial computer models and he enjoyed every minute. The company kept increasing his salary to ensure he would not be bid away by a competitor.

Numbers were so precise! Mathematics was so pure!

After several years of training and hard work, Clark

achieved the highest level of certification from the Actuarial Institute of Tennessee. It was the greatest day of his life.

He was soon promoted to a team leader position at the insurance company. For his first project as leader, his team calculated the general-liability insurance premium for Sherman Management Consulting, a firm that employed 2,000 women in the United States.

The firm owner and founder, Mr. Sherman, had a brilliant business strategy. He had determined that the market salary for qualified male management consultants was $100,000 per year compared with $80,000 for qualified female management consultants. Therefore, he could arbitrage this difference to undercut his competitors.

He went on an aggressive hiring binge to entice the 2,000 professionals. All across America, his recruiters found female consultants with $80,000 salaries and offered them $90,000 salaries.

Then, with this force of 2,000 women with $90,000 salaries, the firm offered equal service at lower cost compared with competitors that were paying $100,000 salaries to men. Sherman himself, the only man employed by his firm, received a salary of $1,000,000. He also distributed all profit to himself each year as dividends, and lawfully transferred that money out of the United States to an offshore trust. Sherman had explained to Clark that the money in the offshore trust was safe from frivolous lawsuits. Clark had wondered at the time, how frivolous could lawsuits be since it would be irrational for the United States to have a justice system like a random lottery?

Business went very well for Sherman Management Consulting. The firm and its clients thrived. The general-liability insurance premium was paid each year as agreed and Clark's boss was overjoyed with his work.

That was when disaster struck. The year was 2009.

A group of one hundred *pro bono* lawyers from the nonprofit organization "Socialists for Equality" filed a class-action lawsuit against Sherman Management Consulting.

After bribing one of the 2,000 female consultants to be a plaintiff, the *pro bono* lawyers sued Sherman Management Consulting on behalf of all of the female consultants. The lawsuit claimed they were victims of discrimination.

Clark remembered back to the day when he received a copy of the complaint and reviewed the figures.

The socialist lawyers had looked at the following salaries: $1,000,000, $100,000, $90,000, $80,000. They took the highest one and subtracted the lowest one, arriving at $920,000. Then, they multiplied this amount by 2,000 for the number of consultants. They tripled the result just for good measure. Thus, they arrived at a damage amount of $5,520,000,000.

They said this was the correct measure of the amount of financial suffering endured by the female consultants because of discrimination.

Clark started shaking and twitching as he sat on the airplane thinking about the idiocy of this calculation. He had a larger sip of the Swiss wine. The female consultants did not suffer financial damages. In fact, they made more money than they would have if Sherman never hired them!

Clark remembered laughing when he first heard about the lawsuit. It was so irrational! How could anyone argue such a ridiculous case and keep a straight face? And, why was this being undertaken by volunteers? Of course it was impossible that any court would award damages to the plaintiffs.

But the socialist lawyers did their magic. They only allowed poor and jealous people to be members of the jury. Then, the lawyers blabbed on for weeks with sob stories about the unfairness of inequality.

Clark had been sitting in the Tennessee court room watching when the jury delivered the verdict in 2010. Sherman Management Consulting was found guilty and liable for the full damage request.

Clark's insurance company was bankrupted by the judgment. Sherman Management Consulting was bankrupted by the judgment. All employees from both companies lost their jobs.

The assets of both companies were squandered in the bankruptcy process, and therefore the female consultants received payouts of less than one year of what their salaries had been. And, of course, the *pro bono* lawyers received nothing, as was their intention from the beginning.

Sherman, who had pulled down his pants and mooned the members of the jury when they delivered the court verdict, moved to the Caribbean where his trust was domiciled.

Clark's body convulsions intensified as he thought back to the pain from his final day of work. He remembered running around the office showing mathematical formulas to his colleagues to prove that his actuarial work was not incorrect. But anyway, he had to pack up his personal belongings and head home, just like everyone else at the insurance company.

As he slogged home on that sad day four years ago, he had called "Socialists for Equality" on his mobile phone. He asked the secretary why they destroyed two productive companies thus putting thousands of people out on the street. The secretary gave a remarkable explanation. She said they did this to alleviate poverty.

Alleviate poverty? By destroying productive companies? That made no sense whatsoever. These "Socialists for Equality" were the dumbest people on Planet Earth! Clark had pledged revenge against the socialists on that day. He would punish them for their irrationality. He would rescue America in the process.

Clark turned his attention back to the present. He finished his wine and put the empty glass on the table. Then, he looked out the window of *Air Force Two*. Three thousand meters below him was San Francisco Bay. He had asked the pilot to do a flyover before landing at Oakland Airport.

Although the sun had set, and the electricity was off in the urban areas in accordance with the rolling blackout policy of the California National Guard, Clark was able to see the Bay because of the lights from ships going in and out past the wreckage of the Golden Gate Bridge.

He assumed the ships going out were former United States Navy vessels now operated by the California National Guard. The fleet included many obsolete vessels that were previously designated for scrapping. Since the function of the military was now to attack civilian cargo vessels to enforce the Great Deal import blockade, every armed ship was useful.

He assumed the ships coming in were oil tankers from Russia. This oil was the only legal import in Great Deal America. The tankers were bound for the refineries at Richmond, Rodeo, Benicia, and Martinez, all of which were now run by the California National Guard.

Clark laughed when he thought about the self-destructive stupidity of the socialists. They were always spreading propaganda about how capitalism was evil because, under capitalist government, the environment was damaged in the process of providing goods to consumers.

But under socialism, the environment was damaged even more and the consumers didn't even get anything in return! All of the refined oil products were for military use and the function of the military was to oppress the citizens.

He had been working four years on his ultimate scheme for the socialists. He had put up with their irrationality long enough. In fact, he could barely stand it anymore. But, he was relieved to be so close to completion. It was difficult for him to imagine how anyone would be able to stop him.

He looked at the framed photo on the ovular table. It was a small and cozy cottage nestled deep in the forest in

Tennessee, far from any cities. He had purchased it back when he got his first promotion as an actuary. The secret cottage was well stocked with computer equipment and had its own power generator. Under the cottage was a cellar filled with fine alcoholic beverages. He was eager to finish what he had to do to defend himself and his country from the socialists. Then, he would move back to his simple Tennessee home and drop out of public life completely.

Saturday, November 1, 2014
(8) Morning at the Sea Hotel and Spa, Arabia

Captain Jack Cannon had a good view through the helmet visor and cockpit canopy of the shimmering Red Sea and towering 3,000-meter peak of the *Jebel Soudah*—the 'Black Mountain'—as he eased the *Flying Yankee* into its landing vector.

He had a great deal of experience landing in dangerous locations and therefore the easy, sweeping landing at the Sea Hotel and Spa did not provide any challenge to him. The landing strip was 3,000 meters long, designed to handle the largest airplanes in the world. This was not in anticipation of commercial jets with hundreds of tourists, but rather in anticipation of tycoon guests having private planes so large that they would require the full length.

Jack was determined to succeed with his first assignment as a member of the Democracy Society. The socialists had attacked his family and his property. And now he had the opportunity to contribute to a group effort to combat the socialist threat. His actions to defend himself would have an additional beneficial effect of helping America.

However, he did have a reservation about one aspect of the assignment. He was concerned about the woman waiting for him here in Arabia. She was not a soldier. She was a journalist. Would she be tough enough to handle a dangerous mission?

And, she was not American. She was Russian. Everything Jack read about current events in Russia indicated to him that the Russian people had a culture of extreme and masochistic dishonesty and corruption, much worse than the people of other nations.

Was it really a good idea to join forces with this mystery woman on a mission where the stakes were so high?

At this point, he was determined to carry out the mission as instructed. He acknowledged to himself that the Democracy Society had to conduct specific scientific research and needed Doctor Zaicev for that and the Democracy Society had to collect certain intelligence from Russia and needed Valentina Zaiceva for that.

However, Jack made a mental note to be cautious. He knew he would be able to rely on himself in a life-or-death situation. But could he rely on Valentina?

The jet rolled to a gentle stop along the brand-new, smooth-as-silk, landing strip. When the cockpit canopy opened, Jack saw a rolling stairway pushed up to the side of the aircraft. Servants in exotic Arabian uniforms helped him climb from his seat and descend the short staircase to where a beautiful carpet had been placed.

He removed his helmet and took a deep breath. He expected hot desert air, but instead drew in cool air blown toward him from a tall air-conditioning device with solar panels which had been wheeled up next to the carpet.

He accepted a fresh juice from one of the attractive female attendants wrapped in colorful silk.

Then, he walked forward toward a curious vehicle. The tall buggy with a clear plastic bubble for a passenger compartment was open, and he hopped in.

He relaxed on the plush couch in the air-conditioned vehicle as the bubble closed automatically. He could see the dark-skinned driver, neatly clad in a white robe, in the rear-view mirror. "Captain Cannon, welcome as a guest of the King to the Sea Hotel and Spa. The first eight-star hotel in the world! Please know that you are just on time. The press conference will begin in an hour."

The driver maneuvered the buggy along a raised and carpeted pathway into a cluster of black tents that were the size of houses, arranged in a beautiful oasis of palm trees. Jack guessed there were three hundred residential tents in the compound.

The driver pulled up next to a tent and Jack exited the buggy, still in his flight suit. Servants dressed in white robes drew open the entrance flaps to the tent, revealing a colorful interior. One of the servants switched on an air-conditioning device to keep Jack cool in between the buggy and the tent.

"I will get ready for the press conference as fast as possible," Jack told the buggy driver. "Please wait here."

"Your wish is my command, sir."

Jack approached the entrance and noticed a mat for shoes near the door. He removed his flight boots and placed them on the mat.

He stepped into the tent to find a large and opulent entry room. He was amazed by what the designers had created in this desert tent. Floors and walls were covered with gorgeous hand-woven carpets and tapestries, some with tribal marks and some with Islamic designs. Each carpet looked to be the lifetime's work of a master artisan.

A framed mahogany structure divided the space into rooms, with dressing and eating areas below and, just visible on the upper level of the structure, a massive bedroom suite and bath area open to the stars.

The aromatic smoke of frankincense wafted from brass pots and distributed around the room, proving to be a source of pure pleasure. Jack now understood why ancient camel caravans from southern Arabia found it worthwhile to spend years bringing frankincense across thousands of kilometers of desert for export to the West.

He also noticed the aroma coming from a hearth in the center of the entrance room. Servants prepared coffee using a brass pot over a fire. One servant presented Jack with a

73

freshly brewed coffee as another servant used a pestle and mortar to prepare beans for the next pot.

As Jack stood and sipped the delicious coffee, he was immediately surrounded by a team of tailors taking measurements. He guessed they were from India, Bangladesh, or Pakistan. "We have been instructed to create business attire for this morning's press conference, comfortable sportswear for the middle of the day, and evening wear for tonight's reception," said the lead tailor. "The press conference attire shall be completed in half an hour. You will have time to bathe and shave upstairs."

Jack unzipped his flight suit as he followed a servant up the mahogany stairs toward the bath.

When Jack stepped out of the tent half an hour later, he felt like a new man. He was clean, fresh, and well-dressed. He had replaced the flight suit with a custom-fitted tan linen business suit and a blue tie selected by the tailors to match the glacier hue of his eyes. Every detail, right down to the bespoke leather shoes, was perfect.

The buggy driver took Jack to the larger and equally beautiful Bedouin tent where the press conference was already underway.

*

Valentina Zaiceva sipped a fresh juice in the huge tent that would soon be venue for the King of Arabia's announcement of the opening of the Sea Hotel and Spa.

She had a good view as she strolled through the mingling international journalists since she was taller than most of them, even the men. She was looking out for her American contact. He had been described as a tall and athletic 35-year-old with a blond crew cut.

She needed to meet the American agent to give him the file of information that she had collected from Russia for the

Democracy Society. Hopefully, the eventual release of this information would help to repair the defective democracies in Russia and America.

However, she was skeptical about the man who would arrive. Although her father, secretly employed by the mysterious Democracy Society for several years, always spoke highly of that organization, she still had reservations.

Valentina hoped for the best. She hoped her partner on this mission would be smart, and therefore honest and dependable. However, it was hard for her to get excited about meeting someone new when every man she ever met, with the sole exception of her father, had turned out to be a disappointment.

She raised her hands to flip her long blond hair away from her eyes and that was when she noticed two Russian men standing nearby.

They looked like brothers, perhaps twins, in their late 20's. Both had shiny, bald heads. Both were very muscular, probably from heavy steroid use. Both wore ridiculous silk-and-foil matching lavender suits.

The lavender suits, incredibly, were not the most gaudy adornment on these Slavic thugs. Valentina could not help but stare at their boots. The brothers wore matching boots covered with shiny holograms which changed between 3-D images depending on the angle of the viewer. The final images were fluttering pirate flags.

As Valentina stepped closer, she wondered if her business suit was not conservative enough since the men whistled as they did lewd head-to-toe stares at her body.

She read identification tags indicating that the brothers were named Vladislav and Vyachislav and worked for the Independent Russian Press, which meant they were anything-but-independent flunkies from corrupt Russian President Ivan Ivanov's media company.

"*Dobry den*," said Valentina.

Vladislav spoke in Russian as he read Valentina's name tag out loud. "Valentina Zaiceva, Informed Voter News Service. We know who you are."

"Are you a fan of my work?" Valentina asked in Russian. "I am happy some people in Russia are reading my articles about corruption."

"You exposed the Moscow Microchip fraud some years ago," replied Vladislav. "Our impoverished pensioner parents and grandparents put every kopek they had into Moscow Microchip securities when Ivan Ivanov had agents selling those papers on street corners. Our family lost everything in the fraud—all stolen by Ivanov."

Valentina felt saddened, "I am very sorry to hear that. So I assume your family did not vote for Ivanov when he won his landslide election after the fraud was revealed?"

Suddenly Vyachislav blurted out, "Are you kidding? We love Ivanov! We all voted for him! I had to carry granny to the voting station because she pawned her wheelchair to buy stock in Moscow Microchip. Ivanov is a very smart and strong businessman since he stole so much money from so many people. I understood from your article that Moscow Microchip never existed at all and Ivanov just put all of the cash from selling the fake stock straight into his pocket. He is a great man! Russia needs a leader like him!"

Valentina's mood instantly switched from sadness to shock. "Again, I am very sorry to hear that. Not so sorry to hear that he robbed you but sorry that we all vote in the same democratic country since you have an irrational love of thieves and I have a rational hatred of thieves."

Vladislav scowled as he spoke. "The Independent Russian Press offered money to you last year to shut down your Informed Voter News Service and join with us. You should have taken the offer."

"You would have lots of cash now," added Vyachislav. "And, you would have President Ivanov on your side."

Valentina put her hands on her hips as she lectured the brothers. "I stand by my decision. I do not want to destroy my journalism career by churning out false propaganda articles for your corrupt organization. Obviously, my credibility would be ruined. And, I am not interested in having President Ivanov on my side. He is a liar and a cheater. Only idiots would join a team led by such a man."

Vladislav sneered. "Look, lady. The Independent Russian Press is a responsible media organization because we work for President Ivanov and we properly identify him as a businessman in our articles. Your Informed Voter News Service is an irresponsible media organization because your articles identify Ivanov as a violent thief."

"Ivanov is a violent thief," Valentina replied with confidence. "All of his wealth was stolen. None of it was earned."

Vyachislav shook his head slowly. "There are two things you should know about President Ivanov. First, he isn't a violent thief. Second, if you say he's a violent thief then he'll use his stolen money to pay his assassins to kill you."

"I run the Informed Voter News Service and Ivanov is a violent thief and therefore the Informed Voter News Service will continue to describe him as a violent thief," said Valentina. "The Informed Voter News Service will not describe him as a businessman because he is not a businessman."

Vladislav frowned, then his eyes lit up and he changed the subject. "Hey babe, why don't you come back with us after the press conference and have a vodka party in our suite." He made a pumping movement with his pelvis.

Valentina cringed and turned away. She noticed a handsome man walking toward her. He was blond with blue eyes and strong features. He looked great in his tan linen suit and blue necktie. Valentina spotted the golden badge on his chest and breathed a sigh of relief. It was the wild turkey badge of the Democracy Society.

Valentina waved to the man. He came closer.

"Thank you for the invitation," Valentina said to the brothers in loud English. "However my husband and I will go scuba diving today. No vodka for us."

With that, she grabbed the tall Westerner's arm and pulled him next to her.

"That's a shame for you, lady," said Vladislav, also in English. "We could have had a good time together."

"My name is Jack," said the Westerner to the brothers. "I am impressed by your English. Have you lived in America before?"

Vyachislav laughed, "The volunteer director of the Russian shelter where we grew up with our poor parents and grandparents was American. She spoke English, like when she yelled at us for beating her and lighting fires in the shelter."

Jack's smile drooped into a frown. "Why did you beat her and light fires in the shelter?"

Vladislav answered, "The shelter lady was nice, and therefore weak. Since she was weak, we were cruel to her."

Vyachislav added, "It is the opposite way with President Ivanov. Ivanov is cruel, and therefore strong. Since he is strong, we are completely devoted to him."

Jack confronted the brothers as he raised a fist. "What you just said is totally stupid. Do you mean I should hit you and steal your money and then you will be devoted to me?"

Valentina pulled on Jack's arm. She switched back to Russian language. "The King's presentation will begin soon. My husband and I will go to find our seats."

As Valentina led Jack away, she could understand the brothers calling out in Russian.

Vyachislav spoke first. "Valentina, you're a coward fool do-gooder fighting against corruption! If you were brave and smart, then you'd join the criminals, like we did! Liars win and

78

honest people lose. Always trust the liars!"

Vladislav spoke next. "Vyachislav is wrong, Valentina. I know what's going on. You are corrupt yourself! But you are a hypocrite because you pretend like you are a do-gooder. You make me sick!"

Just then, a guard at the front of the room made an announcement. The guard, dressed in a neatly pressed khaki uniform with a bright green beret, called out, "His Royal Highness King Abyad is arriving. Please find your seats."

Valentina turned to the man next to her as they sat in the front row near the podium. So, this was the man sent from the Democracy Society to be her partner. He was certainly good looking. And, she was impressed that he was a member of an organization that was actively fighting to restore proper republican government to his country.

However, Valentina had her doubts. She had learned long ago that most men were worthless. Most men were petty factionalists concerned with narrow special-interests. Since they did not live their lives in rational accordance to logical principles, they wound up frustrated failures. Why was it so difficult to find rational men? Such men were bound to succeed as a result of rational behavior. But, alas, such men were exceedingly rare.

*

Jack Cannon looked at Valentina Zaiceva seated next to him. She was tall with a sexy, lean body. Her emerald-green eyes were widely spaced and slanted like a lynx. Her facial features were the most beautiful he had ever seen. He surmised that she might be smart also since her dad was a famous scientist and she was an investigative journalist. Intelligence would imply integrity as well. Anyway, he still had doubts and reservations about her.

He turned toward the center aisle and podium. A phalanx

79

of uniformed guards wearing bright green berets escorted King Abyad into the conference tent, along the aisle, and onto the stage behind the podium. The King was an impressive sight, with long flowing white robes and a headdress ornamented with patterned gold leaf along the fringes.

The King smoothed his well-groomed dark beard with one hand while adjusting the microphone with the other.

He lifted his head to reveal powerful, piercing eyes shining from below the embroidered rim of the *shimagh* headdress. "Distinguished representatives of the world press, thank you for accepting my invitation to the grand opening celebration for the Sea Hotel and Spa—the first eight-star hotel in the world.

"When I became the leader of Arabia two years ago, it was not because I got elected by telling lies to voters. And I did not take control because of violent acts on my part. Rather, I owe my ascension to the throne of the Kingdom of Arabia to my birth. My great great grandfather was the hereditary ruler in a region of Arabia prior to the takeover of most of the peninsula by the Al Saud family in 1934, at which time my family went into exile in the United States. Now that I have been crowned as the king, it is in my long-term self-interest to promote rule of law in Arabia so that the people will prosper and my descendants will be the future kings.

"During the Saudi years, the economic focus of the government was on oil production. The tourism sector was not developed. Tourism happens to be my specialty. I am a graduate of the hotel management school at Cornell University in the United States and I worked in hotel management in Dubai until I was notified that I was to be crowned King of Arabia. We have opened the country to visa-free travel for guests from many countries. We have relaxed the restrictions on property ownership by foreign investors. Therefore we are witnessing a surge of investment in tourism infrastructure."

Jack paid attention to every word. He had read a lot about the King and accepted that in many societies, monarchical government was superior to democratic government for the purpose of promoting peace and prosperity.

The King stepped to the side of the podium and approached the audience in a friendly manner, holding the microphone in his hand. "The opening of the Sea Hotel and Spa, the most luxurious hotel in the world, represents a huge economic achievement for Arabia as our nation heals from the Democracy Experiment.

"As the world witnessed, Arabia experienced tragic times during the one-year experiment in democracy which replaced the former Saudi Arabian kingdom with a parliamentary democracy. The ignorant, factional, left-wing, micro-populist, ethnocentric representatives who got elected to the democratic parliament only cared about handouts for narrow special-interest groups and corruption opportunities for themselves. None of them cared about protection of property and equal rights under the law for the whole nation. The result was widespread violent destruction which did not stop until we re-established peace by abolishing democracy.

"Of course the first step in healing our land was to declare void all acts of ethnic, racial, class, and religious discrimination and economic control, favoritism, and isolationism which had been passed by the parliament.

"The next step was to order the execution, decapitation by sword, of the entire parliament and all lobbyists. The televised executions had the highest viewer ratings of any program in the history of our nation.

"Since the transition from democracy back to monarchy, our economic program has been an outstanding success. Investment is pouring in. The people of Arabia are becoming more and more prosperous, despite the suspension of trade with 37 states of the United States."

The King wore a proud expression. He scanned his eyes across the audience before continuing.

"I am pleased to be opening the Sea Hotel and Spa, which is the largest investment to date in the tourism sector in Arabia. The thousands of shareholders who invested in the Sea Hotel and Spa Corporation are an international consortium, including Europeans and Japanese as well as Arabs. What the investors and employees have created is a marvel of modern hospitality science featuring luxury guest tents plus social and conference facilities in a unique resort. Recreational activities include scuba diving on reefs teaming with colorful sea life, horseback riding in mountain forests, falconry in expansive deserts, and golfing in a lush estuary course designed by the finest golf architects from Spain and Japan. All recreation has been designed to minimize negative environmental impact and a breeding program has been introduced to bring certain local bird and animal species back from the verge of extinction because the corporation will benefit financially by promoting a clean and beautiful environment.

"The investors spent two billion euros developing the resort, forecasting an unlevered yield of 21% from the start. Since modern resorts in countries that protect property rights currently sell at a market yield of 14%, this means that the resort was worth three billion euros upon completion. Therefore the investors created one billion euros of additional wealth immediately, before the resort began to operate."

Jack was impressed by the excellent return that the hotel investors forecasted. He understood that the more profitable an investment was, the more value was being created for society. He became increasingly motivated to fight to restore property rights in Connecticut so that he could resume making capital investments at his farm.

The King was again speaking from behind the podium. "Of course in a universal-suffrage democracy, where workers

82

by law can extort money from their employers by refusing to work and blocking access to private property, the project would not have been feasible. No one would have invested because they would know that profit would never materialize. And therefore no jobs would have been created.

"Under my rule, all foreigners applying for work permits in the kingdom must sign acknowledgments that selling their labor to whoever pays the highest wage is lawful, but blocking private property to extort money is theft and is punished by immediate mandatory beheading.

"This acknowledgment requirement has not slowed down immigration at all. In fact, the rate of immigration is increasing. All of the non-managerial jobs at the hotel are held by foreigners, coming entirely from democratic countries in south Asia where unions and strikes are legal. These workers have fled their home countries, where few jobs are available and salaries are very low, to come to Arabia where jobs are plentiful and salaries are bid higher and higher every year. Of course the irony is that these workers have effectively forced themselves to leave their own home countries by voting for socialist politicians. We are happy to have them working here on mutually voluntary and thus mutually beneficial employment contracts, but you can be assured these people will never be permitted to vote in my country!

"Adam Smith wrote that the purpose of government is to protect the rich from the poor. We abide by this wisdom in Arabia, and as a result the so-called 'poor' in our country are richer than 99% of people in the world. We have the most unequal distribution of wealth in the world, and at the same time we have the most prosperous working class.

"I am maximizing economic freedom, maximizing profit for investors, maximizing protection of property rights, and giving people the right to work instead of the right to strike. Arabia has the fastest growing economy in the world because of this policy.

"Enjoy the hospitality of the Sea Hotel and Spa and witness the rebuilding of a nation."

The King stepped back from the podium and descended from the stage with a circle of guards around him.

Jack, having enjoyed the speech, stood and applauded enthusiastically. He noticed that Valentina did the same.

The King and guards stopped at the first row of seats. The guards ushered Jack and Valentina into the circle next to the King.

The King lifted and kissed Valentina's hand as he whispered, "Ms. Zaiceva, welcome to Arabia and I hope you have a nice stay. I have read some of your anti-corruption journalism work and I am impressed. I wish you luck in changing the way democracy works in Russia. I have been in contact with the Democracy Society and therefore I am aware that you have a file for me."

Valentina's eyes sparkled, "Your Majesty, it is a pleasure and an honor to attend this presentation and best wishes for success with the further development of your nation."

The King turned toward Jack, "And you must be Captain Jack Cannon. Welcome to Arabia. The Director of the Democracy Society informed me that you would be with Ms. Zaiceva. Say hello to the Director for me when you are back in the States. He and I know each other well, not only from our official duties in the United States Armed Forces during the Gulf Wars, but also from some fun times we had on breaks in Dubai. I do not know the details about the Democracy Society, but I believe its responsibility as the property manager at Mount Vernon is only a cover for a more important covert responsibility."

Jack replied, "It is nice to meet you and thank you for your hospitality. I have read a lot about your policies, but reading is no substitute for actually visiting here to see the economic development taking place. Best wishes for future success."

Valentina raised her mobile phone and spoke in a hushed tone. "Your Majesty, if you and Jack both hold out your mobile phones, I will send you an encrypted file by infrared. It is the findings of my research into the Trans Pacific Trading Company, the intermediary between the United States and Russia for all oil trades. It is well known that the United States is paying for this oil with all of the foreign currency and precious metals that used to comprise the reserves of the Federal Reserve System. It is also well known that Russia sells oil to Trans Pacific for 100 euros per barrel and the United States buys oil from Trans Pacific at 200 euros per barrel. The information I found indicates that the true owners of the intermediary, hiding behind a nominee owner, are Russian President Ivanov and American Vice President Clark themselves. I could not send this file to you over the Internet because of security concerns."

Jack and the King held out their mobile phones and received the file.

The King kissed Valentina and shook hands with Jack. "Thank you for the information. I will give it to my forensic financial experts right away to determine where the stolen money has gone and how to recover it and return it to the victims, the American and Russian people. This effort could destabilize the corrupt power structures in America and Russia, although experience has shown that most voters are tolerant and even supportive of corrupt politicians.

"I understand we have a critical deadline. If nobody stops the Great Deal Party before Wednesday, then the Bill of Rights will be repealed and the Great Deal Party will have unlimited power to implement destructive policies. Fatalists are expecting the worst—another landslide for Rojo and Clark followed by repeal of the Bill of Rights. But I believe determined individuals can fight to produce a better outcome."

(9) Afternoon at the Red Sea coast by the Sea Hotel and Spa

Jack Cannon let out a relaxed breath as he absorbed the view of the scenery. It was a beautiful afternoon on the Tihamah, the strip of desert that separated the Red Sea from the mountains here on the west coast of Arabia. There was not a cloud in the sky and the bright mid-afternoon sunshine lit up the sparkling sand between the turquoise water and the sharp granite mountains. A light breeze kept the air moving, but not so much as to disturb the sand.

He heard Valentina Zaiceva's voice behind him. "Ready for action?"

He spun around and saw that Valentina had joined him on the wooden platform suspended above the sand dunes. She wore a light-blue cotton training suit that matched his, not surprisingly since the hotel provided the wardrobe.

"I'm ready," said Jack. "I am told this walkway leads down to the sea and the boat station. Follow me."

They walked along the platform over a row of gentle wind-softened dunes and eventually arrived on the beach.

Jack was happy that several free hours were available for recreation. He was an avid scuba diver, however he had never visited the Red Sea until now. As it so happened, Valentina was also a diver and therefore he had an opportunity to get to know her better as they enjoyed a dive together.

Once on the beach, on the wet sand by the water, the couple paused to take in the view of the Red Sea stretched out before them. To the left, the shimmering sea was interrupted by the mysterious sand-colored coral humps of the Farasan Islands. To the right, the sea seemed to go on forever since the coast of Eritrea was not visible from this distance. The wide rolling swells on the water were barely noticeable, so conditions seemed excellent for scuba diving.

Jack and Valentina removed their matching leather sandals and made their way along the beach until they came to a row of twenty boats. The rigid inflatable boats, or RIBs, were all new. Each was a four-seater with a shiny outboard engine. Everything was colored bright orange for safety. Jack loved fast cruising in a RIB. This would be an enjoyable afternoon.

An attendant, smartly dressed in a long white robe with a checkered-red *ghutrah* folded on his head, approached. His broad smile revealed bright white teeth against sun-darkened skin. "Good afternoon sir and madam. Welcome to the boat station for the Sea Hotel and Spa. Please know that the continental shelf extends from the shore approximately 20 kilometers in this area. The depth of the water approaches 50 meters until the edge of the shelf, where the depth drops off to 600 meters. The shelf is ideal for snorkeling and scuba diving, with beautiful coral reefs and abundant marine life."

"That sounds wonderful," said Valentina.

"Would you like to make use of a boat? And will you be needing snorkeling or scuba gear?"

"We would like a boat with scuba gear," said Jack. "Which one should we take?"

The attendant led Jack and Valentina to one of the RIBs. "This boat is loaded up with scuba gear for two. I trust you are both certified divers."

Jack nodded.

The attendant pointed across the water. "If you motor in that direction, you will come to a long and diverse stretch of reef approximately 1000 meters from the shore. The GPS system on this boat is already programmed for a coral feature called Urchin Tower just on the periphery of that reef. I recommend it as the highlight of the near reef, only surpassed if you arrive earlier in the day and give yourself time to motor out in a larger craft to the underwater national park encompassing the Farasan Islands.

"Once over Urchin Tower, you will find the tower peak five meters down. The sandy bottom is fifty meters down, however I recommend not going deeper than twenty meters."

The attendant strapped small consoles onto Jack and Valentina's forearms. "The resort has been designed for maximum privacy, even while diving. As a substitute for having a professional diver and boat pilot accompany you to the dive site, we offer these panic-button consoles. A scuba rescue team is always on standby and can respond in seconds if you press the button. We have medical facilities including a re-compression chamber on site. We have thought of everything in the creation of the resort.

"The electric engines with GPS minimize environmental impact. The smart engine will find the destination by the most efficient path, then hover over the reef without dropping anchor in order to avoid damaging the coral. There is only one potential problem with the engines. The batteries contain a highly potent acid and therefore the old batteries must be sent to a special recycling plant.

"And, please know we will soon expand our diving offerings. The King is bringing his yacht, the *Royal Arabia*, the second longest pleasure yacht in the world, for scuttling in an area with a sandy bottom not far from the beach. He already had all of the hazardous materials removed from the yacht. He says the yacht, which he inherited, is a fuel-guzzling monstrosity that serves no function other than pointless conspicuous consumption. He says it embarrasses him and that is why he wants to allocate it toward a new purpose—a protective habitat for rare marine life and an attraction for considerate scuba tourists."

"That's wonderful," said Valentina. "I like the King more and more as I learn new things about him. And, you can be assured we will be responsible divers and we intend only to view, not disturb, the natural environment."

Jack nodded approvingly as he pushed the orange boat knee-deep into the calm water. He helped Valentina aboard and then climbed in himself. He pushed a button to start the engine. The boat began to power and steer itself toward Urchin Tower.

Valentina removed her training suit revealing her fit body clad in a bikini with an athletic cut. Jack noticed the nice tone of her legs and abdomen as she leaned over. He wondered how she could have time to keep in such great shape with her busy journalism career.

"Wow. It is boiling hot out here!" said Valentina. "I am so happy for the freedom of diving in my bikini today. This is a welcome change from my last dive trip, when I was confined in a heavy drysuit while diving under the ice off Archangel with my Moscow dive club."

Jack was impressed. It was not easy to find a woman tough enough to stick her toe in the water off Archangel, let alone take a vacation diving up there.

He took off his own training suit revealing swim trunks with the same color. The sun felt nice on his broad, muscular back.

As the boat approached Urchin Tower, Jack inspected the scuba gear. "I see they have the latest high-tech gear for us. Double-pressure, half-size, titanium tanks. Gaugeless, except for plasma readouts directly in front of us on the masks."

Valentina began to put on her mask and fins. "Yeah, this is a good step up from the second-hand Russian military gear that I'm used to!"

The boat stopped moving and the GPS indicated that they were floating just above Urchin Tower.

Having put on and adjusted his fins and mask, Jack slid his arms through the buoyancy vest attached to his tank and helped Valentina to do the same. Both inflated their vests and put their regulators in their mouths. Valentina gave the 'O.K.' hand signal and both rolled back into the warm sea.

Jack felt slightly bothered by the distant speck of orange he spotted—coming from the shore toward Urchin Tower—just before he submerged. It seemed some other tourists were in a RIB and perhaps would be diving nearby. Oh, well, that's how it was at tourist resorts. He was thankful that Valentina and he would have the tower to themselves for at least thirty minutes before the new divers descended. That was much better than the situation at more heavily trafficked scuba tourist areas at larger resorts where over a hundred divers might be exploring the same area.

Jack smiled and looked Valentina in the eyes as they descended into the clear blue water, holding their noses to pressurize their ears on the way down to Urchin Tower.

The wide tower was a formation of hard coral with fascinating irregularities including indentations, protrusions, caves, and shelves providing myriad hiding places for sea life.

The colors of the coral were bright and varied. Jack found the purple, red, and yellow gorgonian fan corals to be the most beautiful.

Dropping to twenty meters, the maximum depth of their planned dive, Jack and Valentina found themselves engulfed by a school of countless striated fusiliers. What a dazzling sight. The silvery fish with light blue stripes surrounded them for a few seconds before moving past, leaving Jack and Valentina with a perfect view of a variety of reef fish swimming near the tower.

A shiny blue parrot fish pecked at the coral on one side as several cute clownfish played in the multicolored anemones just in front. A group of stunning yellowbar angelfish swam gracefully on the left.

Jack gave a quick 'O.K.' signal to Valentina who replied with her own 'O.K.' signal, then Jack pointed the way for the couple to begin a clockwise spiral around the tower, which they planned to enjoy in detail for the duration of their forty-minute dive.

Jack kicked repeatedly to propel himself alongside the tower. He loved diving with this hi-tech equipment, compact and with few tubes getting in the way.

Valentina glided alongside Jack, fluttering kicks produced by well-toned thighs and calves.

Jack became momentarily distracted by Valentina's gorgeous streamlined form before shifting his attention to movement further from the coral tower. A giant sea turtle was visible. As the turtle approached, Jack realized it was of the endangered hawksbill variety. He enjoyed watching the turtle lumber through the water on its life-long struggle to find its next meal.

Jack noticed Valentina gesturing toward a nook in the tower. He looked in the nook and saw a moray eel sticking its head out. He was amazed Valentina spotted the eel because its coloring blended in closely with the surroundings.

Jack and Valentina kept playfully pointing and smiling as they swam about. Jack was impressed that each time he found an example of highly camouflaged marine life, Valentina matched him by finding another interesting creature. He had met a woman with some common interests not only in government but also in outdoor recreation.

Jack noticed a flash in the corner of the plasma display on his mask lens. It was time to begin a slow ascent.

Finishing a revolution around the coral mass, Jack pointed out two lionfish resting on a shelf of fire coral otherwise covered with sea urchins. The sea urchins alone could do quite a bit of damage to any human who touched the coral shelf with bare skin. The black venomous spines of the urchins could cause hours of redness and pain.

But the urchins were a minor concern compared with the lionfish, each with eighteen dramatically flared spikes having the power to inflict excruciating pain on a level most humans would find incomprehensible. Jack could remember that level of pain as a result of a dive long ago in Florida when he was stabbed by a single lionfish spike which broke off in his arm.

He had tremendous respect for the lionfish and approached them with caution to admire the dangerous beauty of their red and white-striped football-sized bodies.

That was when he spotted the glint of something that had fallen into a cave that snaked into the tower behind the fire coral shelf. Concentrating on the orange object, he identified it as a boat battery that some clod must have thrown onto the reef. Jack knew the potent acid in the battery would eventually leak out and damage the fragile living coral. He wanted the seas to be beautiful for his whole life, and he hoped to have a family someday with kids who could enjoy the beauty of the sea, and therefore he was disturbed by the prospect of leaking acid.

Jack could not allow the reef to be damaged. He signaled to Valentina to stop and wait and he saw she complied.

He then engaged in a delicate maneuver only possible for an expert diver. He removed his air tank and held it in front of him to streamline his body so that he drifted, barely clearing the lionfish and sea urchins, into the narrow cave where it penetrated at a downward angle into the coral tower. He estimated he had to swim that way a couple meters into the cave to where it opened up wider and where the battery was visible sitting on another coral shelf.

Being extremely careful not to touch any coral, he deftly glided downward into the cave. Upon arriving at the more open area, he was able to curl in such a way that he faced upward again and could see Valentina hovering above the fire coral shelf, staring back at him.

He picked up the battery carefully so as not to agitate the acid inside. Now he had the difficult task of holding both the battery and his air tank in front of him while gently kicking to pass back up through the tunnel. He was worried about releasing the battery acid. And, he was aware that he could not waste time because he and Valentina were supposed to be ascending.

But suddenly, a new and even more immediate danger came to his attention. Two muscular men, also with scuba gear, had descended behind Valentina and were wrestling with her. They were wrapping a cord around her, attached to a heavy outboard engine!

*

As Vladislav fought to wind the nylon cord around Valentina, he could not help but think about how sexy she looked in a bikini. It was a shame to have to kill a bitch with such a great body. And to think she must be checking out his huge muscles and getting hot for him since he'd selected the skimpiest swimsuit he could find for this dive!

But Vladislav knew President Ivanov wanted Valentina dead. Ivanov promised to pay a huge bonus for this at the yacht cruise for top employees, coming up in just a couple days.

Vladislav expected the cash would be enough to buy a hundred beautiful girls back in Moscow—better girls than Valentina because they'd know to keep quiet instead of blabbing about hypocritical ideas.

Valentina always stuck her nose in where it didn't belong in Ivanov's biggest business deals. It was her fault that he had a contract out on her life. She didn't understand the way the system worked! You don't mess with the Big Man. If he wanted to take something from society, he took it. If you were in the way, he'd run you over.

Vladislav laughed through his mouthpiece and turned to check that Vyachislav was still hanging on to the other end of the cord and the outboard engine from the RIB. The engine would sink Valentina to the bottom of the sea forever.

But wait a minute. Where was Valentina's annoying husband? Maybe that hypocrite was already in a shark's belly.

Vladislav laughed louder. Valentina would definitely die a horrible death. Escape for her was impossible!

That was when he noticed a slender outcropping of bright red rare and exquisite coral. He guessed this coral structure had taken at least 1,000 years to sprout from the side of the tower just over a cave opening where two ugly fish were sitting.

He paused for one second in his effort with the cord and reached out to crush the slender coral just for fun. He laughed into his mouthpiece again and he noticed that Vyachislav laughed, too.

*

Jack relaxed his heart rate and calmed his mind through the quick use of stress control exercises he had learned in the military.

He could see the flashing warning on his mask indicating that he must surface because his air was running out and his blood was becoming saturated with nitrogen. He knew Valentina was in the same predicament.

He could see the fire coral, two lionfish, and a colony of black spiny urchins in the foreground. And just outside the cave opening he could see the two thugs wrestling with Valentina. The thugs were next to the cave opening, but he didn't know why.

Jack chose to act immediately to rescue his partner. He burst out of the cave and in one quick motion tossed the tank and battery up a bit and used both free hands to smash the faces of the two thugs into the spiny urchins and fire coral.

He then scooped up the two lionfish from their harmless undersides and jammed them spikes-first into the groins of the two attackers.

He accomplished all of this in a couple seconds before safely catching the tank and battery.

Jack knew getting hit by a single lionfish spike was exceedingly painful. He could stretch his imagination to think how getting hit with eighteen spikes might feel. But it was impossible for him to imagine how the thugs must feel now with all eighteen spikes drilled directly into the testicles, where at least half of the spike tips broke off and lodged.

Now completely out of the cave mouth, he could see both thugs incapacitated with pain. Their red, bulging facial muscles were locked in silent screams. Blood flowed out from their mouthpieces. He flipped the air tank onto his back and, while holding the battery, used his other hand to help Valentina unwrap herself from the cord.

He and Valentina looped the cord around the necks and tanks of the two thugs, easy to do since they were both stunned, and made sure it was attached to the outboard engine that one of the thugs still miraculously grasped.

Then, Jack calmly pulled his sharp metal dive tool out from the sheath on his calf and used it to puncture the buoyancy vests on both thugs. He yanked the battery off of the outboard engine as bubbles flowed out from the punctured vests and both thugs sank straight toward the sandy bottom far below.

Jack and Valentina ascended at proper speed and conducted an abbreviated safety stop at five meters to out-gas nitrogen from their blood before surfacing.

He helped her climb back into their RIB. He then handed the two batteries to her and climbed into the boat himself.

Both breathed hard as they sprawled back with legs dangling over the rubber bumper that was the side of the boat.

"Those were the Russians we met at the conference this morning! Vladislav and Vyachislav!" Valentina said. "I knew there was something wrong about them. They are clearly not

95

journalists, and if someone sent them here with the specific purpose of killing me, or you, or both of us, I wouldn't be surprised if it was that scumball President Ivanov himself!"

"We don't have to worry about those gangsters anymore," said Jack. "I expect they will push the panic buttons on their wrist consoles and get rescued by the hotel staff. But, since they are pinned down at fifty-meters depth, they will be confined in the hotel's re-compression chamber for at least a week. They can pass the time by pulling poisoned spines and spikes out of their faces and groins.

"What I am wondering about is your journalism career. I guess you made some enemies in Russia? What is it exactly that you write about?"

"I guess I do have some enemies in Russia," replied Valentina. "I am not an ordinary journalist who writes articles by rehashing the words of government spokespeople. I am an investigative journalist and I have my own news service with a team of employees. We publish evidence of crimes committed by Russia's top politicians. These people will never be prosecuted in Russia because they are bribing the prosecutors, but my dream is that I can get the electorate to wake up to what is going on."

"You are a brave woman," replied Jack.

"I don't consider myself brave," sighed Valentina. "Rather, I consider myself to have made a rational choice to defend myself against a government that is robbing and oppressing me."

The relieved pair removed their scuba gear and pushed a button on the RIB control panel to head back to the boat station.

Jack found the woman beside him intriguing. In order for a journalist to be the target of assassins, she must be publishing hard-hitting articles that the other journalists were afraid to publish.

However, he had just had to rescue her. Would this

happen again? Was she suited for the mission? Would she slow him down?

The more dangerous the mission became, the more determined he became to succeed. If the Democracy Society did not prevail in its battle against the forces of socialism, and men like Vladislav and Vyachislav became the leaders of mankind, then the destruction of civilization would not be far away.

(10) Morning in Hyde Park, New York

Maria Diaz stood in the large living room. She loved some things about the decor. The Persian carpets were beautiful. The nautical prints were interesting. However, she was a bit disturbed by the stuffed bird collection.

She was pleased to see that her late night of overtime work had resulted in successful preparation for the media event.

The GFN crewmen, under her supervision, had moved most of the furniture out of the living room and constructed a stage. They arranged cameras and microphones at different angles to the stage with cables leading to the satellite up-link dish set outdoors on a bluff high above the Hudson River. Members of the crew had gotten up early and were testing all of the sound and lighting equipment to ensure a high quality production.

She felt that her cashmere jacket and skirt fit perfectly as she approached the stage. She remembered her happiness some years ago when her career was taking off and she was purchasing nice clothing for herself with the money she earned. She looked down at her gold bracelet and smiled. It was her reward to herself when she earned a bonus for breaking the corruption story that brought down the Democratic and Republican Parties.

The star of today's television event, President Roberto Rojo, stepped into the room. Maria was stunned. He was such a handsome man and such a powerful political leader! She had never seen him in person before.

He looked calm and confident when he entered. But, he quickly turned red in the face and began to tremble as he glared at Maria and the GFN crew. "You are scabs! You are rats! You are making America poor by doing hard and efficient work! You have been up all night arranging this equipment—you worked over thirty hours this week. You violated the Great Deal Act!"

Maria had expected praise for the good work she had done with the crew and she felt shocked by this outburst from Rojo.

Rojo paced around angrily, then started to calm down. "I must remain vigilant to protect the majority people of America against economic criminals. The work of the president is never finished. Except, of course, that it's limited to thirty hours per week by the Great Deal Act along with all other work except forced labor in rehabilitation camps."

He shut his eyes and took some deep breaths.

Maria introduced herself, "Mr. President, I'm Maria Diaz from the GFN. I'll be the commentator for your public appearances up through the election."

Rojo opened his eyes and shook hands with Maria.

Maria's anger melted when she looked up close into Rojo's mesmerizing oaken-brown eyes. "Thank you for providing us with accommodations here in the main house."

"It was not a problem at all," replied Rojo. "We have plenty of space here at Springwood. My accommodations are in Val-Kill Cottage, and the Great Deal Party offices are in the former museum building."

Maria gazed at Rojo for a long moment without speaking as she wished her accommodations were at Val-Kill Cottage also—in the same bed with Rojo.

She regained composure and pointed at her watch. "We go on the air in one minute. Please everyone step into position."

Maria joined Rojo on the stage where taped lines indicated standing positions.

When the crewmen gave the signal to begin, Maria

flashed her best smile at the millions of viewers, "Welcome to the Springwood Estate in Dutchess County, New York. Today we are with President Roberto Rojo who is announcing details on how the election will be conducted on Tuesday."

The crewmen signaled to Rojo.

Rojo exuded charisma as he spoke. "Majority people of America, greetings from Springwood, New York, the campaign headquarters for the Great Deal Party, where we're fighting every day to give America a Great Deal!

"I could not think of a more appropriate venue to introduce the latest strategy developed by the Great Deal Party to give Americans more human rights.

"It was right here at Springwood that Franklin and Eleanor Roosevelt had the idea of making a fundamental expansion in the human rights pioneered by the Founding Fathers of America, including George Washington and James Madison. The Roosevelts believed the original human rights were so wonderful that the list of rights should be expanded and I fully agree.

"Specifically, human rights were expanded to include the right to force other humans to do things for you. This concept was introduced in the "Four Freedoms" speech by Franklin Roosevelt and reinforced in the Universal Declaration of Human Rights by Eleanor Roosevelt.

"I'm following in the footsteps of Franklin and Eleanor Roosevelt.

"So the question that comes to my mind is this: 'Why, since America has had democracy since the Eighteenth Century, is it only today that we're beginning to realize full human rights?' And I have an answer to that question. The problem is that America's democracy was not inclusive enough to allow the American people to select a government that provided for all of their rights."

Maria became concerned when Rojo stopped speaking

for a moment. Had something gone wrong? But then a presidential aide off the stage held up a sign board that read, "property-1856, blacks-15th-1870, women-19th-1920." Rojo began speaking again.

"In the beginning of our nation's history, only white men who owned property could vote. Property requirements were dropped slowly state-by-state and were gone completely by 1856. The federal government then expanded voting further with amendments to the Constitution. The Fifteenth Amendment was ratified in 1870, giving blacks the right to vote. The Nineteenth Amendment was ratified in 1920, giving women the right to vote. But, restrictions remained. The Democracy Amendment was ratified in 2012, giving absolutely everyone the right to vote with no restrictions.

"So far, so good. The expansion in voting has resulted in more and more progressive government and expansion in human rights. But we're still not finished bringing full democracy to America.

"Everyone knows there has been a difference up through the last election two years ago how the different classes have voted. The 80% of Americans who are the generous socialists have supported expanded human rights—specifically increased free stuff confiscated from other humans. And the 20% of Americans who are the evil capitalists have been against this expansion because they are tightwads. Now you might argue that the 80% will always win in democracy and the 20% will always lose and therefore no one needs to worry about the capitalist scrooges.

"However, the reality has been different, and even today the political party that represents the miser minority, the Property Rights Party, controls the governments of thirteen states. The Property Rights Party is preventing the Great Deal Party from repealing the Bill of Rights and therefore the American majority cannot realize the full redistribution benefits of the Great Deal Act.

"Why did the Property Rights Party win in thirteen states with a platform that is only for the minority miser rich people? It's because a much higher percentage of misers go to polling stations and vote.

"A Great Deal Party think tank studied this problem and determined that a lot of majority people have no interest whatsoever in politics and therefore they don't vote. They don't read the news. They don't watch the news. They aren't interested in government or business. They don't know what the issues are. They don't know who the candidates are. They will not bother to go to a polling station on election day.

"The Democracy Amendment helped Americans to reach full democracy, but now we have a fresh strategy, within existing law, to make the most of the provisions of the Democracy Amendment. I introduce to you the Democracy Machine!"

Maria watched as an attendant in a red, white, and blue uniform stepped onto the stage wearing a super-thin monitor screen on his chest. The monitor screen showed images of two men.

The cameras focused in on the Democracy Machine. Maria saw it was the same as the polling machines used in the 2012 election except in a chest-mounted monitor.

On one side of the screen there was a vibrant and colorful video of Roberto Rojo smiling and throwing handfuls of hundred-dollar bills into the air. The other side of the screen showed a black-and-white static picture of David Goldstein scowling in a dark smock and huddling protectively over a hoard of coins.

Maria turned back toward Rojo.

He continued his speech. "Voting won't just be for the elite people who know what's happening in the world and show up at the polling stations, but rather voting will be for EVERYONE. Of course this means the best candidates will win.

"Volunteers wearing Democracy Machines such as this one will walk along every street and knock on every door on Tuesday and EVERYONE will be encouraged to press all of their fingers on the preferred candidate on the touch screen. Computer wizardry is able to analyze fingerprints in a matter of seconds to confirm that each voter only votes once.

"Voting will take place in the Property Rights States and in the rehabilitation camps in the Great Deal States as well, to show we're still a united democratic country. Like before, the only people who will not vote will be people not present in the United States on Tuesday, who obviously must be traitors or else they wouldn't be gone."

Rojo waved to a second attendant. "Please bring out Ms. Summer!"

The second attendant, also in a red, white, and blue uniform, stepped forward onto the stage guiding a woman in her mid-thirties.

The woman looked to be of mixed race, some combination of European and African and Asian ancestry. She wore a simple t-shirt and jeans and her dark hair was tied back into a bun. She was skinny, not surprisingly since Americans in the Great Deal States had been on a crash diet all year. She was average height and didn't wear makeup. Overall she looked quite plain and ordinary.

Summer was now on one side of the stage waving to the cameras. Her image was broadcast across the country. Rojo and Maria were on the other side of the stage, with no cameras pointed at them for a moment.

Maria suddenly realized Rojo was holding her hand! She wondered for a split second if he was attracted to her and making some kind of sexual advance. But then he yanked off her gold bracelet!

"I need to redistribute this for the program," he whispered. "I'm sure you consent because Ms. Summer needs this more than you do and because Ms. Summer and I outnumber you."

The cameras followed as Summer walked across the stage toward Rojo.

He put his arm around the woman and she looked up into his eyes. Rojo spoke, "This American citizen is named Ms. Summer. She was born in America and has been an American citizen since birth. She has never voted and has been cheated out of her opportunity to benefit from democracy. Ms. Summer has made a life choice never to do any work so she spends her days sitting on a couch in an apartment in a public housing project in New York City watching television serials. Her favorite serial is 'Pirate Heroes.'

"Although she was taught to read as a child in public school, she forgot how to read because she has no interest in anything. When we found her walking in the housing project courtyard during a blackout which caused her television to switch off, we asked for her opinion about the upcoming election and she said she had no idea there was an upcoming election. So, we put her in a limousine and brought her up to Springwood.

"If it were not for the wonderful new Democracy Machine, the voice of majority people everywhere, who are just like Ms. Summer, would never be heard."

The attendant wearing the Democracy Machine stepped just in front of Rojo and Summer.

Rojo gestured toward the Democracy Machine. "Ms. Summer, please have the honor of voting for the first time in your life by casting the first ballot in the 2014 election. If you touch my picture on the monitor, you'll vote straight-ticket for the Great Deal Party. If you push David Goldstein's picture, you'll vote straight-ticket for the Property Rights Party. But I really don't expect you to understand all that."

Rojo waved Maria's gold bracelet in front of Summer with one hand while pointing at his picture with the other hand. "Justice, rights, equality, liberty!"

Summer gleefully leaped forward and not only pushed Rojo's picture, but also grabbed Rojo and gave him a hug and a kiss. Then she grabbed the bracelet from his hand and ran off the stage.

Rojo exclaimed in jubilation, "A great victory for democracy!"

(11) Daytime flying from White Plains Airport to Dulles Airport

President Roberto Rojo leaned back in his easy chair aboard the Virginia National Guard jumbo jet known as *Air Force One*. He noticed Maria Diaz had fallen asleep on a chair at the far end of the main cabin.

He stared out the window deep in thought as the plane flew over Washington, D.C. It was a sunny day and he could see the smoke plumes rising all across the city from where socialist mobs were burning buildings.

Ah, how great democracy was! Greedy landlords used to oppress people by renting out those buildings. Now the buildings were being burned into ashes and could never again be tools of exploitation.

He knew his ancestors would be proud of his accomplishments. His mother's ancestors were socialists in Greece and fled to the United States when socialism was implemented in Greece and the economy was destroyed—of course not by socialism itself but rather by the reaction of people to socialism. His father's ancestors were socialists in Cuba and fled to the United States when socialism was implemented in Cuba and the economy was destroyed—again for the same reason. It was a tough battle trying to get people to embrace love instead of greed!

Rojo sensed that the jet had begun its descent to Dulles Airport.

He was aware that Dulles Airport was the only airport functioning in the Washington, D.C. metropolitan area since the other airports had been shut down and demolished by labor unionists shortly after passage of the Great Deal Act.

Dulles only functioned because it was operated by the Virginia National Guard.

He looked again at the urban area below. He thought he could make out the military corridor from the central government buildings in Washington, continuing westward into Virginia through Tysons Corner to Dulles Airport. The modern office buildings at Tysons Corner had been swiftly abandoned by the private sector after passage of the Great Deal Act. The federal government now used the office space for many thousands of socialist administrators comprising the Central Planning Bureau and Fair Price Agency. These administrators, because of the extreme importance of their work, were designated as Virginia National Guard and paid accordingly.

Rojo did not feel happy about spending the upcoming night in his own bed at home in the White House. He was lonely living there as a widower, even with many staff members running around.

He missed his late wife very much. The love they shared was the highlight of his life.

He remembered when they met in 2003 in Pershing, Illinois when he worked at Bedford Glassware Corporation and his father, Hugo, was sole proprietor of a bakery on Main Street. Dad introduced Roberto to the beautiful young assistant just hired at the bakery. Her name was Lolita.

It was love at first sight. Marriage came quickly, as did their first and only child, Augusto. Roberto had wanted to name the child Fidel, but Lolita had insisted on Augusto. Roberto had never heard that name before, but anyway allowed Lolita to make the decision.

Those were blissful days, being in love and taking care of a baby son!

Since that time, Roberto's family had been completely shattered.

After he blew up the Bedford Glassware factory in 2006,

a crisis ensued at the family bakery.

The economy of Pershing had been driven by Bedford Glassware Corporation for decades. When the factory was vaporized, the small retail businesses on Main Street were soon bankrupted.

Hugo had always given Roberto morality lectures against 'selling out' to consumers, and set an example by intentionally baking sizes and flavors of bread according to personal taste rather than customer demand.

Despite this strategy, the bakery managed to turn a modest profit in the boom years in Pershing when Bedford Glassware kept everyone employed.

But, after the destruction of the factory, money was scarce and the bakery no longer had revenues sufficient to cover basic expenses such as utilities and baking ingredients.

Hugo went to First Illinois Bank for a loan. He explained to the bank loan officer that he never wanted a loan when his business was profitable and believed no profitable companies should ever receive loans. He explained that his bakery was losing money and he needed a loan to make up for the shortfall. This was proper banking.

The bank loan officer said this was fine with him. He said he was happy to approve the loan and did not care whether it was paid back or not. He said he only cared about his short term bonus, which was a percentage of loan originations, and he did not care if the bank failed in a year or two.

But then, just before the loan documents were signed, the bank hired a profitability consultant named David Goldstein, a famous economics professor from University of Chicago.

Goldstein advised First Illinois Bank to allocate loans to profitable businesses that would pay back the loans in order to maximize the profitability of the bank. He recommended cutbacks in loans to shrinking sectors with weak profitability and increases in loans to growing sectors with strong profitability. The loan officer's decision was reversed and the loan to the bakery was rejected.

Roberto's heart beat so fast it almost jumped out of his chest. The advice from Goldstein was completely backward! Obviously, banks should operate for the benefit of stakeholders, not shareholders. Banks should provide cash for all unprofitable businesses!

Roberto shook with rage. Goldstein was so cruel! What went on inside the head of that thieving monster? Roberto could not begin to imagine any reasons except ignorance and cruelty as to why a person would support an economy based on capitalist competition rather than socialist bail-out.

Lolita had suggested saving the bakery by changing the product selection to match customer demand. Roberto and his father were horrified by this suggestion since both agreed that providing customers with what they wanted was exploitation—taking advantage of other people's needs. They thought Lolita was a nice person and wondered why she suggested this perverse plan. They hoped she wasn't teaching baby Augusto terrible ideas like this.

Then tragedy struck. The sheriff delivered notice that the bakery was to be evicted for non-payment of rent. Hugo did not want to surrender the property to the owner, as a matter of principle, so he destroyed the property and killed himself in a gas explosion.

Roberto felt certain his father must have killed Lolita by mistake. She'd already worked the ethical maximum of thirty hours that week, therefore Hugo wouldn't have suspected she was in the back room doing extra work in a secret effort to save the business by making it more efficient.

Roberto and his son had been left all alone. Roberto fell into a deep depression and could not imagine any way that his suffering could be worse. But, over the years, things did get worse.

The problems centered on his son.

Roberto and Augusto lived in a small apartment in

Pershing in the beginning of 2012, living off of government handouts. Augusto was a student at Pershing Elementary School.

Roberto tried to raise his son with certain core ethical values: the majority had the right to dictate to the minority, altruism was good, and self-interest was evil.

The economy of Pershing had recovered a bit. Roberto and Augusto went to the grand opening of the Easy Cheap discount superstore that had been constructed on the former site of the Bedford Glassware factory.

At the grand opening, Augusto saw a bicycle for sale for $100. He announced at home that very evening an intention to earn $100 and purchase the bicycle.

Roberto brought his son to the government welfare office and showed him that he could apply for a handout. Roberto taught his son that this was the ethical way to get money. George Washington and James Madison founded the United States on the principle of democracy—the majority rules over the minority. The majority of Americans voted that the government should use force to confiscate and redistribute money. By refusing to accept cash from the welfare center, Augusto fought against the core values of the United States and insulted the memory of the Founding Fathers.

And then it happened—Augusto embarked on a rebellion against his father and against society that continued to this day.

Augusto announced that he refused to take $100 from the taxpayers and described this lawful redistribution as 'stealing.' Next, he announced his intention to get the money required for the bicycle by working after school, bagging groceries at Easy Cheap.

Roberto remembered his fury when Augusto announced this. His own son had turned into a thief without morals! Augusto planned to find people with needs and then satisfy those needs. He wanted to exploit people.

Augusto went to Easy Cheap every day after school and worked for a couple hours. He saved every nickel and dime tip for a month until he accumulated $100. Then, he bought his dream bicycle.

He absolutely loved his bicycle and took diligent care of it, cleaning and oiling it every day.

One day, Roberto had a conversation with Augusto's teacher. The teacher said Augusto was running a business. He was letting other students ride his bicycle in the playground in return for chocolate bars.

Roberto could not understand where he'd gone wrong. His son was evil, oppressing the other students by charging rent—unearned income! Roberto came to school the next day and hid behind a bush beside the playground. When the children came out to play, he witnessed a terrible scene.

The majority of children in the class surrounded Augusto and demanded that he should let them ride his bicycle for free. So far, so good. Obviously, the majority had a human right to take the bicycle.

But, did young Augusto do the ethical thing and give his bicycle to the majority? No! Instead, Augusto started hitting and kicking the other children.

Roberto was not able to keep quiet. He jumped out from the bush and ran across the playground. He told the children to take the bicycle as their communal property. They immediately destroyed it, as was their right.

He grabbed his son by the ear and dragged him home.

Since that dreadful incident two-and-a-half years ago, Roberto had been spanking and scolding his son almost every day—ordering him to understand that the majority had a human right from God to take things from the minority.

But Augusto wasn't learning. He was still saying that the kids had no right to take the bicycle. He said the toy he bought with the money he earned was for himself only.

Roberto tried to relax by thinking of other things. He

counted backward from ten. He reminded himself that after his certain election victory on Tuesday and the repeal of the Bill of Rights on Wednesday, his socialist reforms would be unstoppable.

He cheered up at the thought of the Democracy Machine and that nice woman Ms. Summer. She was a typical supporter of the Great Deal Party: she cared about the community more than she cared about herself, she cared about long term sustainability more than she cared about short term gratification, and she was more interested in giving than she was in taking.

(12) Daytime driving to Midway Airport, Chicago

"I don't give a crap about anyone except myself. I don't give a crap about any time except the present. I steal everything I can grab! That's why I'm a typical supporter of the Great Deal Party."

David Goldstein listened in silent horror as the driver of the Illinois National Guard van spoke. The driver then slammed down the gas pedal and sent the vehicle lurching forward, just failing to hit an elderly lady who was making her way across the garbage-strewn street.

Goldstein tried to pat down a curl of red hair that suddenly became unruly. He always felt uncomfortable when his still-enduring belief in universal-suffrage democracy was tested. This was one of those times, as he was being driven from Robie House through the South Side of Chicago to Midway Airport.

While thoroughly disgusted by the driver's behavior, Goldstein seized on the opportunity to converse with an ordinary citizen who apparently had no idea that Goldstein was one of the two presidential candidates. He spoke to the driver without being able to see much of him from the back seat except the long, brown, greasy hair. "May I ask your name?"

The driver balanced his lit cigarette on the dashboard's overflowing ashtray and extended his thick and hairy left arm toward the elderly lady who lay panting on the sidewalk. He extended his middle finger high in the air. "My friends call me Lefty!"

Lefty took the ashtray in his hand. "I'm not trying to save the world like some fools. I only care about myself!" He tossed the ashes and cigarette butts out of the window, but a gust of wind blew everything back in his face as he coughed and hacked.

"And I can't help but ask, Mr. Lefty, how did you get this job with the Illinois National Guard?"

Lefty stopped coughing and resumed speaking. "Originally, I was an unemployed bum scrounging off the government, trying to cheat and rob everyone I met. Then my cousin clued me into a great racket.

"He was a labor unionist employed by a private company at Midway Airport to operate heavy vehicles for construction and aircraft servicing. He said they got paid double what average people in Chicago earned and they only worked half as much. He said I could join the racket if I paid bribes to the union leaders."

"You paid bribes to get a job?" Goldstein asked. "That doesn't make sense. Having a job means choosing to perform a productive function in return for a negotiated salary."

Lefty laughed out loud. "You don't know anything about economics. Funny, since your house is right next to the University of Chicago."

Goldstein's confusion turned to annoyance. "I was a professor in the Economics Department!"

Lefty turned his face a bit and smirked. "Well, you have a lot to learn about how the job market works. Anyway, I paid the bribes and the next thing I knew I was in uniform, twenty hours per week, driving a truck at the airport. I got paid $100,000 per year when ordinary people were earning $50,000 per year for working forty hours per week.

"Then we went on strike. All the labor unionists, including my cousin and me, decided we wanted our salaries increased to $200,000 per year and hours reduced to ten per week.

"The tightwads who owned the company decided to shut down the business instead of coming out of pocket to fund

114

the losses that would result from agreeing to our terms.

"Since Midway Airport is very important to the City of Chicago and we blocked the runways with our trucks, the City of Chicago decided to start paying us using tax money.

"We started working again for a compromise of $150,000 per year for fifteen hours per week. Since we felt cheated that we didn't get our full demands, we worked as slowly as possible except when we stole and vandalized airport property.

"And that's when the Great Deal Party came to power. At first, all work at the airport stopped because everyone went on strike. Of course the same thing happened at every other airport in the Great Deal States.

"Then, the Great Deal Party announced the militarization of one airport in each Great Deal State for essential government flights."

Goldstein nodded, "I know about that. Midway was chosen for Illinois. White Plains for New York. Dulles for Virginia. Orlando for Florida. Oakland for …"

Lefty interrupted, "All airport employees at Midway, including me, were told that we were now Illinois National Guard employees which was bad since we had to start coming to work, but good since we got statutory salaries of $200,000 per year compared to $100,000 for civilians. Also, I got corruption opportunities, like siphoning the gasoline out of this van."

Goldstein looked out the window of the speeding van at the smoldering remains of a factory. "Can you see that the way the economy is under the Great Deal Party is unsustainable?"

"Unsustainable? What does that mean?"

"If everyone in America gets money today by robbing everyone else and producing nothing, then tomorrow everyone is going to be poor."

"Tomorrow? Who cares about tomorrow? I don't think

115

even one second into the future. Everyone I know thinks the same way."

"So you don't detect that anything has gone wrong in Chicago? How about the trashing of every neighborhood and torching of thousands of buildings? How about the emptying of all stores and reversion to a black market barter economy to find basic goods? Surely you must be thinking that you made a mistake voting for Rojo and you were better off before all the looting started."

Lefty pulled a strand of greasy hair back behind his ear. "Look, I had big problems before Rojo got elected. I wanted to buy a really cool pick-up truck and I couldn't afford it."

"How is it possible you couldn't afford a pick-up truck? You were getting a salary of $150,000 per year!"

"It's because of my cousin. When he got me into the racket and I started making lots of cash, he talked me into investing with him. He stole everything. He sure is smart! My cousin is a really cool guy.

"But now back to my big problems. My next door neighbor, Ernest, was a thief. He did hard honest work managing the local Easy Cheap store. We all know Easy Cheap was evil because President Rojo said so.

"Ernest bought a fancy pickup truck and kept it parked in front of his house. This pissed me off every day because it was unfair that he had a cool truck and I didn't.

"I wanted a simple human right. I don't give a crap about a right to free speech or free religion or free press. I wanted a new right. I wanted the right to go to Ernest's house, kick his butt, and take his truck.

"And so here comes Roberto Rojo, promising he'll shower everyone with free cash and give us the right to take anything we want. Obviously I voted for him. When Rojo signed the Great Deal Act, I grabbed a baseball bat out of my closet and ran to Ernest's house to exercise my new right."

Goldstein, feeling a bit uncomfortable, unzipped his

jacket and unbuttoned the top button of his short-sleeved light-blue polyester shirt. "And what happened? Did you get the truck?"

Lefty scowled. "That loser Ernest packed up all his valuables in the truck and gathered his wife and kid and drove away to Iowa just before I got to his house. There was nothing left to steal.

"Knowing that Ernest was gone, I ran to the Easy Cheap store to join in the looting. I helped the mob smash out the windows. I managed to bring home twenty frozen pizzas without paying! It was great.

"Look, President Rojo is the perfect leader for me. I want to steal things. Rojo says redistribution is okay. Redistribution is exactly the same as stealing."

Goldstein probed deeper. "Do you think other people should have the right to steal things from you? If a street thug tried to take the twenty frozen pizzas from you, what would you have done?"

Lefty gave a quick and enraged reply. "One scumball tried to steal my pizzas and I hit him with my bat!"

"Very interesting," said Goldstein, sighing. He thought it must be impossible that most Americans could be so dumb and cruel.

Lefty turned up the volume on the stereo as the van entered Midway Airport through a gate guarded by heavily armed Illinois National Guardsmen.

Bang bang bangabanga bang bang clang, "Take What's Yours!"

Goldstein did not like this overplayed song and was eager to get out of the van and board his flight to Virginia. He had one public appearance plus a lot of preparation work to do before the presidential election debate at Mount Vernon.

Lefty stopped the car and turned his contorted and angry face toward the back seat. "Now what are you going to give me for my service?"

117

"What are you talking about? I was invited by the government to come to the airport and the government sent this government-owned car and the government is paying you a salary. This isn't a private taxi."

"Yeah, but I couldn't siphon out the gasoline since I had to drive you. So how are you going to make it up to me? I'll accept euros or Canadian dollars."

Goldstein slid open his door and stepped out of the van with his briefcase. "Of course I am not going to give you any money."

Lefty jumped out of the van. He was a very large man. He pulled Goldstein's briefcase. "Gimme your briefcase! It's mine! I'm redistributing it to myself!"

Goldstein resisted by pulling back. "This is not your briefcase! This is mine! I bought it with money that I earned!"

"Don't deny my human rights!" said Lefty as he pulled harder and harder.

Goldstein rarely used his judo skills outside of his practice studio. However, he did believe in self-defense and he was not about to let Lefty take the briefcase. Although the philosophy behind judo was "the way of gentleness," this martial art was used by police and included strikes to disable an aggressor.

With a whirling motion and a coordinated arm and leg movement, Goldstein sent Lefty flying down onto the pavement several meters away.

Then, Goldstein walked, still holding his briefcase, into the airport terminal as he reflected on the encounter. Were most voters similar to Lefty?

Goldstein was suddenly deep in thought. He understood the importance of the upcoming election: his Property Rights Party had to triumph and save the Bill of Rights and repeal the Great Deal Act and Temporary Police State Act or else America was doomed.

Sure, he could try to boost his popularity briefly by lying

that he could make everyone rich by allowing everyone to rob everyone else. He could start by renaming his party. Instead of the "Property Rights Party," it could be the "Steal Anything You Want Party."

However, he was determined to win the election honestly. He would tell the truth to voters. He would tell them that wealth comes from productive work and wise investment. Wealth does not come from neighbors robbing each other.

Goldstein strengthened in his resolve. He reflected back on his career. His career was, without exaggeration, one of the most stellar success stories in the entire nation. He had become the foremost economist in America. He earned millions of dollars as a bank consultant. He earned millions more from investing. He was one of the two presidential candidates.

How did he get to where he was? Honesty and long-term thinking! He was not going to change course now.

(13) Morning at Yosemite National Park, California

The California National Guard helicopter designated *Marine Two* whisked Vice President Clarence Clark from Oakland Airport, where he had slept in the luxurious bedroom on *Air Force Two*, to Yosemite National Park.

Marine Two landed in a clearing in a mountain valley. As Clark stepped out, he saw a large sign proclaiming "Welcome to Yosemite National Park—Mariposa Grove."

A television crew from the West Coast branch office of the GFN had arranged lighting, sound, and camera equipment at the edge of the clearing. Everyone was waiting for the Vice President.

Clark climbed down from the helicopter and made his way across muddy ground past a series of gigantic tree stumps to where the television crew waited. He had already been briefed on the content of today's propaganda program.

A make-up assistant ran forward and performed some quick work to make Clark's plump face less shiny. He straightened his American flag tie himself and struggled to suck in his gut and close the top button on his pin-stripe suit jacket.

At the edge of the clearing stood a line of the largest trees he had ever seen: the famous Giant Sequoia trees of Yosemite. For generations, nature lovers, a small minority of humanity, came to this spot to gaze upon the majestic trees, rising sixty meters into the sky. Friends could gather to try to hold hands and encircle the tree trunks, reaching eight meters in diameter. Mariposa Grove alone had two hundred of these amazing trees.

Not any more! Roughly half of the trees had already been

chopped down.

Clark surveyed left and right to see groups hacking away at ten more trees. California National Guardsmen armed with assault rifles supervised the work.

He knew that the guardsmen here were formerly with the Second Infantry Division of the United States Army, stationed at Camp Casey in South Korea. From the original force of 30 thousand soldiers, 24 thousand had been socialists and now wore the uniforms of the California National Guard. They were dispersed throughout the park.

He thought that the enthusiasm the socialists had for destroying the environment was remarkable. While it was true that he was the author of the Great Deal Act and Temporary Police State Act, he was not the person who decided to clear-cut Yosemite National Park. That command must have come from an altruistic do-gooder in the Central Planning Bureau. And, the California National Guard was acting on that command.

Clark did not enjoy seeing natural areas despoiled. However, he accepted that some environmental damage would be a side effect of the implementation of his ultimate scheme. And, he confirmed silently to himself, the ends justified the means.

The prisoners were chained to their work stations with metal cuffs around their ankles. Each prisoner was equipped only with an ax, and was busy chopping into a thick tree trunk.

Clark knew that the prisoners were entrepreneurs from California's 14th congressional district, around Palo Alto, where they used to have multimillion-dollar homes. They had been rounded up by the California National Guard because they obtained income from interest, rent, and profit and they felt guilty about it and wanted rehabilitation rather than exile.

The television crew aimed the cameras at a particularly large tree that Clark guessed must be two thousand years old, based on the briefing paper he had read.

He positioned himself next to the featured subjects of the propaganda program: the two prisoners who were swinging their axes at this tree. He noted with pleasure that both subjects were just as short as he was. The folks at the GFN had done a good job, since Clark knew that height was one of the most important attributes for a politician in a universal-suffrage election and therefore he liked to make himself seem taller than he really was.

Clark gestured to the nearby California National Guard soldier to lower his assault rifle. The prisoners paused in their work and looked up toward the cameras.

A GFN employee quickly attached microphones to Clark and the two prisoners. Oddly, the prisoners were wearing wool business suits and ties, similar to Clark's, although worn and beaten.

A cameraman signaled the start of the live television broadcast.

Clark forced a smile for the camera and began the propaganda program with a greeting in his squeaky voice. "Good morning America and welcome to the Yosemite National Park Rehabilitation Camp. I am honored to be here today to question inmates and ensure that the rehabilitation camp is functioning properly.

"You, the majority people of America who are watching this program, can see the high-quality services your government is providing."

Clark stepped toward one of the prisoners, a fair-skinned man with scraggly hair who looked to be in his mid-40's.

"Greetings, Prisoner Williams," began Clark. "I have read something about you from your file. You founded a software company in 1992. By the time the Great Deal Party came to power in 2012, you were a multimillionaire living in a luxury home in Palo Alto.

"I read that your software company had approximately

122

one hundred employees, thousands of customers, annual revenues of $50 million, and annual net income of $10 million in its final years of operation.

"Do you feel guilty about this?"

Williams stared into Clark's eyes with an expression of simultaneous shock and offense. "Of course I do not feel guilty about this. Why should I feel guilty about creating jobs and producing products?"

Clark nodded slowly. "Don't you feel guilty that you made a profit off the backs of other people who entered into voluntary contracts to do the work at market salaries? Don't you feel guilty that you were gouging consumers by selling your products with voluntary contracts at market prices?"

Williams stepped back, still staring at Clark. "Of course I don't feel guilty. I feel proud! I created competitive jobs and I created competitive products!"

Clark clapped his hands and signaled to the nearby soldier. The command Clark issued sounded awkward given his high-pitched speaking voice. "Banish this man immediately. I can see that he is evil through and through and is not remorseful about his crimes. He must be exiled from the Great Deal States so that he can suffer in the cruel world of greedy capitalism. March him to the border of Nevada and force him to walk across to the other side! When the majority victory parties happen on Wednesday in San Francisco and Los Angeles, all California socialists are welcome. The government will drop free surprises on the revelers. Capitalist people don't deserve these surprises and therefore must be removed from the state!"

The soldier unchained Williams and began marching him away at gunpoint. The banished prisoner shouted over his shoulder. "You're right I don't deserve anything free from the government! Nobody deserves anything free from the government! People only deserve what they earn!"

Clark now addressed the second prisoner, a dark-skinned

man with a shaved head who also seemed to be in his mid-40's.

"Greetings, Prisoner Patel. I have also read your file. You started a company in 1992. The company originally operated an illegal free website that facilitated piracy of music files. You ran it yourself with no employees. Then, in 2002, you were ordered by a court to obey copyright laws. You reacted by selling music files on your website and remitting royalties to copyright owners. By 2012, your company had grown to approximately the same size as Prisoner Williams' firm, in terms of employees, revenues, and net profit. You also moved into an expensive home in Palo Alto.

"Do you feel guilty about this?"

Tears appeared in the corners of Patel's eyes. "I feel terrible! I am guilty! I am an exploiter! I apologize to my employees! I apologize to my customers! I apologize to America! I never wanted to make profits; I only wanted to facilitate piracy for altruistic reasons …

"When I graduated from UC Berkeley, I received two job offers. One offer was a large salary from a company that needed me very much. The other offer was a small salary from a company that did not need me very much. I made the ethical decision. I purposefully took the lower salary so that I would not be guilty of the sin of greed!

"The website was only supposed to be a hobby. I never intended to make profits. Oh, how did I let my greed get so out of control!"

Patel hunched his shoulders and began sobbing.

A spasm ran through Clark's body, and he feared it must have been noticed by the television audience. Anyway, he needn't be concerned. The big punishment was coming soon for Patel and all of the other irrational American socialists.

Clark tried to relax and patted Patel on the back. "It is good that you feel remorse for your crimes. This means it is possible for you to be rehabilitated. You will not be banished from the paradise of Great Deal California. Instead, you will be permitted to continue as a forced laborer. And, you will be permitted to join the guardsmen and the other remorseful prisoners on Wednesday and travel to San Francisco for the majority victory party. You will all get the free gift that you deserve from the government."

Clark held up a bright-red ribbon from which hung a shining medallion stamped symbolically with an 'equal' sign.

"Prisoner Patel, I am proud on behalf of the entire nation to bestow upon you the highest honor in the land, the award recently created by President Roberto Rojo to make examples of Americans who used to be self-interested capitalists and who now are altruistic socialists: the Socialist Freedom Award. You have become free, no longer enslaved by voluntary work, and you have freed others, by ceasing to exploit them."

Patel stood up straight. He was completely overcome with emotion. He burst into an ear-to-ear smile as tears rolled down his cheeks. He stepped forward and received the Socialist Freedom Award.

SPLAAATTT!

Only to fall flat on his face in the mud, apparently forgetting that his ankles had been chained to his work station.

The GFN team signaled to Clark that the cameras were now switched off, and he staggered as quickly as possible toward his helicopter as his body convulsed in extreme spasms.

He thought to himself as soldiers helped him to climb back into the helicopter. Today was Saturday. The election would be Tuesday. His horrible revenge would be Wednesday. Nobody could stop his ultimate scheme! He only had to tolerate the irrational people for a couple more days. Then, he would relieve them of their misery. He would deal a final and decisive blow to all of the American socialists.

(14) Evening at the Sea Hotel and Spa

Valentina Zaiceva breathed in the cool evening air and looked up at the stars that filled the clear desert sky.

Then she looked down. She was overjoyed with the beauty of the clothes that hung perfectly from her shoulders all the way down her lean frame. The flowing gown was decorated with Bedouin tribal motifs, as well as coins and sequins sewn into the fabric. The matching long cloak, the *abaya*, was an appropriate garment for the grand opening party. Her long blond hair was not visible through the hood, however her eyes peeked out from a light veil, or *niqab*, designed more for style than for concealment. Everything had been handmade by the hotel staff that day.

She stood on the seaside walkway, in the same place where she met Jack just before their scuba adventure. From the quiet walkway on top of the dunes, she had a clear view of the grand opening party with hundreds of guests mingling on the beach.

She saw a fascinating collection of international people wearing stylish dress ranging from Western business suits to Arab robes to Japanese kimonos. The party tonight included not only journalists, but also business leaders and cultural celebrities from various countries.

Several fires blazed, with lambs on spits handled by small teams of chefs. Also, she could see waitresses in colorful dress walking through the crowd and offering food and drinks to the guests.

She turned toward her companion on the walkway. She noticed that Jack Cannon looked very handsome wearing an Arab robe and a headdress that complemented her own outfit.

She recalled the ratty two-star hotels where she typically stayed during her years of hard work getting her investigative journalism practice established. "I will never stay in a hotel with less than eight stars ever again!" she exclaimed with a laugh.

Jack smiled and nodded. "Ha, ha, ha. It seems you don't have to. Not this week anyway."

Valentina looked Jack in the eyes. Then, she reached out and touched the gold-and-diamond turkey badge on Jack's robe. "Now that we finally have a chance to chat, maybe I can learn something about you. What is your story? How did you come to be on an international spy mission? What is the full story behind this organization where my father has been working: the Democracy Society?

"I have heard hushed and vague endorsements from my father, and I trust him absolutely because he has always been honest with me. That is why I accepted the job with the Democracy Society to investigate Trans Pacific Trading Company and bring the file to you and the King. But still the Democracy Society and the Director remain mysterious. What I know is the same as what the King knows—your organization's public role as the management company for Mount Vernon must be a front for a more important function."

Jack spoke in a subdued voice. "Very good questions. I became a member of the Democracy Society only yesterday and I am learning about the organization myself. I cannot tell details, however you have already deduced that the Democracy Society is doing something more than managing Mount Vernon.

"My father told me something about the Democracy Society yesterday. The Director showed me documentation indicating that the Democracy Society was lawfully chartered.

"And, this information tied in with some things I already

knew.

"For example, I now understand there was a reason why my father put so much emphasis on certain aspects of my education and physical training when I was younger. Already in elementary school, my father had me reading treatises on government and economics and practicing martial arts. He encouraged me from an early age to have a career in the United States Armed Services.

"And, there was a specific clue about the Democracy Society in my father's career.

"My father often talked about a project in his past and I knew it was his proudest achievement. But the story did not entirely make sense until I learned of the Democracy Society.

"The attack against humanity by the government of the Soviet Union began in 1939 with the Molotov Ribbentrop Pact and did not end until that government collapsed in 1991. A generation of Americans had to live under the constant terror threat of nuclear bombardment. The reason why America waited so long to put a stop to the terrorism was because of a string of presidents who tried to befriend or appease the Soviet government."

Valentina was fully absorbed. "Yes, the Soviet government was certainly assaulting the whole world, and the biggest victims were the Soviet people themselves who were treated like disposible slaves by their own government."

Jack nodded and continued. "America needed a president who understood that wealth was created by profit-motived businesses serving the marketplace, appeasement always backfired, and the only way to defeat the Soviet government was through military showdown. The Democracy Society members observed that most American voters knew nothing about policy and selected candidates based on charm. Therefore the members, including my father, arranged for a particular movie star to enter politics and take control of the country.

"After Ronald Reagan's 1964 speech "A Time for Choosing," my father worked with a circle of businessmen to get Reagan to run for Governor of California in 1966. In 1980, Reagan was elected President of the United States. In 1991, the Soviet government collapsed. Now I have concluded that this must have been a Democracy Society project.

"I am confident the Democracy Society is a lawful organization working in the best interest of America and the world," concluded Jack. "However, I admit I still don't understand everything about the Democracy Society. For example, I don't understand how the Director derives his authority."

"The Russian people owe thanks to America for helping to bring down the Soviet government," observed Valentina. "My hope is that America will help the Russian people again by bringing down the corrupt mafia that currently controls the democratic system in Russia. The whole world should be nervous because this corrupt mafia is armed with thousands of nuclear missiles."

A waitress passed by on the walkway and handed glasses of fresh juice to Jack and Valentina. A second waitress held a wide silver tray with an assortment of artfully rendered edibles.

Valentina watched as Jack selected two small pastries with a sticky sauce on top.

"Palm syrup," said Jack. "I was hoping this would be offered tonight. I have never tasted it fresh." He gave one to Valentina and they both tasted the exotic dessert.

"Okay, enough about the Democracy Society," said Valentina. "I know the Democracy Society is fighting Ivanov and Clark and that is enough reason for me to be involved. Tell me about yourself!"

"I was brought up in an exceptionally patriotic American family," said Jack. "The Cannons have been based in

Connecticut since before the American Revolution. Our family business for three centuries has been managing a maple forest and producing syrup."

Valentina now understood why he was so interested in syrup.

"My father and both grandfathers were graduates of the United States Naval Academy," continued Jack. "My first toy was a stuffed goat, the mascot of the Naval Academy, as it was expected when I was still in the cradle that I would one day graduate from that institution. That is exactly what I did, although I became a pilot in the Marines rather than a Navy officer.

"My overseas posting was in the Pacific Ocean flying jets off an aircraft carrier. Our job was to prevent a North Korean military strike on South Korea, Japan, or the United States. There were some violent skirmishes. I was proud to be part of the force that was containing the North Korean socialists."

A cool breeze blew across the Tihamah. Valentina moved a step closer to Jack.

Jack continued with his story. "But then, in November 2012, we received orders to withdraw to California and merge with the California National Guard. Our new function was to blockade ourselves because the platform of the Great Deal Party included prohibition of all imports."

Valentina was very interested. She had read extensively about the shift the United States Armed Forces had undertaken just after merging into the state national guards. She had always wondered what the officers thought about abandoning their old function of defending against rogue states to accept a new function of attacking themselves. Now she was hearing directly from an American officer who witnessed the shift.

"The California National Guard people liked me and offered me a huge promotion," explained Jack. "However, enforcing a self-imposed and self-destructive embargo was a job I could not imagine doing. I requested to serve in the Connecticut Air National Guard, even with a lower rank and fewer perks, arguing that Connecticut was my home state. I moved home to Connecticut, where the Property Rights Party had majority voter support.

"In the short run, I would have done better in California. But since the Great Deal Party's policies were obviously a road to serfdom in the long run, I am confident I made the right decision by choosing Connecticut."

Valentina sensed that the shift was an emotional topic. "The change in American policy must have been heartbreaking for every patriotic soldier with a rational mind."

She heard a drum beat and chant coming from the beach. The couple turned away from each other to look out at the party on the beach. Two rows of Arab drummers and swordsmen had assembled. They were singing and dancing. Valentina recognized this as the *ardha* ritual, the national dance of Arabia.

Valentina turned her attention back toward Jack. She moved closer. She was touching him. "But why do you keep fighting? What motivates you? Why do you care? Rojo was democratically elected! Most people who voted for him did so because of his promise to steal money from the most productive Americans and redistribute it to the least productive Americans. Now, the people who stayed in the Great Deal States are suffering for that decision. And maybe they deserve that. Why don't you just retreat into New Hampshire? Or Canada? Start a new life?"

"Yeah, it is certainly frustrating to protect America from socialist suffering when most Americans themselves are socialists. But anyway, I will keep fighting to save my democratic republic because fighting is better than submitting to slavery. Surrendering to the socialists is the same as committing suicide. But how about you? What keeps you

131

fighting?"

"The same concept keeps me motivated in Russia," replied Valentina. "Even though most Russians have chosen to submit to the authority of Ivanov, I refuse. He is using his position to loot my country and therefore he is not a legitimate president even if fools vote for him. I will fight him as long as he is in power because it is a matter of self-defense and surrender would be, like you said, submission to slavery or suicide."

Valentina and Jack were standing exactly together, looking into each other's eyes. Jack took hold of Valentina's hands. The drumming of the swordsmen on the beach grew louder.

"I don't think the situation in the world is completely hopeless," said Jack. "One reason is because socialism eventually destroys itself. An economy ceases to function when people get money from redistribution instead of production.

"But the other reason is because there were times in the past when mainstream thinking was different. Much of the problem now comes from prominent people in recent history who have convinced the majority to adopt a definition of equality that contradicts the original definition of that term.

"Historically, Americans believed in equality of rules. Rule of law. Level playing field. Everyone could work within these rules to earn money and some people would earn more because they provided more to society and some people would earn less because they provided less to society.

"Most Americans have switched over to a belief in equality of results. Government confiscates property from the most productive people, causing them to stop being productive and instead fight the government. The result is violence and poverty.

"It is possible that mainstream thinking, with help from intelligent politicians supported by intelligent voters informed by honest media, can migrate back to the old definition of equality."

Valentina interrupted. "Intelligent voters? We are talking about universal-suffrage democracy. Even infants are voting now by pushing a screen to select their favorite candidate."

Jack smiled. "The infants are not the most dangerous voters since their votes are random. The most dangerous voters are the adults who have been brainwashed with the concept that stealing is good and earning is evil. They purposefully vote for thieves. It is a difficult situation to solve.

"But our mission now with the Democracy Society is not to solve all of the problems of humanity. Your immediate assignment was to research the Trans Pacific Trading Company. And, this is part of a larger mission to save the Bill of Rights.

"When this mission is completed successfully, I will be content to spend the rest of my career on the farm. I hope to have kids some day. I will teach them the correct definition of equality and it will be their responsibility in the future to maintain a society based on capitalist rule of law instead of socialist law of the jungle."

Valentina was wildly attracted to the man next to her. Not only was he incredibly good looking, but also he was smart and therefore principled.

She looked at Jack's moonlit profile as he turned to face upward toward the peak of the *Jebel Soudah*. She studied his strong jaw and determined gaze peering out from the *ghutrah* that covered the rest of his head. An amazing fireworks display erupted in the sky and reflected in his glacier-blue eyes.

He turned back and kissed her. A single gentle kiss on the lips that made her feel like the fireworks above were exploding in her heart.

And then they both took a step back from each other,

while their eyes were still locked together.

Valentina spoke first. "It's been an exciting day and a wonderful evening. I say we get some sleep so we are ready for a big day in Russia tomorrow."

"I look forward to tomorrow, when we can continue the battle!" And with that, Jack released her hands.

She returned to her tent alone.

Tucking herself into bed, Valentina reflected on her last couple years working in Moscow. Always busy. Always running around. No time for dating. Never meeting any unattached men who fit her exacting standards. Could it be that meeting Jack was the romantic breakthrough she needed in her life?

But first things first. They had to fly to Russia in the morning to spy on Ivan Ivanov and Clarence Clark—the most powerful criminals in the world.

Sunday, November 2, 2014
(15) Daytime flying over the Pacific Ocean

Vice President Clarence Clark sat alone in the main cabin of *Air Force Two* savoring a sip of Japanese *saké*. He had purchased the *saké* from a Japanese smuggler in exchange for yen. It was Clark's favorite kind of *saké*, brewed from Yamadanishiki rice. It was not as expensive as *saké* brewed from Miyamanishiki rice, but in his personal opinion it had a better flavor.

As the jet flew above the clouds, Clark thought back to his first revenge attack against the irrational American socialists after they ruined his actuarial career.

His initial scheme back then in 2010, like his ultimate scheme now, was to harness the irrationality of the socialists against themselves. In a sense, it was unnecessary to do this because socialists hurt themselves every day with their irrationality. But, at that time, Clark thought that by increasing the pain the socialists were inflicting upon themselves, he would be able to show them the errors in their logic so that they would change their behavior.

Since Clark had achieved the top percentile in every math and logic test that he had ever taken, he was able to devise a brilliant initial scheme. He organized the largest frivolous lawsuit in history.

He got the idea from an article about how doctors estimated a third of Americans were obese. One hundred million people. They were to become his plaintiffs.

He decided to launch a lawsuit against the entire fast-food industry demanding one million dollars of damages for each of one hundred million plaintiffs—a total of one hundred trillion dollars! This amount was substantially larger than the entire GDP of the United States, approximately fifteen trillion dollars back then. But he was quite certain that a typical American jury would not notice or care about this mathematical imbalance.

He went to the headquarters of "Socialists for Equality" in Washington, D.C. and asked if they wanted to help with a lawsuit against greedy corporations. They agreed to provide one hundred *pro bono* lawyers. These lawyers were mostly the same people who were involved in the Sherman Management Consulting lawsuit.

The lawyers worked day and night for months until they managed to fill an entire Washington warehouse with documents evidencing Americans becoming obese after patronizing fast food restaurants.

Clark then invited the CEOs of the ten largest fast food chains to visit the warehouse and negotiate a settlement.

The settlement terms went as follows: (1) the *pro bono* lawyers got nothing except, of course, the warm fuzzy feeling of helping bring justice to the world, (2) Clark got one billion dollars in cash, (3) all obese Americans were put on a mailing list to receive compensation in the form of coupons. Clark worked with the CEOs to design coupons that would in fact increase the amount the obese people spent at the fast food restaurants, by offering free fries with the purchase of every deluxe burger.

Clark remembered his feeling of triumph when he emerged from the warehouse with the signed settlement agreement and waved his check for a billion dollars at the television news crews as he sneered at the millions of viewers, all of whom were his victims.

He marched proudly to Tasty Burger, with television cameras behind him focused on his large backside, and purchased a Double Decker Delight and Sugar Smoothie. He demanded free fries in accordance with the settlement agreement.

Then, he took the food to the hotel where he was staying. He flipped on the television and plopped down on the bed to eat. Finally alone, he could not wait to watch the millions of crying victims on the television.

He expected to be demonized by the media. He expected a call to go out for reform of law to abolish frivolous lawsuits. He expected that mainstream socialist viewers would be horrified by one man shamelessly using the irrational legal system to take a billion dollars from society while making the poorest Americans fatter at the same time.

But then, something occurred that was totally unpredictable to him even though he had spent years studying actuarial science.

The most popular news programs made him into a hero! The commentators talked about how great it was that a principled, altruistic individual had punished the evil, profit-motivated corporations.

Irrational obese socialists held celebrations at fast food restaurants across the country. They waved banners with Clark's picture as they ate burgers and fries.

He robbed the socialists and they loved him for it because they were too dumb to understand what he did!

He realized at that moment that the problem of the irrational socialists was much greater than he had originally suspected. It was not a small minority of Americans who were socialists. Actually, most Americans were socialists even though they were not conscious of this themselves. And, these socialists did not learn from experience, but rather clung to their irrational beliefs no matter how much it hurt them to do so.

In a sense, Clark was discouraged by what transpired. But, there was an encouraging aspect to this as well. He saw there was no limit to how much suffering he could inflict on the socialists by using their own irrationality against them because they would support him even while he attacked them.

He had formulated his ultimate scheme while sitting there in the hotel room four years ago, munching on his Double Decker Delight. The first step was to gain political power.

He established a large office in Washington, D.C. and called a meeting of the one hundred lawyers from "Socialists for Equality." He announced that he was donating the billion-dollar settlement for the purpose of founding a new socialist political party with the expectation of dominating national, state, and municipal elections by promising government-provided wealth to the majority. The new party would be called the Great Deal Party.

Clark used the *pro bono* lawyers as the core team for establishment of the new party, including recruitment of thousands of people to hold staff jobs and to run as candidates in all local, state, and federal elections. The process took two years.

The timing was auspicious, because the Democratic Party and Republican Party imploded from corruption, leaving a power vacuum.

But, he sensed something was missing. Nobody from the core team had enough charisma to win a presidential election. They had to conduct a nationwide search to find the perfect headline presidential candidate.

The team of lawyers unanimously recommended a single man: Roberto Rojo. He was a hero for socialists all across America for standing up to the for-profit corporations—the handsome leader who received widespread positive television publicity for having organized the strike against the Bedford Glassware Corporation.

The invitation was sent out to Rojo to please come to Washington, D.C. to interview to become the Great Deal Party's presidential candidate.

Clark conducted the interview himself. The questioning was tricky because he had to confirm that Rojo was a perfectly irrational socialist in every way.

Rojo had to be a socialist because he was an honest altruist and not because he was a dishonest kleptomaniac. The same was true of the other key candidates in the Great Deal Party, most importantly the candidates for Congress. Clark expected most voter support for the Great Deal Party to come from kleptomaniacs, however he did not want these people running the party because they would not carry out his agenda dependably. He had to find people who were moralistic: people who believed in 'good' and 'evil' and who thought that redistributing money was 'good' and earning money was 'evil.'

Clark finished the *saké*. He swiveled in his executive chair and put the empty glass on the walnut table, next to the picture frame. A big smile appeared on his face as he reflected on his cleverness.

The Rojo interview had gone on for hours and covered many topics. He had departed from the Great Deal Party office after passing all of the questioning.

Clark had been ready with the final test. He knew that questioning wasn't enough. People can lie when answering questions. There also had to be a test outside of the questioning. Therefore, he staged an experiment outdoors. He watched on a video monitor since he had a secret camera trained on the sidewalk just outside the office.

Four actors were engaged in a struggle on the sidewalk. One was an elderly lady dressed as if she were very wealthy. The other three were young men dressed as if they were very poor. The three men appeared to be hitting the lady and trying to pull her purse away.

Would Rojo act as expected? Would he act as a brave and heroic champion of socialist justice?

Rojo stepped onto the sidewalk and saw the conflict and did not hesitate. He leaped into the middle of the melee, causing the three men and the elderly lady to become

139

separated while he stood in the middle. He yelled out, "I will fight against crime and ensure justice is realized!"

Then, he grabbed the elderly lady's arms behind her back and spoke to the three men, "While I hold her, you guys take her purse!" The men grabbed the purse and ran away.

He released the lady and stood in front of her, waving his finger and scolding. "You are a criminal. Those men outnumber you three to one. And, they are poor and you are rich. Therefore, they have a human right to take your purse. You are a thief because you tried to stop them!"

He smacked the lady across the face and then stomped away.

Clark smiled at the memory as he looked out the jet window at the clouds. In the two years since that interview, everything had progressed as planned.

His ultimate scheme would be a success. He was going to solve the problem of the irrational people by harnessing their own irrationality to annihilate them. He would point the lemmings to the edge of the cliff and watch them jump off. The end of a long struggle was near. He only had to tolerate irrationality for a short while longer.

Oh sure, there would be collateral casualties among innocent people in his ultimate scheme. He had limited this somewhat, by trying to separate the irrational socialists and rational capitalists. But, as he saw today, some people were still not in the correct places.

He had saved Mr. Williams by sending him to Nevada. Clark chuckled at the idea that the socialists watching the television program were so irrational that they thought banishment to Nevada would be punishment for Mr. Williams!

Still sitting in his executive chair, Clark picked up the photo frame from the ovular table. He studied the image of his countryside cottage in Tennessee. His well-deserved retirement would be very soon.

(16) Late afternoon at an industrial port in Korea

American Vice President Clarence Clark, wearing a dark pinstripe business suit custom-fitted for his round body, forced a smile as he followed the Dear Socialist Leader and a retinue of North Korean soldiers, all clad in khaki, through the gates and into the noisy industrial port.

Clark despised North Korea and therefore this visit was mental torture for him. He had to go through with it as an official duty that came along with his U.S. government position and Great Deal Party leadership position. To make himself feel better about the visit, he had also developed a side objective.

He had a good view of the industrial port over everyone's heads since the skinny North Koreans were even shorter than he was as a result of their self-imposed famine. Only the Dear Socialist Leader himself could look Clark straight in the eyes, and only thanks to a pair of outrageous platform shoes.

The Dear Socialist Leader spoke loudly and clearly. His English was excellent. "Vice President Clark, welcome to the Red Martyr Industrial Port, where we North Koreans sacrifice ourselves every day for the common good. As you know, it is here that the economic cooperation between the United States and North Korea is taking place."

Clark felt a tremor run through his body as he carefully enunciated his rehearsed reply, also trying to speak loudly over the factory noise but with his usual squeaky voice. "We have begun a new era. A more sensible era. In the past, when the United States allowed international commerce, the people of South Korea were evil because they were stealing jobs from Americans by selling competitive products in the United

141

States. The people of North Korea, in contrast, were good because you did not sell anything to the United States. Instead, you got money by printing counterfeit dollars."

"Yes," replied the Dear Socialist Leader, "the time has come for recognition that North Korea is a friend to the United States and South Korea is an enemy. Come see what we have accomplished in agreement with your Great Deal Party."

Clark followed as the group crossed a grimy dock area lined with leaking steel barrels toward a large concrete-paneled structure with smoke belching out from the top and sludge pouring out from the bottom. He thought he might get cancer just from looking at this environmental disaster.

The Dear Socialist Leader pointed to where cranes were lifting tree trunks out of a docked ship. "Witness the first shipment of timber received from Yosemite National Park. We hope the entire states of California, Oregon, and Washington will be clear-cut over the next two years so that we can create sufficient paper to print all of the hundred-dollar bills that we promised, with pictures of President Rojo instead of Benjamin Franklin.

"The election of the Great Deal Party and ascent to power of Rojo and yourself has allowed for the advancement of my socialist economic programs. We have been actively printing United States currency here in North Korea for many years, but previously this was done on a smaller scale because we did not have the friendly cooperation of American authorities."

"This is great," said Clark, "and you should be certain that every time we dump a trillion dollars of this stuff on America that you also reward your people by dumping a trillion dollars on them."

"Everyone will be rich," said the Dear Socialist Leader with a smile. "It is such a simple plan and so beneficial for so many people that it is amazing it was not done a long time ago."

Clark cocked his head as he looked at the Korean autocrat. "Aren't you worried that dumping trillions of dollars of cash might cause inflation? Perhaps the people will not be wealthier since they are not producing more goods and services. For example, are you aware that Nazi Germany had a plan to defeat the British government by printing and distributing huge amounts of British currency? This was not meant to be economic aid to Great Britain, but rather it was a military attack."

The Dear Socialist Leader burst into laughter and almost fell to the ground as he wobbled on his platform shoes. "Ha, ha, ha. We do not have inflation here in my Hermit Kingdom! I have outlawed it by decree! All goods and services are plentiful for my people! Anyone who says there is a shortage is immediately shot!"

Clark's arms and legs began to twitch visibly. He grabbed a flask of Japanese *saké* from his pocket and chugged it. He began to relax.

He found it fascinating that the economic tools used by left-wingers in their own countries in peacetime, such as easy monetary policy and protectionist trade policy, were in fact the same tools an enemy country would use against them in wartime. It was a perfect alliance between the well-intentioned domestic do-gooders and the foreign attackers.

He felt satisfied that his ultimate scheme was exactly on track to cause the socialists to destroy themselves. But he had to keep focused on certain details and contingencies.

He stopped walking and let the soldiers get a few steps ahead, then called out to his companion. "Dear Socialist Leader, please remember we must talk in private for a couple minutes."

The Dear Socialist Leader came closer to Clark. The men had to stand right next to each other for their hushed voices to be audible over the clanging noises of the cranes.

Clark began. "I have specific intelligence regarding a counterrevolutionary attack against the United States which is planned for Wednesday. With your arsenal of five nuclear missiles, you can help to ensure the victory of socialism."

Clark leaned closer to the Dear Socialist Leader and explained further.

(17) Afternoon at Mount Elbrus, Russia

Jack Cannon reviewed the control panel. The *Flying Yankee* was on course from Arabia to the Caucasus Mountains of Russia at a cruising speed of 1,000 kilometers per hour and a lower-than-usual altitude of 8,000 meters.

He spoke into the headset built into his helmet. "Hello Valentina, how are you doing back there?" He felt he had gotten carried away the previous evening by kissing her at a party when in fact they were in the middle of an important and dangerous mission. His hope for today was that they could function properly as work partners and succeed in the next part of the mission.

"I am doing great," said Valentina Zaiceva from the rear tandem seat. "It's a good thing you had some extra gear. This flight suit and helmet are perfect."

"These Connecticut Air National Guard flight suits are great," said Jack. "They are flexible, comfortable, and temperature controlled. They can plug into the jet fighter for oxygen and electrical power, and they have a compact attachable air tank and battery for work outside of the aircraft. The suits also have memory features—like hidden multi-directional video cameras and microphones to record everything that happens on a mission."

The video console on the instrument panel of the jet fighter came to life.

The Director and Doctor Zaicev appeared on the screen. Jack pushed a button to channel the same image to the video console in the tandem seat so that Valentina could participate.

The Director, now wearing a well-tailored silver-colored suit and a tie with the turkey pattern, spoke. "Captain

145

Cannon, please update us on progress."

"Hello Director and Doctor Zaicev," said Jack. "I have Valentina with me and we are in the jet fighter. Soon we will enter Russian airspace."

"We have satellite communication and encryption capability in the jet fighter," said Valentina. "I am sending you the file that I provided to Jack and the King yesterday. There is a lot of evidence to indicate that Trans Pacific Trading Company is secretly owned by Ivan Ivanov and Clarence Clark, but we don't have absolute proof."

Jack saw a message at the bottom of the video console indicating that the file transfer was in progress.

The Director looked to be keenly interested. "We know Ivanov and Clark are the owners, but we can't prove that in court?"

Valentina replied, "Exactly."

The Director typed something on his keyboard. "Okay, we shall continue with the overall mission to prevent the repeal of the Bill of Rights.

"Ivanov and Clark will be at the grand opening of the Peak Hotel and Casino. We want you both to spy on them and try to figure out what they are scheming.

"I am already convinced the Great Deal Act has not come about as a result of the stupidity of Rojo but rather as a result of a deliberate attack against America orchestrated by Clark. We did background research on him and discovered that he has a very high IQ and incredible abilities with mathematical logic. Therefore, he cannot be a socialist because he is stupid, like Rojo. Rather, Clark must be a socialist because he has a perverse objective.

"You must discover what Clark is trying to accomplish. And, you must prevent him from succeeding by any means necessary.

"As for Rojo, we are working on a humane strategy. We must render him harmless because billions of people are suffering. But we recognize that he is a well-meaning person who just happens to have a non-functional mind."

Doctor Zaicev, dressed in white coveralls and twirling a pencil in his hand, elaborated, "The plan for Rojo relates to my scientific work on neurological downloads and uploads in Russia some years ago, work that is being perfected now at Mount Vernon."

Jack was interested. "What do you mean?"

The doctor made a sweeping motion with his arm and stepped back thus giving Jack and Valentina a view of the entire Democracy Society laboratory. The scientific team was there, as before. And now, they had two animals strapped onto the metal beds with electrodes attached to their heads. One animal was a pig and the other was a goat.

The Director quickly stepped in front of the camera, blocking the view of the laboratory. "Let's just say there are some interesting animals here. Pigs who think they are goats. Goats who think they are pigs. We can't reveal any more. Do your duty in Russia and we will do our duty here at Mount Vernon."

Jack nodded and switched off the console as the conference call ended.

Valentina commented over the headset. "This is just like my father—always working on some mysterious science project."

Jack replied as he reviewed the aircraft controls. "I can see that something interesting is going on in the laboratory. I would love to know more, but for now we must focus on our arrival in Russia."

Jack had a great view of Mount Elbrus through the cockpit window. The 5700-meter volcanic cone, where the Peak Hotel and Casino was located, was the highest point in Europe. Jack marveled that it was a kilometer higher than Mont Blanc in the Alps.

He could now see the Peak Hotel and Casino. It looked

to him like an oversized aircraft carrier sitting on top of the rocky peak of the gigantic mountain.

Jack had never seen such a large building before. And not only was it large, it was also ornate. The facade shimmered and glistened brightly even from a far distance.

He presumed that the marble-clad structure to one side of the runway was the hotel, topped with a building that looked like a fairy castle complete with a high tower. That was probably the casino and a penthouse office for President Ivanov.

The snowboard facilities were alongside the hotel with a line of brightly painted helicopters secured on the roof of another marble-clad structure that was the top of a massive cable-car tram, serving an area below the hotel but entirely above the tree-line.

Jack observed that the snow conditions were excellent. Today was sunny, however it appeared the mountain had been covered with a fresh blanket of powder snow overnight. He was aware that they would have some free hours before the critical evening meeting. His fantasy was a ride through the powder on a snowboard.

Alas, it was unlikely to happen. Sure, Valentina was an experienced scuba diver. But was she likely to be an experienced snowboarder as well?

Jack recalled a woman he had dated back in America. He had brought her to Wyoming for a snowboarding holiday that turned into a disaster. She could never keep up with him and he had to rescue her again and again in areas that were not even particularly difficult.

Just then, Valentina spoke over the headset. "Do you ride?"

Jack snapped out of his daydream and replied, "Ride?"

Valentina sounded impatient. "Do you snowboard? We have a couple hours free before the important evening reception. Let's go snowboarding."

148

Jack replied as he looked out the window at the slopes, "You read my mind. I would love to go snowboarding!"

Valentina summarized the situation. "I see the snowboarding area is different from how it was when I was a teenager coming here with my father. The Old Viewpoint cable-car station, at 2900 meters, has been reconstructed and appears to be the bottom of the snowboarding area. It used to be the top of the snowboarding area. I assume they disconnected Old Viewpoint from the valley when they built the new hotel on the summit because President Ivanov is at war with the minority ethnic groups living in the valley."

Jack was delighted to hear Valentina was a snowboarder. "You have snowboarded here before? With your father?"

"Yes, I snowboarded here many times when I was a teenager. Back then, the resort did not offer any safety or comfort. We reached the best slopes above the rickety lift system by flying up in an old Soviet military helicopter. We faced constant risk of death from avalanche or falling into unmarked crevasses. I had to rescue my father once. He was hanging off the edge of a crevasse that was almost impossible to see from above. Good thing I was prepared with a safety rope. The snowboard area today appears to be better organized with new lifts and marked trails. I'm not interested in marked trails, however. I want to go off-piste to get away from the amateur riders."

Jack thought to himself. Could it be true? Was Valentina really such a daring and accomplished snowboarder? He loved to snowboard and he knew the most beautiful spots were often dangerous. He was experienced in mitigating the danger. It sounded like Valentina was similarly experienced.

Jack looked at her on the video screen. She was staring out the canopy with her lynx-like eyes. She was an incredible woman. Not only was she stunningly beautiful, but she was an accomplished journalist and she knew her way around a coral reef. Now it turned out she was a snowboarder as well.

"Ready for action!" he exclaimed into the headset as the *Flying Yankee* approached the hotel landing strip.

He sighed. This was too good to be true. She must have a flaw, but he hadn't found it yet. All his life he wanted to find the perfect woman. However, he doubted such a woman existed.

*

Valentina stood at the upper end of the Bolshoi Azau Glacier as she inhaled deeply from her oxygen supply and prepared for the descent. She brushed the powder snow off of her snowboard and snapped her boots into the bindings. She was excited to try this brand-new, high-quality equipment provided by the hotel.

Jack had been correct in advising her that the flight suits and helmets were perfect for snowboarding. She was warm in the suit and she appreciated the flexibility of the fabric. The helmet had a visor that changed tint in accordance with the brightness. The sun was shining brightly today, and therefore the visor was at its darkest tint. The headset in the helmet allowed her to talk with Jack. And, on top of all that, the suits and helmets looked nice, she thought as she checked out Jack stretching out his legs and snapping his boots into his snowboard.

Valentina scanned the scenery. They were at a height of 4200 meters with the glacier stretching down below them at a moderate pitch. Kupol Peak towered above them at 5000 meters.

Snow conditions were perfect since light powder snow had fallen overnight. And, the ride would be a thrilling mix of open areas for carving plus rolling ridges to jump off of.

She looked to her side and saw that Jack was ready to begin.

The setting was beautiful and would be tranquil as well,

except for some reason the helicopter that dropped them off was still hovering nearby. Although painted in bright cheery colors to please tourists, it was the latest model of Russian military helicopter and it was very loud since it had a special engine for high-altitude flying. Valentina wished it would return to the hotel and leave them in peace.

The couple snowboarded smoothly through the fresh powder snow. Valentina was impressed by Jack's graceful style as he led them downward. They glided over a series of rolling rises and dips and the feeling was pure exhilaration each time another turn sent a wave of powder flying in the air.

They both stopped at the top of the Khotiutau Snow Plateau at 3600 meters. They could see more rolling ridges of the snowfield extending all the way down to the 2900-meter level, which is where they would traverse a lake area to reach the bottom of the resort lift system.

The high peak of Ullukambash was visible with an enormous snow cornice on top. The peak was at 3700 meters, which put it about 400 meters higher than the level of the snowfield in front of it.

Valentina was again disturbed by the helicopter. It was still hovering nearby. In fact, it was near the snow cornice overhang. What were the pilots thinking? Didn't they know about the avalanche danger from creating a loud noise under such an overhang?

A voice boomed out from the helicopter loudspeaker, "Die do-gooders!"

Suddenly, a different voice called out from the loudspeaker, "Die hypocrites!"

Valentina spoke urgently into the headset. "Vladislav and Vyachislav are flying the helicopter! They will try to kill us again!"

She could see that Jack was also looking at the helicopter. He replied over the headset. "Let's go!"

Valentina and Jack began to snowboard down the mountain as fast as possible just when ten black-clad soldiers on skis popped out from behind a ridge and pursued while firing machine guns.

Valentina spoke into her headset as bullets flew past, "Follow me exactly! Hidden deep crevasse at the far side of the snowfield! We can lose the soldiers there!"

Valentina swooped ahead of Jack and cut an arching turn through the snow. Jack followed. They were on their way across the snowfield.

Bullets threw up puffs of powder snow all around Valentina and Jack as they glided at full speed.

Valentina heard Jack's voice through the headset. "Valentina, are you sure you know what you're doing?"

She didn't respond, but instead crouched and extended her arms to snowboard as fast as she could over the slight ridge that extended above the hidden crevasse, making it invisible to riders approaching from this angle.

With snow flying across her helmet visor, she had to rely a bit on feel to choose the moment to cut back in the other direction. "Now!" she yelled as she leaped and turned the snowboard and raced back the other way with Jack following her trail exactly.

As Valentina slowed down, the snow spray was reduced and her visibility improved. She looked behind and confirmed that Jack was there.

Both looked back and upward and saw what they had just missed—a huge gaping crevasse. The shear ice walls dropped straight down into the glacier further than they could see.

As Valentina and Jack came to a stop, ten black-clad, machine-gun-toting skiers launched over the ridge and fell straight down the crevasse. Screams and gunfire were audible as the soldiers disappeared, plunging into the abyss.

But Valentina did not relax for a moment. She took a quick look at the helicopter before resuming the snowboard descent together with Jack.

*

Vladislav leveled out the helicopter in a strategic position, 200 meters above the snowfield just in front of Ullukambash Peak under an enormous snow cornice.

He found it convenient that when he served briefly in the Russian army, he had not only learned about scuba diving, but also how to pilot helicopters.

This particular helicopter, a super-charged, high-altitude version of a Russian military helicopter, was new to him. But he was able to figure it out well enough.

He watched as the last of the black-clad soldiers plunged into the deadly crevasse and then turned toward his brother in the co-pilot seat. They spoke to each other with lisps since both had lost their front teeth.

"Ha, ha, ha. Fools," said Vladislav. "This saves us some work because President Ivanov said that after the soldiers killed Valentina and Jack, we were supposed to kill the soldiers to eliminate witnesses."

"Dead men don't tell tales!" laughed Vyachislav.

"But this means we need to kill Valentina and Jack ourselves," deduced Vladislav.

"Jack is very annoying because he seemed like he was honest and not a criminal," said Vyachislav. "People like that must be cowardly fools. They're not like us—brave smart people who side with criminals because we know criminals always win."

"Foolish brother," laughed Vladislav. "When will you learn? Everyone has a corrupt angle to everything they do. I know that because I have a corrupt angle to everything I do. Valentina and Jack must have dark, ulterior motives."

Vyachislav shrugged, "Anyway it's great we can kill them today. It should be a lot of fun."

Vladislav was now looking at Vyachislav and could not help but be disturbed. His face looked like a checkerboard with red splotches where the sea urchin spines had hit. And, his front teeth were missing having been bashed out on the fire coral.

Alas, thought Vladislav, he probably looked the same. And they probably suffered similar brain damage from the nitrogen bubbles in their bloodstreams since they refused to go into the re-compression chamber in Arabia, as advised by the scuba rescue team at the Sea Hotel and Spa.

But it didn't matter because they would have plenty of girlfriends after they got their bonus from Ivanov. The bonus party was coming up soon!

Vladislav fumbled around in between the pilot and co-pilot seat to find the binoculars. Vyachislav helped by moving some junk out of the way—empty vodka bottle, empty cigarette pack, and the mirrored helmets they had been wearing when they flew Jack and Valentina to the glacier.

Vladislav finally found the binoculars on the floor under the heels of his pirate boots. He picked up the binoculars and used them to focus on the two targets down on the snowfield.

He had known all along that Valentina would come to the Peak Hotel and Casino opening. Ivanov invited her for the sole purpose of arranging her assassination. In fact, Vladislav had not expected her to be in Arabia. He and his brother were only in Arabia to spy on the King.

Since Jack appeared to be working in cooperation with Valentina, President Ivanov had added him to the assassination list as well.

Vladislav scanned the mountains. He saw a lot of snow in the mountain valleys in every direction. He hoped that later he could stuff some snow into his pants to provide pain relief for the infected welts where the lionfish spines had lacerated his testicles.

It was time for what he called revenge: committing an unprovoked cruelty against an innocent victim a second time after failing the first time.

Vladislav lowered the binoculars as the helicopter automatically hovered in place.

The brothers then pulled two large black cases out from behind their seats. They opened the cases on their laps and assembled their bazookas.

Discarding the cases back behind the seats, they pushed controllers that opened the windows on either side of the cabin. They each leaned out a window and aimed their bazookas at Jack and Valentina.

But what was that just ahead, running across the snowfield? It was a giant leopard! Vladislav never saw one of those before, except on television. Therefore, he assumed the leopard must be extremely rare, from an endangered species. That was why he wanted to kill it. He pointed the leopard out to his brother. They switched their aim away from Jack and Valentina and toward the leopard.

*

Jack carved another broad turn as he raced through the fresh powder on his snowboard. As he rode through the snow, he got a good view of Valentina snowboarding alongside him, just a bit behind. She had beautiful form. She was clearly a gifted athlete. Also, she had exhibited bravery and intelligence when she rescued them from the ten soldiers.

Jack looked upward at the continuing threat—the helicopter. It was hovering under a nearby peak. Vladislav and Vyachislav were visible hanging out of the windows armed with large bazookas. For some reason, the brothers seemed to be aiming in the wrong direction, at a target further downhill.

As Jack jumped his snowboard over a small ridge, he got

a view downward at the target. It was a Caucasian leopard! He could not believe his good luck. He had read that the beautiful and magnificent Caucasian leopard was near extinction with only a couple dozen still living in the mountains.

Jack and Valentina created a blinding spray of snow when they carved a sharp turn to avoid the leopard. When they came to a stop, they had a perfect view of the leopard on the snowfield below them and the helicopter under the snow cornice above them.

BLAMMM!!!

The bazookas fired. There was a black smoldering hole where the leopard had been standing. But fortunately, the leopard had darted away just an instant before and was running down the slope unharmed.

As the noise of the firing bazookas reverberated and echoed off of the cliffs, a new rumbling noise became audible. Jack and Valentina looked up toward the helicopter.

The bazooka noise had started an avalanche! Snow was pouring off the top of the peak onto the hovering helicopter. Then, the entire snow cornice overhang collapsed.

When the snow cornice hit the helicopter, the fuel tank exploded in a giant fireball. The helicopter was smashed straight down to the surface of the snowfield. And, the fire was immediately extinguished as the plummeting cornice buried the helicopter completely.

Jack and Valentina lifted their helmet visors and turned to each other, panting.

"Good thing the leopard got away!" said Valentina. "And this time I really think we have seen the last of Vladislav and Vyachislav."

"Let's enjoy the rest of the ride," said Jack. "We should build up some speed for the traverse to the cable car at Old Viewpoint!"

(18) Late morning at Washington National Cathedral, Washington, D.C.

David Goldstein was skeptical about the publicity event that his Property Rights Party staff had scheduled for the last day before the presidential election debate. Even though he was not religious at all himself, and his ancestors had been Jewish, the staff strongly encouraged him to accept an invitation from Reverend Monk to attend a youth educational service at Washington National Cathedral in the presence of television cameras.

As Goldstein rode in the back of the Virginia National Guard van toward the event, he thought about the situation with education in the Great Deal States. All schools had been shut down since June 2013 by the teacher strike and, since then, the only education available was provided by volunteers in churches.

Reverend Monk, once Goldstein's nemesis in Chicago, had written to the Property Rights Party on multiple occasions in what seemed like a genuine effort to restart his relationship with Goldstein on a new basis.

Monk claimed he was teaching economics to young Americans. He was no longer opposed to the study of economics, but rather had embraced it and become an academic himself. He wrote that he wanted to show off his new economics school to Goldstein and thus the two men, with mutual interest in the study of economics, could become friends.

Goldstein had been worried about the youth of the Great Deal States ever since the schools shut down. Therefore, he was relieved to hear that some young people were getting a

157

proper education. Yet, he had vivid memories of past encounters with Monk.

When Goldstein was a bank profitability consultant, back before the "Subprime Mortgage Crisis" of 2007, Monk, a firebrand community activist in Chicago, was leading street protests to pressure banks to make 100% loans to unqualified borrowers to purchase overpriced homes. Goldstein was opposed to these loans because he believed banks should function only for the purpose of maximizing profit and he expected that under-collateralized loans to unqualified borrowers would cause huge losses to shareholders.

History proved Goldstein to be correct. And, not only did shareholders suffer from the altruistic practice of lending to unqualified borrowers, but the borrowers also suffered. Monk probably learned from his mistake and that was why he switched from left-wing activism to teaching economics.

As Goldstein stepped out of the van and beheld the soaring Gothic facade of the cathedral, he reminded himself that it might be friendly territory. He had been here once before, ten years earlier for the funeral of Ronald Reagan. The cathedral, by reputation, was a place that welcomed conservatives.

Goldstein walked into the cathedral with two Virginia National Guardsmen. They stepped into the impressive nave with a thirty-meter ceiling and beautiful stained-glass windows.

Just as Goldstein had been briefed, the congregation was comprised of roughly one hundred children. They were all seated in the pews on either side of him.

Suddenly, he heard a voice emanating from the loudspeaker system. "All children listen to God's word: earning money is evil!"

Goldstein looked up at the man behind the lectern. It was Reverend Monk, hooded and dressed in an ornamental white robe, who was speaking into the microphone.

158

"Everyone here today is guilty," continued Monk. "You are all sinners. You are all guilty of the sin of greed. You must repent!"

The children all withdrew leather whips that were provided in wooden pockets behind each pew. The children began whipping their own backs in unison as they cried in pain.

Goldstein wondered. What was going on? This sounded like the old community-firebrand Monk. This did not sound like a new economically literate Monk.

"We have a very important guest today," announced Monk. "The presidential candidate from the Property Rights Party, Professor David Goldstein!"

The children stopped whipping themselves and applauded politely. Goldstein stood stunned in the middle of the aisle.

"Now children, begin your activities," said Monk.

The children gathered together in groups of four and began their projects.

Monk stepped down from the lectern and walked along the aisle toward Goldstein. Monk flipped back his hood, revealing a shaved head, bright blue eyes, and an eager smile. He welcomed Goldstein with a hearty handshake as a GFN television camera focused in. "Welcome to Washington National Cathedral, David. I am so happy you accepted my invitation!"

Goldstein was worried as he replied, "Thank you for the invitation. I am happy to hear that you are educating children about economics. But I am confused. Why did you just make a speech about how earning money is evil?"

"Ha, ha, ha," laughed Monk. "Obviously, we cannot have the children conducting business in greedy and self-interested ways. Rather, they must conduct business in ethical ways. Here, let me show you."

Goldstein groaned, but tried to maintain a friendly smile

as he followed Monk to the first group of children. The group was comprised of four boys and each held a can of soup. A GFN cameraman followed and focused in on the group.

Monk explained, "David, take a look at these children. They are learning about free market trade."

Goldstein felt a bit relieved as he replied, "That is wonderful. Free market trade is very important for maximizing human wealth."

"I agree completely," replied Monk, who then turned toward the boys. "Okay, just like I taught you—begin trading!"

The children all studied each other's soup cans and the pictures of the ingredients. The soup cans were each different: onion soup, garlic soup, mushroom soup, and chicken soup.

The kids had a silly and childish discussion for a minute as they grabbed soup cans away from each other. Finally, each child had a soup can different from the one that he started with.

One little boy was crying. He held the can of chicken soup.

Monk explained, "You see, David, I have trained these children well. Each brings a can of soup from home. Soup cans, of course, are the only food still available in the city since all of the grocery stores were emptied in June 2013. Families are running low on supplies. Therefore, we only usually see the least desirable flavors of soup in here.

"The children do have opinions about different flavors. For example, Tommy brought onion soup and Joey brought mushroom soup. Tommy and Joey both hate onion soup and mushroom soup, however Tommy dislikes mushroom soup even more and therefore he traded his onion soup for mushroom soup. Likewise, Joey dislikes onion soup even more and therefore he traded his mushroom soup for onion soup."

"But that is totally backward!" exclaimed Goldstein. "Free trade means each individual makes a voluntary decision to trade an asset for a different asset that he values more highly! That is how wealth is created!"

"Don't forget, I am teaching the children to trade ethically," said Monk. "If a child traded his soup to get a soup that he liked better, then he would be exploiting his trading partner. I don't tolerate exploitation here in the cathedral and therefore everyone is required to make trades against their own self-interest for the sake of the common good."

Goldstein looked down at the smiling boy holding the garlic soup, but was distracted by the wailing cries of the boy with the chicken soup.

Monk explained, "Garlic soup is the best one because all of the children hate it. Therefore, a child can never exploit another child by trading something to get garlic soup.

"However, I see we have a problem today. Somebody brought chicken soup. This doesn't usually happen because chicken soup is scarce these days. You see, all of the children like chicken soup. Chicken soup is their favorite."

Goldstein was confused, "That isn't a problem. That is a good thing. If this boy has chicken soup and he likes chicken soup, then he should be happy!"

The boy with the chicken soup, still crying, now resumed whipping himself.

Monk spoke in a soothing voice as he took the chicken soup from the boy. "Johnny, don't worry. We will do something to reduce the value of this soup so that nobody will be exploited."

Monk stepped toward the next group of children and Goldstein followed. The GFN television camera was right behind them.

Monk stopped where a group of four girls was gathered by a mixing pot. One of the girls was stirring the water in the pot. The other three girls were pouring ingredients into the pot.

One girl poured salt into the pot. One girl poured sugar into the pot. One girl poured vinegar into the pot.

Monk pulled a can opener from a pocket in his robe and opened the chicken soup. He poured it into the pot. "Okay Suzy, mix everything up."

Goldstein stared as the mixing girl swirled all of the incompatible ingredients together. "This is absurd. You have taken four valuable inputs and mixed them together to create something worthless. Why did you do that?"

Monk looked at Goldstein and explained. "This is all about ethical economics, David. Are you saying that University of Chicago didn't teach ethics?

"If we mixed four ingredients of low value together to create something of high value, then the result would be profit. According to God, profit is evil. Therefore, we are mixing together four ingredients of high value to create something with no value.

"This is what has always been done in countries with socialist economic systems. For example, the Soviet Union burned enormous amounts of valuable oil and gas to manufacture products that were worthless. Since the Soviet people became very poor from this, they were behaving in a good selfless way instead of an evil self-interested way."

"Self-interest is natural," said Goldstein, his red hair curling up as he became more and more annoyed. "It is not evil. Try to give me any rational reason why these children should intentionally strive against their self-interest when self-interest is beneficial to society when property rights are protected. Why should these children go through life refusing to earn money when earning money means efficient production of goods and services for consumers? Give me a rational reason!"

Reverend Monk put his hand on Goldstein's shoulder.

"David, David, David. There is no rational reason. You must look to faith! You must look to God!"

Goldstein turned toward the television camera and forced a final smile. Then he spun around and stomped back down the aisle toward the exit. He was flanked by the Virginia National Guardsmen and followed by the GFN crew as he passed the one-hundred crying children.

His logical mind was seriously concerned as he left the cathedral. What was going on in America? Had everyone gone crazy and become socialist? Could he save his country?

(19) Daytime at Everglades National Park, Florida

President Roberto Rojo stood in the middle of an enormous expanse of monoculture plantation, dressed as usual in a business suit. He had taken *Air Force One* from Dulles Airport down to Florida in order to make a campaign appearance at Everglades National Park.

He beamed with pride at yet another example of the great work he had done for America. He remembered a family vacation to Everglades National Park when he was a child. At that time, the park was completely useless: a big swamp filled with weeds, mosquitoes, and alligators.

Now, as he viewed the drained and denuded land, replanted with sugarcane, he felt a sense of accomplishment.

Rojo had the details on a briefing paper right in front of him. In November 2012, when he became president, Everglades National Park comprised 1,509,000 acres or 611,000 hectares. This was approximately a quarter of the original Everglades area. The other three-quarters had already been drained by a series of government actions.

He considered the most brilliant step to have been the introduction of sugar import quotas in 1934. Franklin Delano Roosevelt believed Americans would become richer if they were prohibited from buying affordable sugar, and this made perfect sense to Rojo.

In 2012, the American people were spending approximately $5 billion per year on sugar protection. This included the direct cost of subsidies and the indirect cost of an above-market sugar price to consumers. This did not include the additional resources that had to be spent on economic aid and drug-law enforcement aid for dozens of so-

164

called "developing" countries that were hurt by the sugar quotas.

Rojo had ordered the draining of the last remaining swampy hectares as one of his first actions when he became president.

Then came the Great Deal Act and Temporary Police State Act. Sugar import quotas were replaced by a total ban on imports. The Florida National Guard brought unpaid prisoners to Everglades National Park to perform all labor.

Early in 2014, the draining had been completed. The final wetland hectares were converted to sugarcane cultivation. Rojo had finished what FDR had started.

And the result was now here before Rojo's eyes. He held a stalk of sugarcane and licked the sweet sugar. His face lit up with a smile.

He thought how nice it would be in the future if an altruistic retail chain could be set up in America so that consumers could purchase this sugar at the low price that had been set by the Fair Price Agency. The current practice of bulldozing all of the harvest into the sea seemed wasteful, but it was better than the unethical alternative of allowing for-profit retailers to sell the harvest.

He snapped out of his daydream when he noticed Maria Diaz waving to get his attention. He walked to where the cameras and sound equipment were directed at two men.

One man was dressed only in boxer shorts, black socks, and muddy wingtip shoes. He was drenched in sweat as he staggered between the rows of sugarcane pulling a huge plastic tank on wheels while pointing a spray tube at any plants that appeared between the cane rows. His skin was sunburned with painful-looking lash stripes across his back.

The other man was a Florida National Guard private who stood nearby with a bullwhip. He was wearing combat fatigues and a helmet.

Rojo positioned himself next to the subjects. His briefing

paper indicated that their names were Prisoner Clancy and Private Lombardi.

Maria addressed the cameras first. "Good morning to all GFN viewers. We are in Florida today with coverage of President Roberto Rojo's visit to the Everglades National Park Rehabilitation Camp."

The cameras swiveled and pointed at Rojo, who began his speech. "Good morning majority people of America! I'm visiting the Everglades National Park Rehabilitation Camp today to present the Socialist Freedom Award to an inmate who has rehabilitated himself from being a profit-making parasite to being a money-losing altruist. I'd like to introduce the nation to Prisoner Clancy!"

The toiling laborer stopped pulling the tank cart and looked at the camera as he panted in exhaustion.

Rojo stepped beside him, "Prisoner Clancy, you were an evil thief. You owned a company that developed an apartment complex in Miami. After you invested all your money in the construction of this apartment complex, you rented the apartment units to families at market prices. You were an evil thief because it is unethical to charge rent. Families have a human right to live wherever they want without paying rent. When you spent all of your money building the apartment complex, you should have foregone all revenue and allowed people to live in the apartments for free.

"Can you explain your rehabilitation program to the television audience?"

Prisoner Clancy's voice was dry and raspy. "I am suffering the punishment I deserve for having charged rent in the past. My job is to pull this tank across this field from sunrise to sunset and spray Agent Orange herbicide on any invasive indigenous plant that I see."

Rojo was happy to hear this because he'd made a personal contribution to the day-to-day effort to improve the Everglades. When he was told that herbicides were

166

unavailable because all producers were on strike, he remembered the military had a massive supply of Agent Orange that was sitting unused, awaiting destruction. Why destroy such a useful chemical when it could be sprayed into one of America's major watersheds for the purpose of losing money? Advisers told him the chemical was extremely hazardous to humans. But, Rojo knew Americans had to make sacrifices in the implementation of socialism.

Prisoner Clancy continued, "Since my incarceration, I have succeeded in spraying a million gallons of Agent Orange herbicide into the Florida ecosystem, and by doing so I set a record in my forced labor unit."

Rojo smiled with joy. "Prisoner Clancy, can you say a few words about the purpose of spraying a million gallons of Agent Orange herbicide onto the Everglades?"

Prisoner Clancy replied with a look of pride. "The wise and altruistic people at the Central Planning Bureau studied history to find the most unprofitable economic activity for Florida, and they decided it must be sugarcane cultivation. Of course, profit is not a meaningful word when labor is done at gunpoint and prices of inputs and outputs are set by government mandate. However, the bureaucrats knew that sugarcane cultivation was unprofitable in past years, and therefore must be non-exploitative.

"I have learned here at the Everglades that in my previous life as an apartment developer I was cruel and I hurt a lot of people by providing them with homes that were not free. Now I am in the process of repenting with hard labor duties."

Rojo made a final statement to Prisoner Clancy. "I sincerely hope that after your ten-year term at the camp you'll be able to go into society as a reformed man, never producing rental housing again. Congratulations on being awarded the Socialist Freedom Award."

"I have taken an oath many times in front of the lecturers from the Central Planning Bureau that I promise never to do anything which generates a profit," said Prisoner Clancy.

Rojo withdrew a long red ribbon and shining medal from his pocket. Prisoner Clancy smiled and bowed as Rojo placed the red ribbon and medal bearing the 'equal' sign over Prisoner Clancy's head.

Private Lombardi suddenly spoke. "We in the Florida National Guard are proud of our work giving freedom to the American people!"

The sharp crack of the whip sounded as Private Lombardi lashed a red stripe across Prisoner Clancy's back.

Rojo turned toward Private Lombardi, impressed by the good work the soldier was doing. "Private Lombardi, please give me and the television audience some background about your role at Everglades National Park Rehabilitation Camp."

Private Lombardi tilted his helmet up to reveal dark hair and observant brown eyes. He replied, "I was with the U. S. Army 172nd Infantry Brigade in Germany. We were withdrawn to Florida in 2012 and merged with the Florida National Guard.

"When the Temporary Police State Act became law in 2013, we were ordered to round up the profit-mongers in the 22nd congressional district, around Boca Raton. That used to be the richest district in Florida.

"All prisoners were questioned about whether they felt guilty about obtaining money through interest, rent, or profit.

"Prisoners who felt guilty came here to the Everglades to begin ten-year rehabilitation sentences.

"Prisoners who did not feel guilty were exiled. We loaded them up on boats and sent them to the Bahamas, where they will suffer for the rest of their lives under capitalist government, according to official Great Deal Party propaganda."

"Private Lombardi, not only should you be proud of yourself for helping Prisoner Clancy to be free, but also you should be happy you are part of the team producing sugar in

168

a manner that is completely uncompetitive and inefficient and thus beneficial to society because nobody gets profit."

"Actually I'm confused about the whole sugar strategy," said Private Lombardi. "None of our produce ever gets to market. And anyway, what's the point? Why don't we just purchase sugar from countries that produce sugar more efficiently, such as Brazil? Then the Everglades could be restored as a natural wetland. I used to enjoy canoe trips here as a child."

Rojo was shocked. Obviously something had gone badly wrong when the GFN people vetted candidates for this television spot. He shot an accusative glance at Maria. They'd selected a soldier with some ideas that sounded to Rojo not only capitalist, but quite possibly fascist or even feudal! Rojo lunged forward and snatched the whip out of the soldier's hand.

Rojo stood in the ready position with the whip wound up for a strike. "Private Lombardi, I'll tell your superiors that you should watch the evening propaganda movies together with the prisoners until you learn something about ethics!"

CRACK went the whip!

"You'll learn not to question the central planners because they are the most benevolent authorities in America!"

CRACK went the whip!

Rojo then regained his composure as he turned back toward the cameras. In his peripheral vision he saw Prisoner Clancy and Private Lombardi limping away grasping their sore backsides.

"All of America sees the huge progress that has been made by the Great Deal Party," announced Rojo. "We are changing America from a nation of capitalist slaves motivated by money into a nation of socialist free people motivated by love. Vote for the Great Deal Party on Tuesday! And, if you believe you deserve something for free from the government, please come to the majority victory party in Orlando on

Wednesday. Get a surprise from the government!"

*

Maria Diaz gazed out the window of the smooth-flying helicopter from the Florida National Guard designated *Marine One* as it crossed the seemingly endless field of monoculture sugarcane. Then, she swiveled her seat toward her traveling companion, Roberto Rojo.

Rojo spoke loudly over the noise of the helicopter. "Maria, I hope you're enjoying the helicopter flight and I hope you're not working too much. You know we have a law against that."

"You have reminded me several times about the thirty-hour rule and I'll try to comply," said Maria. "But I admit I did a bit of extra work prior to the Everglades event. I reviewed preliminary footage for the Great Deal propaganda video that is to be aired starting today on the West Coast, and I noticed a problem you should be aware of. The video is supposed to show a family living in luxury in Great Deal California and another family living in squalor in Property Rights Nevada. However, crashing waves of the California coast are behind the Nevada family and the skyline of Las Vegas is behind the California family. How can this be?"

"Maria, Maria, Maria. You must be familiar with the universally accepted saying 'the ends justify the means.' Simply ask the GFN people to do some magic with their computers. Put the waves behind the Nevada family and put the skyline behind the California family."

"But that's deceptive! You mean the rich happy family is really in Property Rights Nevada and the poor miserable family is really in Great Deal California? And you want to trick viewers that it's the other way around?"

"Of course! We did the same switch with the New York versus Connecticut propaganda documentary. We just need to keep the deception going until Wednesday so that we can repeal the Bill of Rights and give unlimited power to the Great Deal Party congressmen."

Maria's jaw dropped. She swiveled her chair so that she looked out the window, away from Rojo.

What kind of scam was she participating in? Her intention was to be an honest television presenter. Was she being used as the face person for a big fraud? She really didn't think this footage switch would make a difference in the election. She was confident Rojo would win regardless. But, she was deeply disturbed by Rojo's action as a matter of principle.

Maria had her doubts about Rojo before. She always sensed that his brain did not function logically. But this was the last straw—deliberate dishonesty! How could she repair her damaged career after learning that she participated in a false propaganda effort?

She knew that after they took *Air Force One* from Orlando to Dulles Airport, she would have time alone in her hotel room to prepare for the presidential election debate. She would be the moderator. The truth must be revealed during the debate! Was it possible for someone to save America from the Great Deal Party? Was it possible for someone to save the Bill of Rights? She feared the worst!

(20) Evening at Mount Elbrus, reception

Jack Cannon made a final adjustment to his 'tie,' which was nothing more than a large and brilliant emerald stud, and straightened the diamond turkey badge on his black dinner jacket.

He turned and saw Valentina Zaiceva looking gorgeous in her watered-silk evening gown. Her custom-tailored gown was the same green color as his emerald and her eyes, making the couple a dazzling and stylish team as they arrived at the reception.

He reflected on the amazing efficiency of the team of Russian tailors in the hotel suite to create such elegant bespoke clothing in just a few hours. Perhaps this hotel did deserve its self-designated nine-star rating.

Jack offered Valentina a cocked elbow and escorted her along the red carpet through a gauntlet of soldiers.

He counted thirty soldiers on either side in black fatigues pointing assault rifles at the guests as they entered the party. President Ivanov was hated by all rational Russians. Even though rational people were the minority in Russia, as in all other nations, they were a potentially powerful group and therefore Ivanov needed heavy security. Jack thought with amusement about the possibility of a gun battle in this entranceway, since the guards would all shoot each other.

After the gauntlet of soldiers was a gauntlet of waitresses. The waitresses alongside the red carpet were all tall and slim with high cheekbones indicating Slavic origin. Each had the body of a dancer and was dressed in skin-tight black pants, topless with painted shark scenes cleverly concealing her breasts.

172

Jack and Valentina received glasses of champagne from one of the waitresses and continued walking.

The couple now stood in the center of a gigantic room where over one thousand VIP guests had gathered for the grand opening party of the Peak Hotel and Casino, the first nine-star hotel in the world.

Jack looked about. The tremendous room was larger than a football field with plush red and blue carpeting and gold trim everywhere. The ten-meter-high ceiling was vaulted in some places, mirrored in some places, and hung with many chandeliers.

An incredible mountainscape could be seen through the panoramic windows, but this was not what held the attention of the guests.

Rather, the guests were gathering around the colossal aquariums. The five aquariums reached from floor to ceiling. Each housed a massive and ferocious live shark.

Valentina seemed mesmerized by the sharks. "Wow. Although I find the decorating to be overdone and less tasteful than the traditional decorating at the Sea Hotel, I've got to admit these shark tanks are fabulous. It seems they have one of each of the largest shark varieties."

The pair approached the largest of the shark tanks, the one containing a six-meter-long hammerhead shark from the Red Sea. They studied the hammerhead as it undulated its body causing it to race smoothly and effortlessly through the water, a blank look in its primitive eyes and its mouth hanging open exposing sharp teeth. They had a good view of the top of the shark also from the mirrored top of the tank.

Jack noticed two men standing at the shark tank. He knew much about them but had never met them. He nudged Valentina.

Russian President Ivan Ivanov was of average height and slender build. He had a full head of wavy brown hair and nondescript eyes. His physical features could only be described as ordinary.

Ivanov wore a close-fitting suit with big diamonds in the buttons and cuff links, a colorful tie with an expensive French brand-name printed in large letters down the middle, shiny shoes made from an unfortunate reptile, and a watch with more diamonds in it than metal. As Jack and Valentina moved closer, large price tags became visible, indicating that Ivanov wanted people to see how much he overpaid for each component of his outrageous outfit.

Meanwhile the American vice president, shorter and younger than Ivanov but much heavier, was dressed in a conservative suit designed to impress a different sort of voter. Clarence Clark probably intended his gray pinstripe suit to make his large belly less noticeable, but he was not successful. The bright red stripes on his American-flag tie matched the color of his puffy cheeks, indicating that he had downed a few champagnes already.

Approaching the two men, Valentina spoke first, in English. "A fascinating creature, the *sphyrna mokarran*, largest of the hammerhead sharks. Sharks evolved 400 million years ago and haven't changed much since then—and therefore they have no intelligence whatsoever. They will immediately eat anything in front of them without regard to the future. They will eat their own offspring and even their own tails.

"It is fortunate that humans have evolved further, or some humans anyway, and have invented such concepts as honesty, cooperation, rule of law, and protection of private property. In short, enlightened self-interest. Humans don't depend on socialist theft to obtain wealth but instead can obtain wealth from capitalist productivity."

Ivanov spun and stared upward, directly into Valentina's eyes. He replied in English. "Ha, ha, ha. I thought it was the other way around. I thought sharks were the capitalists because they steal or kill everything they see. Some years ago I thought humans had evolved past capitalism toward

174

socialism, where people did not compete and instead worked in cooperation for the common good. But recently I have learned that capitalism—lying, cheating, bribing, killing, and stealing—is what people still want. And so sadly I have been compelled be a capitalist myself."

Clark froze for a moment studying Ivanov, then made a dismissive gesture and giggled.

Jack wanted to get involved in the debate. He questioned Ivanov. "Speaking of capitalism, I must admit the hotel is very nice. Did you make a cash flow *pro forma* for the hotel before deciding to have the Russian government spend three hundred billion rubles on its construction?"

Ivanov turned toward Jack. "I made a very simple *pro forma*. The government spent three hundred billion rubles making the hotel. And then I privatized the hotel from the government to myself for one ruble. Therefore, I made two hundred and ninety-nine billion, nine hundred and ninety-nine million, nine hundred and ninety-nice thousand, nine hundred and ninety-nine rubles of what you capitalists call profit."

Jack scratched his head in confusion upon hearing this reply, and also noticed that Clark's giggling grew louder.

Valentina looked briefly at Clark then back at Ivanov. "The fact you used your corrupt government power to steal the hotel from the taxpayers, instead of having the government privatize the hotel in a competitive auction, is well known. I think what Jack was wondering is whether the hotel is projected to have operating income that justifies the initial cost."

Ivanov shrugged his shoulders. "The operating income of this hotel is not something to be expressed in numbers. The hotel is all about competition, which you capitalists love. I knew the King of Arabia was developing the world's first eight-star hotel. And, I knew he would be the greatest person in the world if he had the best hotel in the world. So, I purposefully developed this hotel to be one star better than his hotel. Therefore, I am the greatest person in the world."

Valentina's eyes widened. "But I understood the King of Arabia did not arrange development of the Sea Hotel and Spa for the purpose of showing off how great he is. That hotel belongs to a group of private investors and they put in two billion euros because they want profit. The hotel is projected to have an unlevered yield of 21% starting the first year. Since the market currently demands a 14% return on hotel assets in countries that protect property rights, like Arabia, that means the completed resort is worth three billion euros. So, through wise allocation of capital the investors have created an extra billion euros already."

Ivanov shrugged. "But that doesn't make any sense. Who did they take the extra billion from? The economy is a pizza pie. If one person gets a larger slice, then a different person must get a smaller slice. I didn't have to go to Cornell University, like the King, to learn that. I learned that at the Marxist-Leninist Institute of Dzerzhinsk."

Clark broke into open laughter. Jack was seriously wondering now what was going on between these two criminals.

"You really have no idea what capitalism is, do you," said Jack to Ivanov. "The pizza pie, as you call it, gets larger when capital is allocated for maximum profit. All of society benefits."

Ivanov put his hands on his hips and stared at Jack. "I know exactly what capitalism is about. It is about receiving rewards for taking on risk."

Valentina spoke in a tone of relief. "Well, at least you know that."

Ivanov stood proud, puffing out his chest. "For example, if a Russian entrepreneur approaches a business owner and threatens to shoot him unless protection money of one million euros is delivered, then the entrepreneur has a

176

possibility of a reward, but also has the risk that the business owner will shoot back!"

"Can you believe this guy?" Valentina whispered to Jack. "He is Russia's democratically elected leader!"

Ivanov patted his companion on the shoulder. "Clarence, are you listening to this? These guests have a very interesting idea about how it is possible to create wealth through wise allocation of capital. I wonder if anyone else has ever thought of this idea before. Certainly none of my professors at the Marxist-Leninist Institute of Dzerzhinsk know about this."

Clark laughed so hard now that he had to hold onto his belly.

Ivanov directed his next comment to Jack. "If capitalism is so great, then why do Americans refer to the rich industrialists of the Nineteenth Century as the Robber Barons? The implication is that these people stole the wealth they accumulated."

Jack sighed, "Socialist-leaning Americans often refer to the Nineteenth Century industrialists as Robber Barons, but I would never use that term. The term originated not because these industrialists actually robbed anyone but rather because they hired large numbers of employees at market wages, and in the process drove market wages upward. Socialists perceive hiring people at market wages to be robbery because socialists don't understand that voluntary employment agreements benefit both sides."

Ivanov seemed unimpressed. "And why do Americans say that rich people must give back to society? The implication is that rich people took something from society."

"Again, a leftist might talk like that, but I sure wouldn't," said Jack. "If a rich person's fortune came from efficient provision of goods and services to consumers, then nothing was taken from society and nothing must be given back. Of course he could give something to society if he chooses. But 'giving' something that was not stolen is not the same concept as 'giving back' something that was stolen."

Clark stopped laughing. He nodded his head and seemed calm and relaxed. He finally spoke in his usual squeaky tone. "Ivan, let's stop joking around so that we can properly greet this fine gentleman and lovely lady."

Clark pointed toward the diamond turkey badge on Jack's tuxedo. "Interesting insignia. Is this from an organization I should be familiar with? Have we met before? I am Clarence Clark, Vice President of the United States of America." He put his hand forward to shake hands with Jack.

Jack declined to shake Clark's hand but rather moved straight on to introductions. "Of course we already know who both of you are because we have the misfortune of being citizens of the countries where you have been elected. I would like you to meet Valentina Zaiceva, journalist representing the Informed Voter News Service. I am Jack Cannon, a private American citizen attending tonight's event as Valentina's date."

Jack noticed when Ivanov showed a momentary expression of shock and surprise.

"President Ivanov," said Jack, "while we wish to thank you for your hospitality today, we have noticed some safety deficiencies in the hotel's helicopter snowboard service. If you are able to rescue the two goons buried in the avalanche on the Bolshoi Azau Glacier, they can tell you full details."

Ivanov frowned. At this moment, two bleach-blond bimbos walked up behind him and grabbed his butt. His frown quickly changed back to a smile as he put his arms around the girls.

Valentina alternated hard looks between Clark and Ivanov. "Our little chat was very interesting," she said. "My hope is that in the next elections in your respective countries, the best candidates will win and therefore both of you will have to find new jobs."

Clark, who had been staring at the turkey badge, looked

up and laughed, "Goldstein doesn't have a prayer of winning! Wake up, kids. Most voters are irrational. They have no common sense. They don't understand basic logic. They will vote against their own interests. The best candidates will never win."

In the background, the shark lashed forward with jagged teeth displayed.

Ivanov ignored Jack and Valentina and spoke to Clark. "Let's go play roulette with the girls. Clarence, you and I will have a great night with the girls up in the hot tub tower." Ivanov handed the girls ruby bracelets and wads of cash and led them toward a roulette table.

Clark followed behind, audibly murmuring, "Playing roulette is irrational. Unless you own the casino …"

After Ivanov and Clark were gone, Jack commented to Valentina. "Ivanov seems to be an idiot and Clark seems to be insane."

"It is an absolute disaster that they have been elected to important positions in our countries," Valentina replied.

Jack and Valentina watched the hammerhead as they finished their champagnes.

A waitress came past with a tray of desserts—small pancakes with a light syrup on top.

Valentina pointed at the pancakes and explained. "Here is something to cheer you up, Jack. Syrup from birch trees. A Russian delicacy."

Jack's mood brightened as he sampled the pancakes.

He wrapped his arm gently around Valentina's back and whispered into her ear, "Let's go back to the suite and slip into something more comfortable."

Valentina winked. "Ready for action!"

(21) Evening at Mount Elbrus, tower

American Vice President Clarence Clark was feeling quite drunk. Natasha helped him out of his clothing before she ripped off her own clothing and they splashed naked into the giant hot tub.

He reached up to put his stubby arm around the shoulders of tall Natasha, but this wasn't working and therefore she put her long arm around his shoulders.

He peered out at the fabulous view from the panoramic window surrounding the rotating spa. The mountains looked splendid in the moonlight.

Then, he gazed down and saw that the glass floor of the hot tub was the top of the hammerhead shark tank in the ballroom below. He spoke to Russian President Ivan Ivanov, "This is great, Ivan. You put the hot tub tower on top of one of the aquariums!"

Natasha giggled as she looked into Clark's eyes and spoke in accented English, "Yikes! I hope the one-way glass is very strong!"

Meanwhile, Olga snuggled closer to Ivanov on the far side of the hot tub and Clark assumed they had lost their clothing as well.

Clark was smiling and relaxed as he talked to Ivanov. "It's great that we can hang around together now since the couple times we met in the past were just quick deals with no socializing. You know, it is very difficult for me to find friends since most people make me angry and frustrated. I certainly don't have any friends in the Great Deal Party since I purposefully selected only dumb people to be party members."

JOHN CHRISTMAS

Clark examined the complex chrome device that emerged from the middle of the hot tub. The top of the device was circled with dozens of upside-down bottles, positioned above shiny levers.

He correctly identified a dispenser for champagne flutes and took two of them, one for himself and one for Natasha.

"All this conspicuous consumption with stolen money must make the voters hate you more and more every year," Clark said to Ivanov. "Look at this; a rotating hot tub full of hookers and a champagne fountain on top of a nine-star hotel, all paid for with taxpayer money. You are going to have to cheat a lot in your next election, even more than you cheated in your first election."

Ivanov looked confused. "Who said I cheated when I got elected?"

Clark was astonished. "You didn't cheat? I assumed your thugs were out stuffing ballot boxes when you got elected. How else could you get elected since you robbed the Russian people blind through corrupt privatizations before you became president?"

"Obviously you don't know anything about democracy in this part of the world," said Ivanov. "When I decided to become a politician it was for the usual reasons. I wanted more corruption opportunities and immunity from prosecution. However, I decided to go for the presidency instead of just a seat in the Duma because my supporters told me I was extremely popular *because of* my corruption.

"Do you notice how I spend money as conspicuously as possible, always showing off the most expensive cars, planes, yachts, houses, and clothes? This serves a purpose at election time. The purpose is to win respect from the majority of voters. This is not about my personal enjoyment. It is an important aspect of the job.

"The mentality of the mainstream voter in a poor country is he practically worships people who trick him out of his

181

money because he wishes he could be smart enough to trick others out of their money. If I didn't trick people out of their money, most would perceive me as weak and stupid and wouldn't vote for me."

Olga and Natasha spoke in unison. "We love Ivan!"

Clark looked across at Olga and then turned toward Natasha. He could feel a mild shaking tremble building up in him because of their irrational comment.

However, he realized he had just learned something from Ivanov. Irrationality was different in Russia and America. Most voters were irrational in both countries, however they were irrational in different ways. Interesting.

Clark needed yet another drink to ensure relaxation in case the girls made another stupid comment. He tipped one of the top levers that protruded from the chrome device, expecting bubbly to pour from one of the spouts. He didn't see any bubbly, however he did turn sharply to look out the window at a screeching rocket that fired out of a launcher on the roof. The rocket lit up the sky as it streaked from the top of Elbrus down into the valley. Even from up here on the peak, the explosion was visible when the rocket hit a village in the valley. The sound of the explosion followed twenty seconds later.

Ivanov now giggled along with the whores. "Clarence, the champagne levers are on the bottom row. The levers on the top row are what I call the fireworks. They shoot missiles down on the villages where minority ethnic groups live. We should certainly shoot some missiles tonight since the main party is still going on below and the guests will be entertained by the explosions."

Clark became thoughtful, or at least as thoughtful as he could become given all the champagne he already consumed. "Yes, I remember. The us-versus-them election campaign that helped you to win the presidency. Lying to the ethnic-Russian majority that all of their problems were caused by minority groups living in and around Russia and promising to kill those minority groups."

"Yes, Clarence. I have nothing against the ethnic minorities. However, I oppress and murder them to maintain my popularity with the majority of the electorate. Taking money from the electorate certainly helps to win votes, but I had to introduce the hate-mongering campaign to be certain of victory."

"Aha. Very impressive, Ivan. You really do have a great read on how democracy works and I see it works differently from country to country. In Russia, what works best to gain support from the majority of voters is inciting ethnic warfare while stealing as much money as possible and spending it conspicuously.

"In America, most effective is provocation of class warfare rather than ethnic warfare. Americans don't support the kind of theft that you are talking about where a multi-billionaire politician flaunts his stolen cash. But, Americans have different irrational ideas. For example, they think they can steal money from corporations and this money is not really being stolen from anybody because corporations are not people."

"There is no reason to cheat at the ballot box," reiterated Ivanov. "But, of course, different sorts of corruption are required by democracy. For example, I need to pay a secret cash stipend to all of the representatives in the Duma so that I can dictate laws to them. The stipend money is small, however, compared to the money I am able to take from the taxpayers by this arrangement."

After recovering from the initial shock of learning that Ivanov was elected without cheating in the election, Clark was relieved to learn that at least the Duma was working for bribes. "Ivan, I have something to tell you that might come as a surprise. I don't pay any bribes to the Great Deal congressmen. They voted for the Great Deal Act and

183

Temporary Police State Act because they believe in their hearts that those laws are good."

Ivan was tickling Olga and responded. "I am not surprised to hear that, Clarence. The representatives in the Duma are capitalists, which means they are working for bribes. The Great Deal representatives in Congress are socialists, which means they are sacrificing themselves for the common good."

Clark's body experienced a spasm. He needed more alcohol in order to tolerate the idiots surrounding him.

He studied the lower row of levers. "Ivan, can you please help me out? How can I tell which champagne is which? All I see on this row of lower levers are numbers starting from five thousand and going up to one hundred thousand."

"Simple," said Ivanov. "The champagnes are ranked by price. The champagne that costs the most euros per bottle is obviously the best and for the most discerning connoisseur. The champagne that costs the least is for someone less sophisticated. Originally, the fool who designed this champagne fountain put the names of the champagnes instead of the prices, so it was impossible to see which one was best!"

Clark laughed at the hilarious joke. "My favorite champagne is *blanc de noirs* from *Montagne de Reims*. Experts say the best vintage was 1996, but I personally prefer 1995. Do you have any of that? I sometimes get it in America from a French smuggler in exchange for euros."

Ivanov shrugged and turned his playful attention back to Olga.

Clark looked at the bottles mounted across the top of the metal device and made a selection based on coloring. He drew two full flutes from the spout and handed one to Natasha.

Ivanov pulled a lever on a separate tap at the edge of the hot tub and filled two snifters with a dark liquid. "Clarence,

184

you might be interested to know that I don't drink champagne anymore. I admit that I love the taste of champagne. However, my advisers told me that cognac is more expensive and therefore I switched drinks for the sake of maintaining my image. This cognac costs 200,000 euros for one serving."

Olga got excited and grabbed one snifter from Ivanov. "Wow. This cognac costs 200,000 euros? That is more than my mother will earn in 100 years! And the taxpayers got the bill for it? Ivan, you are very smart. I respect you more and more as I get to know you better."

Ivanov took a sip of the cognac and gagged and spit it into the hot tub.

Clark began to shake more and took a hearty sip of champagne. He was near his breaking point from seeing this display of irrationality. His opinion about his partner-in-crime had changed completely, but he had to act cool and relaxed so that he could accomplish what he needed to accomplish on this visit.

Ivanov smiled at the two ladies as he pointed back and forth between himself and Clark. "I plan to let the press know about the ownership of Trans Pacific Trading Company. It is already publicly known that Trans Pacific buys oil at 100 euros per barrel from the Russian government and sells the oil at 200 euros per barrel to the American government without ever taking possession of the oil. What the public does not know is that we are the real owners behind Trans Pacific and the profit is piling up in our offshore bank accounts. The Federal Reserve System is burning through its assets to pay for this and will be bankrupt soon. Of course the Russian people are getting screwed because the profit is going to me personally even though it is not my oil. I want Russian voters to be informed about this scam because they will respect me for being such a smart businessman."

Clark was in a mental struggle to make himself relax. "That's fascinating, Ivan. But please hold off until after Tuesday's election before you make your press release because American voters think differently and they will be upset at me when they learn about this robbery."

Ivanov responded without hesitation. "Robbery? But Russia is a capitalist country now. Earning money is no longer considered robbery. Earning money is considered business."

Clark chugged his champagne, refilled the flute, and again chugged it. His body was twitching visibly now and Natasha scooted away from him.

"Business?" exclaimed Clark, "This is not business. This is crime! The two of us signed the Trans Pacific deal on behalf of our countries with a nominee owner of an offshore company who was secretly working for us. It was not an arms-length agreement."

"It sure was arms-length!" said Ivanov. "I reached out my arm and shook hands with the nominee as soon as he signed! Universal-suffrage democracy is sleazy and cruel business. But it isn't my fault Russia adopted this form of government. You would have to blame those famous Americans who invented democracy, George Washington and James Madison. We studied them at the Marxist-Leninist Institute back in Dzerzhinsk."

"I have been laughing all evening about your Marxist-Leninist Institute of Dzerzhinsk because I assumed you must be joking," said Clark. "But now I have concluded that you are not joking when you say irrational things. You are in fact irrational yourself and you make your decisions on the basis of irrationality!"

"Look, Clarence. I have no idea what you are talking about when you say that I make my decisions. Do you think I actually have a choice about what to do? I just go along with things as they happen. I just do what society wants me to do."

Clark was infuriated. "That statement was also irrational.

Obviously you can make your own decisions."

Olga wrapped her arms around Ivanov. "Ivan, relax. You guys are so smart talking about government, but I thought we came up here to have fun. Natasha and I don't care about government, we just know we will always vote for you."

Clark stood up in the hot tub and pointed accusingly as he spoke. "Look, Ivan. Let's forget about the friendly chit-chat and talk about crime. Or 'business' if that is what you want to call it. I need to murder Rojo on Wednesday, as soon as he is sworn in as president and I am sworn in as vice president by the Chief Justice of the Supreme Court."

"I think it is a shame that capitalism requires you to kill Rojo," said Ivanov, now sitting with both girls next to him. "I think Rojo is a great moral and ethical leader because he is a devout socialist. Of course I respect the American electorate far more than my own Russian electorate since the American people put ethics ahead of self-interest and voted socialist. What I can't understand is how you got to be the running mate for Rojo since you are a capitalist."

"Can you give me something so that I can kill Rojo?" interrupted Clark. "Blame it on fate, if you like."

"Since you are an Adam Smith-style capitalist," replied Ivanov, "you could probably read how to kill people in the *The Wealth of Nations*. I never read that book, but I am sure it must have many chapters about how to kill people since it is all about capitalism."

"I just need a weapon, Ivan. Please help me."

"I might have just the thing for you," said Ivanov. "My weapons expert found a prototype handgun developed by the KGB thirty years ago. It is a red-hued revolver in excellent condition. It has a distinctive shape, with a barrel and cylinder that seem too long compared to a normal revolver. The KGB called it the 'Hammer and Sickle' and designed it especially for assassinations. I find it odd that the principled socialists from the KGB would have designed such a thing, since its application seems distinctly capitalist to me, but anyway it is a two-way gun."

Clark was baffled and his shaking became more pronounced. "What possible purpose is there for a two-way gun? A weapon like that is totally irrational."

Ivanov smiled as he sank lower into the hot tub bubbles. "As you probably know, it is wise whenever you send out an assassin to kill someone, to send out a second assassin to kill the first assassin and a third assassin to kill the second assassin and a fourth assassin to kill the third assassin, and so on, to make it difficult for anyone to confirm who ordered the first killing."

"I have read that Russian organized crime groups normally hire assassins to kill their own assassins," replied Clark, shaking. "Therefore, I always wondered why anyone would be an assassin for a Russian organized crime group."

"This two-way gun solves the problem," explained Ivanov. "You tell the assassin to kill the target with one shot to the head at point blank range. Then, when the assassin pulls the trigger, he gets a big surprise. Two bullets shoot out from the gun, one killing the target, and the other killing the assassin himself! Shooting backward into the assassin's own eye!"

"The Hammer and Sickle is the dumbest invention I have ever heard of, Ivan. I cannot comprehend why the KGB would design a weapon for the purpose of shooting themselves. What I need is poison. I need something to slip into the natural apple juice that I give to Rojo each day; poison that will give him a quick heart attack, then dissipate. Do you have anything like that?"

"Sure. We will take a little trip later tonight and I will get some for you."

"That would be great. Once I am on my way back to Washington with a vial of poison, my ultimate scheme will be unstoppable!" Clark shut his eyes and dreamed of the near
188

future when he would not have to deal with the socialists anymore.

*

Jack nudged Valentina and spoke to her softly. "Are you comfortable? Are the ropes too tight?" He released a clasp and looped one rope through a different o-ring.

Valentina smiled, giggled, and nudged Jack right back.

They were in harnesses, hanging by ropes wrapped around a decorative gargoyle on the outside of the hotel tower.

Having changed out of their evening wear before scaling the tower, they were now back in flight suits and helmets. The battery-powered heating systems in the flight suits were important now since the nighttime temperature on the mountain peak was frigid.

They spoke through the headsets built into their helmets. Conveniently, the helmets also had enhanced night vision.

"That conversation not only confirmed the Director and King's suspicions of corruption in the oil trade, but also revealed an assassination plot," said Jack. "Good thing we got a clear audio and visual recording of it with our flight suit equipment. I have you to thank for that."

"No need to thank me," replied Valentina. "We are partners in this mission and I will contribute however I can. While you keep up-to-date with aviation technology as a pilot, I keep up-to-date with surveillance and anti-surveillance technology as an investigative journalist." Valentina held up an electronic device the size of an apple. "I knew that this pulse device to disable white noise generators would come in handy when trying to spy on Ivanov."

"The plot we just heard to poison Rojo is so illegal that even the most dense people in America, the congressmen from the Great Deal Party, would find it unacceptable," said

Jack. "I hope we can get into the *Flying Yankee* and transmit the video and audio files to the Director as soon as possible. Maybe he can broadcast the information on television, from Canada, Mexico, and the Property Rights States if the GFN won't air it. Although many facts about the Great Deal Party's destructive socialist policies have been broadcast without denting the popularity of the party among mainstream voters, this murder plot announcement from the founder of the Great Deal Party could finally cause their voter support to collapse. Let's rappel down to the runway."

"Aren't you worried about the snipers on the roof?" queried Valentina.

"No, I'm not worried about them," said Jack. "They will be okay because I made certain the ropes weren't too tight when I tied them up."

Jack and Valentina rappelled rapidly down the tower wall toward the runway. Suddenly, spotlights from the runway shone upon them. They had been discovered!

They ignored every safety rule to speed up their rappel.

Hitting the runway hard, they ran for their lives toward the *Flying Yankee*.

But, they were not quick enough. A spring-loaded trap on the runway shot a net across the path.

The last thing Jack remembered from lying flat on the runway with a net holding him down was the view of two pairs of feet in holographic pirate-flag boots and the sound of laughter as he felt a dart hit him on the back.

Monday, November 3, 2014
(22) Before dawn on the Red Sea, between Eritrea and Arabia

Clarence Clark was having a fabulous dream. He was back in a college lecture hall listening to a professor giving a talk about mathematical logic.

But suddenly, he was awakened by someone who grabbed his shoulder.

"Clarence!" said Ivan Ivanov, "Wake up!"

Clark opened his eyes and looked around. He was reclined on a white leather couch in the passenger compartment of a luxuriously appointed helicopter. The Russian president was sitting on another white leather couch just opposite. They had views of the night sky and dark sea through windows on either side.

Feeling sleepy and upset, Clark spoke to Ivanov. "Where are we? What happened to those annoying women Natasha and Olga?"

"We are flying over the Red Sea. Don't worry about the women. I made a capitalist deal with them. I gave them as bribes to the militia men at the airport in Eritrea. Of course I am sad because I liked those women, however nobody has any choice about what to do in this life and therefore must act as directed by fate."

Clark's mood brightened. "I remember now! The Eritrean militia men were shocked when *Air Force Two* arrived on their landing strip. I am quite sure none of them expected to see that plane in their lifetimes. They were still arguing when we left in the helicopter about who was going to fetch the

191

highest price at the upcoming camel market auction: Natasha or Olga!"

Just then, Clark saw a bright twinkle through his peripheral vision and spun to look out one of the windows. In the blackness, he could see what looked like an enormous, illuminated, blinking Christmas tree.

Ivanov pointed enthusiastically out the window. "My new yacht is coming into view! She is quite a sight when fully lit up. She uses as much energy as a small city. I like to prove how great I am by burning as much fossil fuel as possible.

"She is the largest pleasure yacht in the world, measuring 400 meters from bow to stern. She is superior to the King of Arabia's yacht because she is longer. Therefore, I am superior to the King.

"I christened her the *Universal Suffrage* because I paid for her with my earnings as a democratically elected politician!

"When you examine her, please notice the plank and the pool. Those were special custom features that I requested."

Clark made out some details of the yacht as the helicopter flew closer. He could see that the vessel had a built-up tower at the stern rising ten stories above the deck. The tower was ringed with brightly lit balconies and capped with an impressive array of antennae, radar devices, and missile launchers.

Amidships, a deck with a circle of stadium-light towers surrounded a huge open pool in the center. Clark figured the pool must be 100 meters across given that the yacht was 400 meters long. A shiny plank spanned the pool.

The plank was a walkway bridge to a structure at the bow, rising only four stories above the deck but wider than the aft tower and with a prominent command window jutting out above the bow. The roof of this structure was a helicopter landing area, currently empty.

Ivanov leaned back on the couch and looked at Clark. "I bet the King is extremely jealous that I have such a large and expensive yacht! He must be burning with envy!"

Clark doubted that very much based on what he had read about the King. But Clark knew he could not argue anymore. He had to focus on self-control or else the ultimate scheme for Wednesday would be ruined. He needed to get the poison vial from Ivanov and negotiate the final aspect of the oil deal and get back to *Air Force Two*.

The helicopter landed on the yacht's helipad. Clark barely noticed the touchdown so expertly done by the Russian pilot.

The rotors were still spinning as a sailor in a white uniform ran forward across the helipad and unlatched and pulled open the passenger door, beckoning Clark and Ivanov to exit.

The world oligarchs stood up from their couches and exited the aircraft. They climbed down four short stairs onto an awaiting red carpet and ducked slightly as they moved across the helipad toward the bulkhead. A hot nighttime breeze was a reminder they weren't in Russia anymore.

Clark observed as the sailor opened the helicopter's cargo hold. Two bald men with pirate-flag boots emerged, carrying a pair of unconscious prisoners over their shoulders. The landing pad was not well lighted, however Clark knew who all of these people were. He disliked Vladislav and Vyachislav because they were irrational for being loyal to Ivanov. And, he liked Jack and Valentina because they exhibited rational logic skills.

Clark, however, always believed the ends justified the means. In his battle against irrationality, he had to act in temporary alliance with irrational people and there would be some rational people who would get hurt.

A different uniformed sailor held a bulkhead door open and Clark and Ivanov stepped inside to the air-conditioned and plushly decorated top of a futuristic spiral staircase.

Ivanov led Clark onto the top step of the spiral staircase. "Let me give you a tour of the yacht! We will begin with

Sophistication Hall."

Clark was surprised when the steps began to slowly rotate by their own power. The ornate spiral staircase functioned as an escalator, automatically and gradually lowering the oligarchs into a large hall. The sailor followed behind as an escort. Reaching the bottom, they all stepped off of the escalator and into the hall.

The ceiling of Sophistication Hall was roughly three stories high, and the forward window spanned at least thirty meters, as did the bubble-shaped window looking aft.

Ivanov pointed at a semi-circle of white leather couches with a view through the forward window. "I can sit here with my remote control and move the yacht anywhere I choose." He displayed a silvery remote control device. "I just key in a desired destination, which could be anything from latitude and longitude coordinates to a specific name of a place, such as a harbor.

"But the sea view and remote control are not what I brought you here to see. Observe and enjoy!" Ivanov waved his arms toward the starboard and port walls of Sophistication Hall.

On each wall hung a gigantic canvas stretching most of the way from floor to ceiling and from the one end of the hall to the other. The starboard canvas was all white and the port canvas all black.

Clark gazed briefly at the white canvas and then moved toward the black canvas and studied it more carefully, failing to detect any sort of pattern or texture.

Under each canvas lay a bronze plate with a number. The black canvas: 100,000,000. The white canvas: 200,000,000.

Ivanov was visibly proud. "When I ordered this new yacht, I sent an agent to London to purchase the two finest works of art in the whole world."

Clark was bewildered. "How did your agent know which were the two finest works?"

194

"He just bought the most expensive ones," Ivanov replied. "The prices in British pounds are on the bronze plates. The job turned out to be less straightforward than I had expected, since the art was being offered by an auction house. The people at the auction house told my agent that normally the purchasers strive to pay as little as possible for paintings instead of as much as possible. However, they soon came around to my way of thinking. My agent told the auction house that he was authorized to pay 300,000,000 pounds and the auction house sold us these two works. He made a press release about my purchase so that everyone in the world would know about my excellent taste."

Clark started shaking and twitching as he stared at the all-black canvas. "But obviously, when you participate in an auction, you should try to get the lowest price!"

"That doesn't make any sense," replied Ivanov. "The purpose of buying art is to brag about how much you spent."

"You are totally irrational and you got cheated," concluded Clark, speaking with difficulty since his twitch had become severe.

"Cheated?" replied Ivanov. "Do you mean these are forgeries?"

Clark could not stand it anymore. He saw a large opening from Sophistication Hall, near the bubble window, and he ran outdoors.

He found himself at the upper end of a thick and wide metallic plank spanning a pool that was one hundred meters across. Countless gems and precious metals were set into the plank, and the stadium lights surrounding the pool made these decorations glitter. He took some deep breaths to stop from shaking, but suddenly he heard Ivanov behind him.

"You will see this plank put to good use at my annual staff bonus party tonight. The plank spans the pool, which is filled with hammerhead sharks. We are in the forward tower now. The aft tower is on the other side of the plank and the

195

pool. The aft tower is a luxury hotel. One suite has been prepared for you."

As the oligarchs stood near the top of the plank, they saw Vladislav and Vyachislav on the other side of the pool by the base of the plank tying Jack and Valentina together.

Ivanov yelled down to his henchmen, "Make sure you leave them in the air-conditioned flight suits when you tie them up. They will be hanging in the hot sun all day and I don't want them to die before the bonus party!"

Then, Ivanov spoke quietly to Clark, "I am certain you will want to sleep during the daytime so that you will be rested for the festivities this coming evening." Ivanov turned and said something in Russian to the sailor escort before turning back toward Clark and switching back to English. "The sailor will lead you to your guest suite. Also, a tailor will take quick measurements and he will have a new wardrobe ready for you when you wake up.

"The bonus party is not something I enjoy. It is a necessary purge of my staff. The staff members are all witnesses to the illegal activities that I have been compelled to engage in because of capitalism and democracy. I know they are all criminals because they did what I asked them to do and therefore they cannot be trusted.

"I will bring two hundred staff members onto the pool deck one at a time. I will tell each of them to walk the plank to receive their bribes and kickbacks for devout service. And, they will all fall through a trap door and get eaten by the sharks."

Clark stopped shaking and smiled. He was overjoyed at the idea of two hundred irrational socialists getting fed to the sharks. "That's great! I will sleep soundly in anticipation of the bonus party." Clark then had a silent thought, a fantasy about Ivanov following his employees into the pool.

Ivanov turned and walked back into Sophistication Hall.

Clark followed the sailor down the plank to the pool deck

and paused near the brothers and the prisoners.

Clark leaned down over Jack and Valentina. They were drugged unconscious, their helmets had been removed, and they were tied together. Vladislav and Vyachislav were preparing a nearby crane.

Clark discretely patted the chest pocket of Jack's flight suit. Feeling a hard lump, Clark quickly unzipped the pocket and slipped an object into his hand.

He then followed the sailor into the aft tower to get some sleep. Revenge was coming soon!

*

Ivan Ivanov re-entered Sophistication Hall alone, planning to retire to his private suite here in the forward tower.

As he passed through Sophistication Hall, a uniformed waitress appeared and gave him a glass of the most expensive cognac in the world.

He tried not to show his displeasure as he forced a sip of the nasty cognac down his throat. He could not understand why anyone liked the flavor of cognac. But anyway, he continued drinking the stuff because he knew his powerful image depended on his conspicuous consumption.

Ivanov sat on a white leather couch to nurse the rest of his drink while he stared out at the dark sea. He found Americans to be absolutely baffling.

His closest American peer, Clarence Clark, was the most baffling of them all.

At times Clark seemed so smart, like when he planned business deals. But at other times he seemed so dense and unsophisticated! For example, when selecting champagnes, he didn't choose the most expensive one. When viewing art, he was more interested in Black-on-Black than White-on-White even though the latter was twice as expensive.

Why did Clark criticize Ivanov's business and election

strategies? Ivanov perceived himself to be an excellent businessman and president and had no idea why Clark was laughing about this.

Ivanov forced down another sip of the harsh cognac.

Clark, not Ivanov, was from the British-American culture that created the monsters of capitalism and democracy. The British invented capitalism, where everyone is supposed to be a thief, and the Americans invented democracy, where psychopathic racist kleptomaniacs are routinely elected by large majorities. And now the American vice president was criticizing a Russian who was dragged into capitalism and democracy?

Ivanov always thought that the Marxist-Leninist idea about people working in friendly cooperation for the common good was wonderful and Adam Smith's idea about people stealing from each other was terrible.

Likewise, Ivanov always preferred totalitarianism to democracy. It was clear that Joseph Stalin's idea of strong government providing benefits to all of society was better than George Washington and James Madison's idea about universal-suffrage democratic government where the majority hurt the minority and the majority also hurt itself.

Ivanov reflected on the capitalist and democratic revolution in Russia and how it turned his world upside down.

When he was a young man in Soviet times studying at the Marxist-Leninist Institute of Dzerzhinsk, he had been a devout socialist.

He had been told by the central planners, who assigned students to jobs without any input from the students themselves, that he would be allocated to Factory 127 in Dzerzhinsk upon graduation and could expect to work there for the rest of his life. The factory produced anthrax cluster bombs designed for use against domestic counterrevolutionaries.

He was not sure how the government could use such weapons to conduct a precisely targeted defense against counterrevolutionaries. However, he knew the central planners were intelligent and civic-minded people. It wasn't appropriate for him to question their wisdom. He knew he would have a productive function in the socialist society and he would never earn any profit and therefore would never exploit anyone.

Ivanov graduated from the institute at the same time the Soviet government collapsed. He discovered that Factory 127 had been shut down. All equipment and inventory was gone, presumably stolen by management and shipped to a rogue state somewhere.

Ivanov found employment in Moscow through a newspaper advertisement. He moved to Moscow and began to work.

He had a low-level job in a bank which was controlled by a powerful, dishonest, and violent man named Sergey Sergovich. Sergovich lived surrounded by beautiful women and ugly bodyguards in a huge palace outside Moscow. He had fleets of cars, airplanes, and yachts, all paid for with stolen money.

Ivanov's job at the bank was as a clerk in the payments office. He toiled at this job for a year before an event occurred which caused him to become a successful capitalist.

Sergovich himself summoned Ivanov for a meeting. Ivanov remembered he was so excited that he could barely speak as he sat in Sergovich's giant office. Armed mercenaries in black body armor stood around the desk as Sergovich told Ivanov the plan.

The bank had a special client and this special client had a relationship with a corrupt insider at the Russian Central Bank.

The client planned to remove $10 million from the central bank that afternoon in a fraudulent transfer. The money would be wired into an account held by one of the client's opaque shell companies. Then the client wanted the money wired to an account in Nauru, presumably held by a different opaque shell company controlled by the client.

Sergovich wanted to intercept the payment and wire the money to a different account in Nauru, which presumably was held by one of Sergovich's opaque shell companies. That was Ivanov's assignment.

As for what to do with the soon-to-be-disgruntled client, Sergovich whispered secret instructions to the mercenaries.

A couple of hours later, while Ivanov sat at his desk in the payments office, he received a computer message that the transfer from the central bank had been received. He created a false instruction with false authorization to divert the transfer. However, he did something Sergovich had not anticipated.

Ivanov had a friend who worked at a different Moscow bank and they had a secret meeting over lunch—between the time when Sergovich gave instructions to Ivanov and the time the transfer arrived. As a result of this meeting, he had a different account number to use for the false instruction.

Ivanov did not agree with the principles of capitalism. But, Russia had become capitalist. He could not fight a tidal wave of opinion himself. While morally uncomfortable with his actions, he felt that he must embrace capitalism—by stealing as much money as possible. He began by stealing the $10 million.

At that point, he had not figured out how he would escape with the cash once it was in his own secret account. But, this problem soon solved itself.

The special bank client was enjoying champagne and *foie gras* at the exclusive Moscow restaurant "*La Propriété*," in a premature celebration of his latest transfer from the central bank. As he wished *bon appétit* to his guests, black-clad mercenaries smashed into the restaurant through the windows and shot him at least a hundred times with Kalashnikovs.

And, it turned out, this special client was not without grieving friends. An hour later, as Sergovich sat in another exclusive French restaurant, *"C'est le Vol,"* on the other side of Moscow, raising his champagne glass to prematurely toast his anticipated business victory, a rocket-propelled grenade struck him straight in the gut and exploded, showering his girlfriends and guards with bloody flesh chunks.

So Ivanov became the uncontested owner of the $10 million. His meteoric rise to wealth had begun. Capitalism was certainly a cruel game, but Ivanov found he excelled at it.

Having forced down the last sip of cognac, Ivanov stood from the white leather couch. He walked to his suite with plans to sleep all day and wake up after dark for the bonus party. This year's staff would get the usual necessary treatment at the bonus party. He would be sad to see them go. He would start next year with a new staff and he had plenty of applications sitting in his office back in the Kremlin.

He only looked forward to killing two people at this year's party. He wanted to make Jack and Valentina suffer and die for their meddling and hypocrisy.

(23) Evening at Mount Vernon—The Presidential Election Debate

David Goldstein felt determined this evening as he traveled in the back of the Virginia National Guard van. The headlights were on as the driver navigated the final turn out of the forest and through the west gate. They had arrived at Mount Vernon.

The mansion house was well lit and easily visible at the far end of a field bordered by a careful arrangement of trees.

The serpentine road wound from the gate toward the mansion. The tulip poplars, white ash, and elm trees exhibited fall colors and would soon be losing their leaves. Goldstein looked up to see the inspirational dove-of-peace weather vane atop the cupola on the white mansion house.

Goldstein's life journey for the past two-and-a-half years since he had become a politician had been arduous, but he felt confident his work would be met with reward—a better future for the republic.

The van rounded the elliptical lawn in front of the mansion house and came to a stop. The driver, wearing a Virginia National Guard uniform, hopped out and slid open the side door so that Goldstein could climb out from the passenger compartment.

As he stepped carefully on the gravel driveway to the mansion house doorway, a beautifully plumed wild turkey burst from the willow trees and ran right in front of him, across the grassy ellipse.

The heavy wooden door of the mansion house swung open. Goldstein climbed the steps to the threshold as he heard a greeting.

"Professor Goldstein, we are honored to have the leader of the Property Rights Party as our guest at Mount Vernon."

A tall man stepped forward. He was a powerfully built black man with graying hair. He wore a dark suit with the likeness of a turkey embroidered on one of the breast pockets.

Goldstein, standing only five-feet-five-inches tall, stepped forward and shook hands with the host.

The host, who stood a towering six-feet-three-inches, gave a firm handshake in a manner characteristic of confidence and leadership.

They stepped together into the central passage of the mansion house, passing a Virginia National Guardsman on the way into a parlor with Prussian-blue walls and a cozy fireplace.

The tall man spoke, "I am the Director of the Democracy Society. My organization manages the estate here at Mount Vernon. We are unrelated to the Virginia National Guard. Please follow me into the large dining room, where the camera equipment is set up. As you know, there is no live audience for this televised event. The only people in the large dining room are staff from the GFN."

"Thank you, sir, for your efforts in hosting this event," said Goldstein, who was impressed by this intense yet courteous stranger. "You are making a positive contribution to democracy."

Goldstein followed the Director into the large dining room. On the near side of the tall room, GFN crewmen made final adjustments to an array of cameras.

On the far side, dueling podiums stood mounted on a newly constructed stage. Goldstein had never seen podiums like these. They seemed to be constructed of glass and had a dull gray color.

He saw a large mirror on the wall, next to a Palladian window that offered a view of the dark forest outside. He stopped to check how he looked before this critical television appearance.

He was not sure about his necktie. It did not seem to be tied correctly. He preferred not to wear a tie. In fact he didn't own any ties except for this one, and the last time he recalled using it was for his high school homecoming dance, which he only attended briefly before returning home to finish reading an economics textbook that, to him, was much more fun and interesting than the dance.

Was the tie supposed to loop through once or twice? It kept flipping around backward, revealing the tag '100% polyester, Made in Ohio' between the broad brown stripes on the short fat tie.

He tried to slick back his red hair, but he was unsuccessful as a big curl kept popping up in defiance of his efforts to tame it.

He stared into the mirror at his suit jacket. Did he bring the correct one? For some reason the checkered pattern on the jacket didn't exactly match the checkered pattern on his slacks. Well, there was no time to do anything about that now.

He approached his podium and saw Maria Diaz. "Maria, it is nice to see you. Thank you for the diligent work you have done to prepare the hall. You must have been working non-stop all night and day to get this ready. You should be proud of yourself."

She smiled. "Thanks, David. We've been working very hard and we've received a lot of assistance from the Director."

As she spoke, she took hold of Goldstein's tie and corrected the knot. He felt that she slipped something into his jacket pocket. She whispered, "Take a look at that when you respond to the first question."

He stepped up to his podium with great confidence. He had dedicated many hours to extensive intellectual

204

preparation for the debate, having studied all policy issues thoroughly. Truth and logic were the core of his platform and truth and logic would prevail.

He knew the American people would abandon the nonsensical policies of the Great Deal Party and choose the rational policies of the Property Rights Party. It was impossible to think American voters could be so dumb that they would make the same mistake again and vote for Rojo since almost everyone in the Great Deal States was impoverished and suffering.

Goldstein was ready for the debate.

*

Roberto Rojo entered the large dining room of the Mount Vernon mansion house. He was dressed immaculately in a charcoal gray suit and American flag tie from a famous fashion house. With his rippling hair styled back and his tan just right, he looked like a model from a magazine.

He had dedicated many hours to perfecting his physical appearance, and therefore he was ready to do his duty for America in this debate. His life purpose was altruistic self-sacrifice for the good of the majority people of America and tonight he was going to serve his constituents well as he trounced his opponent.

Of course Rojo spent so much time primping that he didn't have any time to read about the campaign issues. But he knew the majority of voters would not care. Winning the debate would just be a matter of labeling Goldstein as 'greedy' and promising lots of free stuff.

As Rojo walked toward his podium he passed Maria Diaz. He noticed that Maria looked great today in a designer business suit that fit her fabulous body just perfectly. However, he remembered how important it was to always be vigilant in protecting the interests of the majority.

"Hey, Maria! Yes, I'm talking to you. It seems you and your crew were working very hard to prepare this equipment. You should be ashamed of yourselves! Don't you feel guilty about what you've done? By doing hard efficient work you've made labor unionists look bad. Do society a favor and stop working so hard or I'll order your arrest!"

Rojo looked on as Maria turned and stomped away. He wished she would stop breaking the law.

He stepped behind his podium and adjusted his microphone upward. He kept his cool gaze focused on the enemy, David Goldstein, who was smiling and adjusting the other microphone downward.

Rojo shivered with disgust. He assumed that heartless cruelty was hidden behind Goldstein's smile. It was the phony smile of a stingy monster who cared more about property rights than human rights.

Rojo was ready for the debate. He knew he would prevail. The voters wanted a generous president, not a stingy president.

*

Maria Diaz pulled herself together after the verbal abuse from Roberto Rojo. She focused on her duty. Her credibility, and therefore her long-term career possibilities, had been severely damaged since she had unwittingly become a part of Rojo's campaign of false propaganda.

She had an opportunity to repair her credibility now, since she was the moderator for the presidential election debate. She planned to use this opportunity.

She stood between the two candidates at their dull-gray glass podiums and straightened her satin suit. She knew the whole country would be watching tonight, even though most people didn't care about the debate.

The GFN was airing a four-hour special episode of the

wildly popular serial 'Pirate Heroes.' The national guards of all of the Great Deal States turned on the electrical power in their states for this period and therefore everyone could watch on their looted televisions. The GFN sandwiched the twelve-minute presidential election debate into the middle of 'Pirate Heroes' as a way to trap ordinary voters into watching.

The lead cameraman signaled for the debate to begin.

Maria drew back a brunette lock and shined her twinkling chestnut eyes at the cameras. "Welcome to the 2014 Presidential Election Debate. We are broadcasting on the Greed Free Network from the mansion house at Mount Vernon, family residence of the General of the Continental Army and first President of the United States, George Washington. We would like to thank the Democracy Society for providing the venue."

Maria stepped closer to Rojo. "On my left, the 45th President of the United States and presidential candidate of the Great Deal Party, Roberto Rojo!"

She took a long look at Rojo. The way his muscles filled out his suit was incredible. The dignified crow's feet and handsome dimples in his strong and tanned profile were so attractive that she could barely resist running toward the man and wrapping her arms around him. She forced the thought out of her head by reminding herself of Rojo's dishonesty regarding the switched footage in the Great Deal propaganda programs and the way he yelled insults at her crew whenever they were doing a good job.

Next, she took steps toward the other podium. "And on my right, former University of Chicago professor and presidential candidate of the Property Rights Party, David Goldstein!"

Maria noticed a copper-red curl of Goldstein's hair shooting straight upward and she wished she'd had a chance to flatten it prior to the debate.

She began with an explanation for the audience.

"Television viewers are asked to switch on their interactive consoles so that the GFN can monitor audience reaction after the statements made by each candidate.

"I will ask a question to the incumbent and he will have just under two minutes to speak. At the end of his time, his podium will flash green if most of the home viewers are clapping, and it will make an applause sound. If most of the home viewers are booing, then it will flash red and make a booing sound.

"Then, the challenger will have just under two minutes to speak. His podium is programmed in the same way.

"There are three questions and two candidates, and therefore the total time of the debate will be only twelve minutes. 'Pirate Heroes' will resume immediately following the debate, so please pay attention and don't go anywhere."

Maria thought to herself that the people at the Central Planning Bureau were in for a surprise since she was not going to use the questions they prepared for her. It was her way of fighting the system.

She commenced the debate. "And now for the first question. The Great Deal Party, holding the presidency and majorities in both houses of Congress for the past two years, has launched a new television program on the GFN to educate America about how the people of Property Rights Nevada are poor and the people of Great Deal California are rich. The television program shows a horrible home in Nevada and a wonderful home in California. Did the people of Nevada become poor because of the capitalist economy in that state? Did the people of California become rich because of the socialist economy in that state?"

Rojo responded with a voice of comfort and reassurance. "Thank you, Maria. Greetings to the majority of the American people.

"Obviously, the people of Nevada are poor because of capitalism. And, the people of California are rich because of
208

socialism.

"Capitalism is based on greed, and greed is evil. Socialism is based on altruism, and altruism is good. I cannot explain why greed is evil and altruism is good. But it must be that way because that's what everyone says, except evil people.

"The results of the change from greed to altruism speak for themselves. The people in the Great Deal States are much better off. This is not only because we have waived rent and debt payments and lowered prices on all goods by edict.

"You can look at the income statistics. The average salary in America when I took office was $50,000 per year. Now, the minimum salary by law is $100,000. Therefore, GDP has doubled.

"I promise that if I win the election, I'll double the minimum salary again. The minimum salary by law will be $200,000. Therefore, GDP will double again.

"This result is incredible considering no other country has such a high GDP. In fact, some countries do not have any minimum salary law. There's no need to go to those countries and observe the result. The result is predictable. Greedy competitive employers looking for profit will pay their employees nothing. GDP must be zero.

"When you vote tomorrow, please remember the poor family in Property Rights Nevada and the rich family in Great Deal California."

Rojo flashed his best movie-star smile to the cameras, raised his fist, and screamed, "Justice! Rights! Equality! Liberty!"

The dull-gray podium suddenly sparkled with a bright green color. Speakers within the podium made a sound of enthusiastic applause. The majority of Americans loved their president.

Maria stood nodding her head until Rojo's podium quieted down. She noticed the Director standing behind the cameras shaking his head in disappointment.

"And now for the rebuttal, please?" asked Maria as she turned toward Goldstein.

Goldstein spoke with confidence into the microphone. "Thank you, Maria, and greetings to all of the American people.

"Two years ago, the American electorate had a choice between the capitalist platform of my Property Rights Party and the socialist platform of the Great Deal Party.

"The electorate chose socialism. And, the result has been devastation. America used to be one of the most productive, and therefore richest, countries in the world. Now, the people of the Great Deal States produce nothing and are just months away from mass starvation. I am sorry to have to say this result was predictable.

"The old capitalist economic system, where people obtained wealth by competitively providing goods and services to each other, caused prosperity.

"The new socialist economic system, where people obtain wealth by finding someone else with wealth and then confiscating it, causes poverty.

"This has nothing to do with good and evil. When people produce goods and services, then goods and services are produced. When people do not produce goods and services, then goods and services are not produced. This is an irrefutable fact.

"It doesn't matter whether the politicians command that prices must fall 10% or 50% or 100%. It doesn't matter whether the politicians command that incomes must rise 10% or 50% or 100%. What matters is this: what is the output of the economy? What is being produced? If nothing is being produced, then consumers will get nothing.

"All of you, the American electorate, must be able to see that socialism has failed just by walking in any neighborhood in the Great Deal States and observing the destruction. As for the GFN television programs, I really cannot understand ..."
210

Maria made a sudden movement like she was reaching into her jacket pocket. Goldstein saw, and reached into his own jacket pocket. He pulled out the paper that Maria had placed there and scanned it in a couple seconds.

He suddenly announced, "Aha! Just as I thought!"

He held up the paper and spoke forcefully. "The Great Deal television campaign has been a big fraud! In the programs comparing Great Deal New York to Property Rights Connecticut and Great Deal California to Property Rights Nevada, the footage was switched! The people in the Great Deal States are living in the horrible houses and the people in the Property Rights States are living in the wonderful houses. I have the addresses of all of the houses right here and my staff will investigate immediately!

"Please, voters, use your own eyes and use your own minds. You can see suffering all around you. You know you made a mistake voting for the Great Deal Party two years ago. You can turn things around tomorrow! America needs to return to capitalism, and the party ready and able to do that is the Property Rights Party."

He yelled into the microphone. "Honesty! Prudence! Austerity! Forethought!"

Goldstein jumped when a loud booing sound came from his podium, which suddenly turned red and started flashing.

Maria was shocked that the audience was still hostile to Goldstein even after the revelation about the switched footage. Apparently, his attempt to mirror Rojo with the use of buzzwords did not work. She already took her best shot with the first question set-up. Goldstein would have to fend for himself for the rest of the debate.

She faced Rojo and asked the second question. "Mr. President, one of the pledges you made when you got elected in 2012 was that your socialism was going to be completely different from Soviet communism. Yet, Americans who remember or who have read about the Soviet system could list many parallels between Great Deal America and the old USSR. Do you agree that Great Deal America is similar to the old USSR?"

Rojo shook his head in the negative, "It's absolutely not true that socialism and Soviet communism have anything to do with one another. I'm all for socialism and I'm completely against Soviet communism. In fact, I'm completely against all communism, not just Soviet communism.

"Under communism, all decisions are 'top down' or dictated from above. This is bad. Under socialism, all decisions are 'bottom up' or made democratically by all of society. This is good.

"But the worst thing of all about communism is the police state. Communist countries have police and military everywhere. Everyone must follow the commands of the elites, or else get sent to a prison camp.

"Of course the situation in the Great Deal States today is that everyone must follow the commands of the Central Planning Bureau and Fair Price Agency and the only people doing work are soldiers who receive double salaries and prisoners who are being threatened by the soldiers. However, this is only temporary until human nature changes and people become altruistic.

"When people begin to make decisions about work, investment, and consumption without considering self-interest, then socialism will begin to function without coercion. The Temporary Police State Act will be repealed and the Central Planning Bureau and Fair Price Agency, along with all of the state national guards, will be disbanded."

Rojo then smiled his most radiant smile and called out the buzzwords, "Justice! Rights! Equality! Liberty!"

Rojo's podium sounded cheers and flashed green.

Maria could easily resist her animal attraction to Rojo right now. True, he was extremely good looking. However, he was also dangerously stupid.

212

She invited the rebuttal, "Professor Goldstein? Your response?"

Goldstein was visibly angered as he grasped the sides of his podium. "Claiming there is a difference between communism and socialism is ridiculous. It is a fantasy of unrealistic utopians that communism is 'top down' and socialism is 'bottom up.' Clearly, communism and socialism are both 'top down.'

"Under both communism and socialism, reward incentives that motivate productive activity under the natural capitalist economy break down because property rights no longer exist.

"When reward incentives disappear, people stop working. If people stop working, nothing is produced and people starve as soon as inventories of food are used up.

"The government has two choices to avoid starvation. The government can reintroduce reward incentives, thus going back to capitalism. Or, the government can remain communist or socialist by introducing punishment incentives to compel people to work.

"The introduction of punishment incentives means the creation of a police state. And, a government system where the elites control the people through punishment incentives can only be described as 'top down.'

"My opponent believes the police state is only temporary until people cease to be self-interested and begin to do work altruistically, without taking incentive into account. This is impossible. It is the natural result of evolution that people take incentive into account.

"And, there is nothing wrong with people responding to incentive. If government protects private property, thus restoring a reward system, then people will naturally produce goods and services for each other.

"In summary, there is only one 'bottom up' way of running an economy. That is capitalism. Protection of private property. People use the money they earn to buy what they want. Companies produce what the people want because companies are trying to maximize profit. Employees are efficiently allocated between companies because more profitable companies bid to entice self-interested employees away from less profitable companies. No police state is necessary because people act the way they naturally act."

Goldstein paused and took some deep breaths. The red light in the podium started flashing. A booing noise came from the podium.

Maria was disappointed, but not surprised, to see that most people were booing him.

The cameras turned to Maria and she again flipped back her errant brunette lock and smiled.

"Now moving on to the third and final question," she said. "We're standing today in the home of America's first president, George Washington. Both of you profess to be great admirers of Washington and yet you have opposite opinions on all issues. Which one of you is truly striving to reach the goals that Washington set for our country?"

Rojo addressed the cameras. "When the Founding Fathers of America, including George Washington, fought the Revolutionary War, they were fighting for one thing— equality! It was a noble dream and a dream that was worth the lives of hundreds of thousands of American soldiers in that war and later wars. However, the dream was never realized until now.

"Washington never approved of Adam Smith-style capitalism. Smith's idea that everyone should only care about himself and steal everything he can and hurt everyone else in the process was the opposite of what Washington wanted.

"Washington was never interested in Smith's cruel ideas!

"My Great Deal Party is following Washington's example. We are fighting for equality!"

Rojo's podium began flashing green and sounding

applause. When the noise and flashing subsided, Maria turned to Goldstein and asked, "Rebuttal?"

Goldstein focused his gaze on the cameras. "When George Washington and the other Founding Fathers fought for equality, they were not talking about equality in the sense that people can steal anything they want until everyone is equally poor but rather equality in the sense that no one was permitted to steal anything.

"The party that is fighting for equality the way Washington defined equality is my Property Rights Party. We believe in absolute equality.

"And, to say Washington was not interested in Adam Smith's ideas is ridiculous. Washington ran Mount Vernon to earn profit! He was very interested in Adam Smith's *The Wealth of Nations*. Historians know that Washington studied that book right here in this house!"

Maria turned and saw that Rojo started talking into his microphone. No sound came out because it was not his turn to speak and therefore his microphone was switched off. He stomped over to Goldstein's podium, shoving Maria out of the way.

Rojo pushed his way in front of Goldstein's microphone and yelled. "I will not have George Washington slandered in his own home!"

Rojo pointed at Goldstein and continued ranting. "I don't have to read Adam Smith to know what he said. I know he was the inventor of capitalism. He said rich people should steal money from poor people. He said that because he was a cruel monster—just like you!"

Goldstein sprang into action, restraining Rojo with a judo hold. Goldstein recovered control of his microphone and announced, "I can explain Smith to you in one sentence, Roberto, so you don't have to overwork your brain by reading his book: the reason a baker provides bread to society is not because of altruism but because of self-interest. Smith

215

did not try to re-invent human nature but rather he described what he observed. As long as people were not allowed to steal the baker's bread, the baker continued to bake bread and sell it for the purpose of gaining wealth for himself."

Rojo went into a rage and shook off Goldstein. Rojo recovered the microphone and began yelling as his face twisted with anger. "You leave my father out of this, you parasitic, profit-mongering scrooge!"

Maria was baffled. What was Rojo talking about?

"My father was a baker," continued Rojo, "and you insult him by saying he baked bread out of self-interest! I'm certain the reason he baked bread was altruism! And he would have given that bread to his customers for free if it weren't for the misers at First Illinois Bank refusing to fund his losses. And that was your fault since you were advising those bastards!"

Rojo looked upward and raised his fists. "This is for you, Dad!"

He started swinging his fists and jumped onto Goldstein, who was able to defend himself with a judo move.

Maria saw that the time for the rebuttal was over, because both podiums lit up. Rojo's podium was flashing green and applauding. Goldstein's podium was flashing red and booing. Both men were pushing each other behind Goldstein's podium.

She turned toward the GFN crew and signaled with a chopping motion across her neck to end the television broadcast. She observed as the crew shut off the cameras.

As the candidates grappled, they fell on top of Maria, who found herself smashed between the man who attracted her physically and the man who attracted her intellectually.

Rojo yelled, "I'm a patriot! I'm following in the footsteps of George Washington! You're evil!"

Goldstein yelled back, "I'm a patriot! I'm following in the footsteps of George Washington! You're a moron!"

Maria peeked her head out from the wrestling match and

saw the Director adjusting a strange nozzle on a black box near the camera equipment. She figured that he was helping to disassemble the camera equipment since the debate broadcast was finished.

Rojo jumped up from the floor and charged the Director. "I said it a thousand times already! Nobody is allowed to work more than thirty hours per week!"

Maria was sick and tired of hearing this nonsense from Rojo. She saw a power cord taped onto the stage. She yanked it upward just as Rojo began his sprint, catching his foot and sending him flying. The Director finished unscrewing the nozzle.

But what was that nozzle? It certainly wasn't part of the usual equipment set-up.

Maria heard a hissing noise coming from the nozzle and she felt light-headed. She drifted into unconsciousness.

Tuesday, November 4, 2014: Election Day
(24) Before dawn on the Red Sea

Valentina was having the worst nightmare of her life. She was suspended above a blood-red pool. She was swinging from a cable attached to a crane. Her arms and legs were tied up with cords. Vladislav, Vyachislav, President Ivan Ivanov of Russia, and Vice President Clarence Clark of the United States were lined up in front of her on the pool edge.

The brothers were dressed in black jumpsuits and their trademark pirate boots. Ivanov was dressed in a well-tailored white uniform with golden fringes on the jacket that made him look like an admiral. Clark wore a similar, but larger, white uniform without golden fringes.

Valentina shook her head and regained her senses and realized this was not a nightmare. It was real. She could see it was night and she could feel that she was on a ship. She had no idea where she was, except she could feel the air was hot here even in the night. She was still dressed in her flight suit, and it was keeping her body at a comfortable temperature, but her helmet was gone.

Ivanov spoke to her in English. "Did you enjoy your rest? You slept through the entire day and now it is night again. Do you like my yacht? I call her the *Universal Suffrage*. She has many special features that I conceptualized myself, such as the plank spanning the pool. I never made a *pro forma* for these features, however I am confident the cost has been justified today! And, the hammerhead sharks didn't cost anything at all. They live here in the Red Sea and we have hatches below where we lure them in with bait."

Valentina tilted her head downward and studied the blood-red pool, horrified by what she saw. Chunks of human flesh floated everywhere, mixed up by dozens of hammerhead sharks in a feeding frenzy. She wondered what made her fear these sharks most. Was it the huge size of their teeth or the tiny size of their brains?

She then noticed that she was tied together with someone—and the other person was moving. She twisted her head to confirm it was Jack. He was also missing his helmet. She wasn't sure if she should be happy to be with him or sad that he had also been captured. Jack seemed groggy.

Looking upward, she saw huge stadium lights illuminating a dazzling metallic walkway that spanned the pool from the deck where the villains stood to the bow structure.

Valentina looked forward again and studied Vyachislav and Vladislav as they stood a couple meters away from her on the edge of the pool. The faces of the assassins looked gruesome: welts from the sea urchins, scorched flesh from the helicopter explosion, and black frostbite from the avalanche. They both stood uncomfortably with legs spread wide, apparently still hurting from the lionfish spines lodged in their groins.

Despite the plethora of hideous injuries, they appeared to be in a joyous mood. They smiled to reveal they had lost their front teeth.

Vyachislav called out, speaking in English with a lisp. "Hey guess what! The save-the-world do-gooders are awake. Ha, ha, ha! The reason why I am doing so well and you are doing so badly is because I only care about myself and you two are do-gooders trying to save the world!"

Valentina turned her head to give a confused look to Jack, who was also observing the action because his eyes were open and the cable was turning in the wind. The brothers were beaten, bruised, and burnt from head to toe, but Valentina and Jack did not have any injuries at all.

Vladislav also spoke with a lisp. He contradicted his brother. "Do-gooders? What are you talking about, Vyachislav? I'm certain these two had some corrupt plan to extort cash. I know that because I'm always trying to think of a corrupt plan to extort cash."

Valentina spat out her reply, "Why can't you morons get it through your thick skulls? I am Russian and I want Russia to be a nice place. Jack is American and he wants America to be a nice place. This means we must fight to defend ourselves against Ivanov and Clark. We are not altruistic do-gooders. We are not corrupt. We are just defending ourselves."

"Didn't you guys ever hear about the Golden Rule?" said Jack, who still sounded a bit groggy but was improving fast. "It isn't about being an altruistic do-gooder. And, it isn't about corruption. It's about enlightened self-interest."

The brothers scratched their toasted bald heads in confusion.

Ivanov stepped forward between the brothers. "Listen Jack, you don't understand anything about the world. I have heard about the Golden Rule you have in America 'do unto others as you would have them do unto you.' It doesn't make any sense. The reality of Russian society is that if you do something nice to a person, then that person will see you are weak and he will do something cruel to you. What's the point? It is much better to be cruel to people so they will be nice to you."

The brothers spoke simultaneously, "Yeah!"

Valentina felt the need to add something. "Hey there everybody! I am Russian. But I don't believe in being nice to cruel people and cruel to nice people. That is just plain stupid."

Ivanov grabbed a slender metal lever that rose a meter from the deck. "Soon I will pull this lever which releases the cable from the crane. You will fall into the pool. The sharks will rip you apart. I will be rich and alive. You will be poor and dead. Can you please explain to me again who is stupid?"

Clark spoke for the first time. He squeaked, "Whether you should be cruel or nice depends on which group you want to impress: the irrational socialist majority or the rational capitalist minority. One group is large but self-destructive. The other group is small but strong. An argument could be made for either strategy." A shark knocked a human arm onto the deck. Clark burst into laughter and kicked it back into the pool. "I had a great time this evening helping Ivan give bonuses to his socialist staff!"

"We killed my core staff members," Ivanov explained to Jack and Valentina. "Two hundred people, including lawyers, accountants, bankers, judges, prosecutors, and police. We also killed the yacht crew.

"Obviously, it was necessary to kill all of these people because they knew too much about my democratic and capitalist activities, including fraud, bribery, and assassination. I knew that I could not trust any of them because they were all dishonest people or else they could not have carried out the dishonest assignments that I gave to them throughout the year.

"Over a three-hour period, the victims were invited one by one onto the deck. They were each told that they could walk the plank to Sophistication Hall where piles of bonus treasure awaited. Each person saw the murdered humans floating in the pool. And each person anyway decided to trust me and walk the plank. This was not surprising, since all these staff members were, as you said, self-interested."

Clark laughed louder and interrupted. "Self-interested? Only an imbecile could say it is self-interested to trust a person who you know to be a liar and get led onto a trap door over dozens of snapping sharks. Your employees were irrational socialists! And now, they have been eliminated from the human gene pool!"

Valentina thought to herself that Clark had made a good

point. She wondered what he was doing working with Ivanov.

Ivanov looked disturbed as he turned toward Clark. "Clark, what you just said doesn't make any sense. I thought we were partners in this." After a pause, Ivanov turned back toward the rest of the group. "But anyway, I want music and drinks. Vyachislav, turn on the music system and fetch another bottle of the cognac from below since we don't have any waiters anymore."

Clark clarified the order. "Please make it something from the *Borderies cru*. I prefer if it is aged at least ten years but not more than twelve years. And hopefully you can find one made with pure *Folle Blanche* grapes instead of the hybrid."

Ivanov sneered and raised his voice. "I am loosing my patience! Get the best cognac—the one with the highest price tag. And bring me a cola chaser since cognac tastes terrible!"

Vyachislav obediently ran off, pausing to flip on the music switch. "Here's your favorite song, boss, all about capitalism!"

From speakers around the pool, a familiar catchy drum beat could be heard. And Vyachislav was gone.

Bang bang bangabanga bang bang clang!

"Vladislav, why don't you go ahead and get your bonus right now?" said Ivanov, loudly. "You can walk the plank and when you reach Sophistication Hall at the top, you will find a stack of treasure and a dozen beautiful women waiting for you."

"Shouldn't I wait for my brother to come back?"

"Why wait? You can run up there right now and start celebrating. Your brother will join you later. Don't be a fool!"

"I'll go and get what I deserve. I've been working hard for you all year lying to people and killing people. Tonight was the best, killing the whole staff. It was super smart putting the automatic trap door in the plank to drop all your employees into the tank full of sharks just after you promised their bonuses. Ha, ha, ha! Fools!"

Valentina looked at Jack in horror and Jack looked back at her with the same expression.

Ivanov pulled the remote control from the pocket of his admiral uniform and continued speaking loudly as the drum beat pulsed from the speakers. "Yeah, it was a good idea having this remote control with a big red button in the middle for the trap door."

Vladislav couldn't contain his joy and excitement. "And a profitable idea for my brother and me. We will take all the bonus treasure! We're so smart!"

The chorus of the song began and Vladislav sang along, "Take What's Yours!" as he ran up the plank.

Valentina watched as Ivanov calmly pushed the central button on the remote control.

Ivanov had to raise his voice to be heard over the screams as Vladislav was ripped limb from limb by the hammerheads. "It is just terrible the things I am compelled to do because of democracy and capitalism. I really liked Vladislav."

Clark laughed so hard that he was almost doubled over as he held onto his belly.

Valentina remembered that the secret video cameras and microphones in her flight suit and Jack's flight suit were capturing everything.

She spoke carefully and clearly to the American vice president. "Look, Mr. Clark. We know about your plot. We know you will bring a vial of poison back to America and put it into President Rojo's apple juice on Wednesday so that you will be president. But we have no idea what your objective is. Rojo is already your puppet and therefore you already control the Great Deal States."

Clark didn't answer to Valentina. Instead, he spoke to Ivanov. "Look, Ivan. We are partners. We don't agree about anything. We have totally opposite outlooks. But anyway, we are partners. You want to use me to get cash. I want to use you to get what I need.

"And, even though you killed two hundred associates today, I know you will not kill me. You need me to access the bank accounts with the skim from the Russia-USA oil trade.

"So tell me Ivan, do you have the vial of poison for me?"

Ivanov patted the jacket pocket of his white uniform. "It's right here."

Clark nodded and continued. "Therefore, I am going to let you in on the ultimate scheme. Jack and Valentina can listen, too. They might like the scheme.

"When the Great Deal Party wins 38 states in the election and immediately repeals the Bill of Rights, the schism between the Great Deal States and Property Rights States will cease. An Alaska Air National Guard jet will fly to Washington, D.C. with the Supreme Court and the Governor of Alaska. The Chief Justice of the Supreme Court will swear in Rojo as president and me as vice president. Rojo will drink his poisoned apple juice and die. Then, I will be immediately sworn in as president.

"The moment I am president, I will demand that the Governor of Alaska give me the electronic controller for the North American Missile Shield. I will turn off that shield.

"All of this is already arranged and will happen on Wednesday morning.

"On Wednesday morning, Ivan, you must nuke North Korea into oblivion. And on Wednesday afternoon, you must launch nuclear missiles at the American cities where the Great Deal Party is promoting majority victory parties, killing all of the American socialists. The irrational people of America who have been tormenting me for so long will be dead.

"In exchange, I will give you the codes for our offshore bank accounts. You can have all of the money—the former reserves of the Federal Reserve System. I don't want any money myself.

"I will have a couple hours to get out of D.C. I will travel to my cottage deep in the forest in Tennessee and retire anonymously. I will spend the remainder of my life sipping drinks and programming my computer.

"I will be satisfied that by eliminating American socialists, I will be the greatest of all of the American presidents even though I will only serve in that position for a couple hours. The ends will be achieved.

"You, Ivan, will be even richer than you already are. And, you can justify your action by saying you had no choice and it was fate or capitalism or democracy or all three."

Clark let loose with a screeching laugh which sounded like it was coming from the devil himself.

Valentina was very interested to hear Clark's ultimate scheme. It wasn't what she expected. She had thought he was a typical thief with a short-term horizon who wanted to steal lots of money and didn't care that he would suffer for that later.

Ivanov scratched his chin. "But, I like socialists! Maybe I will not shoot all the nukes at the Great Deal States. Maybe I will just kill you right now and make a deal with Rojo to shut off the missile shield on Wednesday and I will nuke the remaining Property Rights States. My advisers tell me there is an inverse relationship between how smart a person is and how much he likes me. I will be obliged to use the nukes to kill smart people.

"And, I am not interested in nuking North Korea. The Dear Socialist Leader is a good friend of mine.

"Regarding the money in the offshore accounts, I already embezzled that. I don't need to get the codes from you."

Clark stopped laughing. He froze and his jaw dropped open.

Valentina kept her concentration on the scene on the pool deck while she could feel Jack becoming stronger behind her. The drug had worn off. He was struggling with the ropes that bound them together.

Just then, Vyachislav appeared, holding a silver tray with an ancient bottle of cognac, a glass already filled with cognac, and a can of cola. "Hey, I heard some screams. Did you guys kill another employee? I didn't know there were any left. That's hilarious. I wish you waited for me. Did my brother get a good view? He loves to watch when the sharks rip our colleagues apart."

Valentina saw a great opportunity to turn Vyachislav. "Your brother got a great view. Right up close. I can't believe you both knew Ivan got all his riches by lying to people and killing people, yet you decided to trust him. Vladislav is in a shark's belly right now."

Vyachislav laughed. "Vladislav is in a shark's belly? Never! President Ivanov would never betray Vladislav. President Ivanov is the best businessman in the world, a man of honor!"

Valentina shook her head sadly. "That is a strange thing to say about a man who has dedicated his political career to corruption. Just look at the ripped body parts floating in the pool to see how he treats his loyal employees."

Vyachislav laughed again. "You don't know anything, Valentina. That is why you're a do-gooder. The employees we killed were replaceable. Vladislav and I are the only important members of President Ivanov's team and he will always treat us well. In fact my brother and I were going to divide all the treasure between ourselves once the rest of the staff was dead. Where is Vladislav? I hope he comes over here soon to hear all of this."

Jack twisted his head toward the last remaining brother. "Forget about it, Vyachislav. Vladislav is dead. Ivanov killed him and will kill you, too. He never planned to give a penny of treasure to anyone except himself."

Ivanov stepped back from the lever and indicated to Vyachislav to take his place. Vyachislav put the cognac tray on the base of the plank and approached the lever, placing one hand on it.

Ivanov pointed to Jack and Valentina. "Vyachislav, I command you to kill these do-gooders to punish them for lying about your brother. I promise that you and your brother will be very rich soon, leaping in a pile of treasure with beautiful women ready to do as you command. You must pull the lever and drop the do-gooders into the pool."

Ivanov opened a white leather belt holster and drew an elongated red revolver, which he handed to Vyachislav. "Next, you will need this special weapon: the 'Hammer and Sickle.' After Jack and Valentina are dead, you must shoot Clark. Kill him with a single shot to the head. Make sure you aim carefully, by looking straight down the barrel."

Vyachislav visibly tensed, holding the metal lever with one hand and the long red revolver with the other hand.

Clark started to cry. A wet spot appeared on his trousers.

Valentina's hopes for a successful resolution were shattered, until she saw an interesting object float to the surface of the pool.

*

Vyachislav glared angrily at Jack and Valentina as he held the crane lever. "I know why you lied that Vladislav is dead. You are cowards and you want to make me feel bad. But the joke is on you! I will get a pile of treasure because I am brave! You will be shark food because you are cowards!"

Vyachislav noticed that Jack and Valentina were staring down at the water.

Vyachislav heard Valentina yell to him in Russian. "Vyachislav! Look! I found your brother!"

Vyachislav examined the pool.

A human leg bobbed up and down in the water. That was no surprise since two hundred men and women had already been devoured by the sharks during the course of the night.

But suddenly Vyachislav got a sick feeling in his stomach. He closed his eyes and opened them again to focus on the leg, and more specifically the boot on the end of the leg.

It couldn't be. But it was. A pirate hologram boot. Vladislav's boot. His brother's boot.

Vyachislav let go of the lever and held the Hammer and Sickle gun high in the air. He screamed in rage and spun around.

Vyachislav had always acted in accordance with the mainstream philosophy, mainstream in Russia anyway, that whenever you met a cruel person, you should submit to that person and follow his orders. And, whenever you met a deeply dishonest person, you should trust him.

Up until now, this philosophy had served him well. He'd enjoyed a nice salary and access to luxury living and easy women.

But now, his philosophy was shattered. His mind was blown. His world was rocked.

He'd been wrong! He chose the wrong side!

Vyachislav stopped screaming and planted his feet at shoulder-width on the deck.

Grasping the Hammer and Sickle with both hands, he pointed it at his enemy.

He looked down the barrel with both eyes and aimed carefully.

"I'll show you I'm not a fool!" he yelled.

The target yelled back, "Nooooo!!!!"

Vyachislav pulled the trigger.

BLAMMMM!!

*

As his ears stopped ringing from the double gunshot, Jack looked onto the deck to see Vyachislav and Ivanov's brains sprayed in opposing directions from where their bodies lay prone.

Jack and Valentina were still dangling from the crane over the shark pool.

Clark's change of mood was immediate. He had been crying just a moment before but now was bursting out with guffaws of laughter. "I was right after all! I have set up the irrational socialists to destroy each other!"

Clark hopped over to the music power switch and turned off the speakers. With the drum rhythm gone, the only sounds were the wind and the chomping sharks.

Jack winked at Valentina and then yelled out an exclamation. "Good riddance socialists! Ha, ha, ha. These New Russians were not different from the Soviets. They all deserved to die! You finished our assignment for us."

Clark froze for a moment, deep in thought. Then, he pulled something out of his jacket pocket and waved it in the air. Jack saw a glint. It was his Democracy Society badge!

"I have figured it all out," said Clark. "You two are in some kind of secret organization. You are fighting against the socialists. I am also fighting against the socialists! I hate them! And, I have been very lonely working on this project myself with no like-minded friends and partners. We can join together, we can be a team, and we can be friends!"

"That's great, Clarence," said Jack. "I can't wait to finish off the rest of the socialists."

"Does your organization have access to manpower and weaponry?" asked Clark. "Can I plug this turkey badge in somewhere and communicate with headquarters?"

Jack responded in his most serious tone. "We can all call headquarters together, Clarence. We can cooperate to destroy the irrational people just as soon as you swing this crane back over the deck and release us."

Clark pinned the turkey badge onto his own jacket. Then he swung the crane around and released Jack and Valentina onto the deck, just centimeters from the edge of the pool and the snapping sharks.

Clark untied Jack and Valentina. While Clark was looking the other way, Jack picked up the remote control from where it was lying near Ivanov's corpse. He also quickly slipped a hand into Ivanov's jacket pocket.

Valentina shook out her sore arms and legs as the men continued to talk.

Jack asked a question. "I am curious, Clarence. With Ivan dead, how can you complete your ultimate scheme?"

Clark seemed like he was trying to be reassuring as he spoke in his squeaky voice. "I already have a backup scheme in motion. I am so smart! I made a deal with the Dear Socialist Leader. He wanted an opportunity to launch his five nuclear missiles at the West Coast. He says that he is in range of Anchorage, Vancouver, Seattle, Portland, and San Francisco. I told him there will be a counterrevolutionary strike on Wednesday. I told him Rojo will be assassinated by the counterrevolutionaries and they will make it look like a heart attack.

"And I know this because I am the one who will kill Rojo! I will be happy to see Rojo screaming in pain when he drinks the poisoned apple juice and has a heart attack! I told the Dear Socialist Leader that the counterrevolutionaries were based in the same five West Coast cities and he could blow them up as soon as I became president and turned off the North American Missile Shield."

Jack put his hands on his hips. "But wait a minute. How can you kill socialists by nuking Anchorage and Vancouver? That is where most of the capitalists who evacuated from Portland and Seattle are now living."

"Yeah," agreed Clark. "My ultimate scheme was to have Russia blow up the 38 socialist states plus North Korea. Having North Korea blow up five West Coast cities was only an imperfect backup scheme in case something went wrong with the ultimate scheme. Anyway, the backup scheme is in

230

motion and it cannot be stopped. As long as I am alive on Wednesday and I poison Rojo and turn off the North American Missile Shield, the Dear Socialist Leader will fire the missiles!"

Jack pondered the situation. "And you aren't too concerned about all of the capitalists who will get killed and the extensive damage to the environment?"

"The ends justify the means!" laughed Clark.

"Aren't there other ways to deal with the socialists?" asked Jack. "For example, banning them from voting? Or, having constitutional limitations to prevent them from using their votes to rob people?"

"I don't care!" answered Clark. "So what if the Bill of Rights is repealed? Its protections were getting eroded over the years. There is only one solution for the socialists. Killing them! Anyway, they make me angry with the stupid things they do."

"Okay, Clarence. You are correct. Let's do what we have to do," said Jack. "Let's walk up to Sophistication Hall. You go first."

Clark nodded in agreement. He turned his back to Jack and Valentina and began walking up the plank. Jack and Valentina were at the base of the plank when Clark reached the spot where the trap door was.

In an instant, Clark stepped on the trap door, Jack pushed the red button on the remote control, Clark leaped back to face Jack, and the trap door fell open. Clark had escaped death by a fraction of a second.

Clark laughed. "You can't trick me! I am too smart. I guessed you might do that. I can see you are too soft to do what must be done to eliminate the socialist threat."

Clark then pulled the Hammer and Sickle revolver out from where it had been hidden in his belt. "When you were sneaking the remote control into your pocket, look what I sneaked into my belt!" He waved the gun in the air, then checked the cylinder, which amazingly had been loaded with more than two bullets. He pointed the gun at Jack and Valentina while holding it to the side, careful that the back of the barrel was not pointed at himself.

"Get back, you two," he said.

Jack and Valentina backed away from the base of the plank as Clark descended.

Clark reached the base and was standing next to the tray of cognac. "I will celebrate my triumph!"

While keeping the Hammer and Sickle trained on Jack and Valentina, Clark used his other hand to grab the glass of cognac and raise it to his mouth. He took a big slurp.

It was only a matter of seconds before he screamed, dropped the glass and the gun, and clutched his chest.

He spun around a couple times at the base of the plank. He teetered on the edge of the shark pool.

Jack leaped forward and yanked the turkey badge off of Clark's jacket.

Clark then spun around once more, flailing his arms. He slipped off of the edge and splashed into the shark pool. He was immediately surrounded by huge hammerhead sharks with gaping jaws and teeth dripping with flesh and blood. The sharks enjoyed their final feast of the evening.

Jack showed the empty poison vial to Valentina, then tossed it aside. He felt a wave of relief at having completed his part of the Democracy Society mission. He hoped everything was progressing according to plan at Mount Vernon as well.

Jack gave Valentina a hug and a kiss. "We have earned a vacation. I know a great hotel nearby. It only has eight stars, but I think it will be more friendly than the nine-star place."

"Ready for action!" said Valentina enthusiastically. "Let's start our travels over again from the beginning, but minus the gangsters!"

Jack typed "Sea Hotel and Spa, Arabia" into the remote

control and showed it to Valentina. He was happy to see her smile and begin to relax.

They walked hand-in-hand up the plank, carefully going around the edge of the open trap door, and ascended the plank all the way to Sophistication Hall, where they saw there was no treasure after all.

(25) After dawn on the Red Sea

Valentina stood in Sophistication Hall in a new bikini with a colorful coral-fan pattern. She saw that Jack was looking handsome in matching swim trunks.

She commented, "The wardrobe in Ivanov's suite is the most outrageous that I have ever seen. The selection of clothing rivals the finest London department stores. Every item is from a top designer, with the price tag still attached."

"Yeah, but that wardrobe was cheap compared to the canvases on the walls," said Jack, pointing to both artworks. "I remember the press release when Ivanov bought Black-on-Black and White-on-White. They are the most expensive artworks in the world. If you can call them artworks."

The couple approached the bow window and sat on a white leather couch. Jack put his arm over Valentina's shoulders.

"The morning sun on the misty sea is a beautiful sight," said Valentina. "And, that must be *Jebel Soudah* in the distance. We are approaching the Sea Hotel and Spa."

The relaxed couple watched the waves and the mist for an hour as the Black Mountain came closer and closer into view. The *Universal Suffrage* had enormous engines and was moving very quickly.

Jack leaned forward. "Valentina, what is that straight ahead? I think we are approaching another large yacht. We had better change our course to avoid a collision."

Valentina held up the remote control and showed it to Jack. The screen prompted them for a password. They started to push buttons at random, but with no success.

Jack stood and flipped up the cushions on the
234

surrounding couches. He pulled out a pair of life vests, handing one to Valentina. "I think we should step outside and prepare to jump overboard."

*

"I hereby re-dedicate the *Royal Arabia* to a higher use. No longer shall she purposelessly consume resources to pollute the sea and the air, but instead she shall provide a comfortable and protected habitat for rare marine life thus enhancing the tourism experience at the Sea Hotel and Spa!"

King Abyad felt proud today as he made the dedication speech. Even prouder than he felt on the opening day of the Sea Hotel and Spa.

He stood at the stern of a 20-meter yacht, dwarfed by the 200-meter *Royal Arabia* yacht anchored nearby. He was accompanied by a pilot and ten guards and officials, all neatly attired in Arab garb or military uniforms.

With the dedication for the new reef complete, the pilot prepared to maneuver the smaller craft away from the soon-to-be-sunk superyacht.

The King held up the remote control for the explosives. He expected that the four small charges, strategically placed by divers, should open up the hull of the *Royal Arabia* and allow it to sink slowly and upright in the chosen spot, a sandy area with a depth of forty meters.

Since efforts had already been made to remove all potentially hazardous materials from the giant yacht, the King expected that a wide variety of marine life would begin to inhabit the wreck almost immediately.

He found it safe to assume that many common reef fish and plants would soon arrive. And, he was hoping the wreck would also become a popular playground for the hawksbill turtles that were multiplying in the area, thanks to a Sea Hotel and Spa project to provide a protected beach area for nesting.

The daydream was interrupted by one of the guards giving him a gentle and respectful tap on the shoulder. "Sir, please brace yourself. Another yacht is approaching from out of the mist. I think it is going to ram the *Royal Arabia*."

The King spun around to look through the mist at the fast approaching super mega yacht: a stinkpot of incredible size and gaudiness. It was twice as large as the *Royal Arabia*! Even King Abyad had never seen anything like it. Its massive engines were churning up wake like a tsunami.

The King recalled that there was only one yacht in the world that this could be—Ivan Ivanov's brand new *Universal Suffrage*. What was it doing here?

CCCCRRRRAAAASSSSSHHHHH!

The *Universal Suffrage* slammed bow first into the port side of the *Royal Arabia*.

The damage to both ships was substantial. The bow of the *Universal Suffrage* and the port side of the *Royal Arabia* were now nothing more than twisted hunks of scrap metal. The two immense yachts began to sink. The King and crewmen stood silently for several minutes gawking in disbelief.

The King heard a familiar voice from behind. "Your Majesty, we hope you don't mind that you will have two shipwrecks instead of one to entertain visiting divers!" He spun around to see his attendants pulling a man and woman from the sea. The man helped to remove the woman's life vest as he continued speaking to the King. "You might be interested to know the most expensive paintings in the world will now be viewed only by divers visiting your resort! And, I recommend getting a dive team down there right away to remove environmentally hazardous material before it leaches out."

The King approached Jack and Valentina, now recognizing them. "Captain Cannon! My heart-felt thanks to the Democracy Society for increasing the size of the reef. Ms. Zaiceva! When I praised you for your fine work in anti-corruption journalism, I had no idea how far you were willing to go with your work. I promise that you will be the recipient of the Kingdom's highest journalism award this year for the boundaries you have broken through.

"Please be my guests again at the Sea Hotel and Spa!"

The King addressed his staff. "Attendants, please radio ahead to prepare a guest suite for our heroes!"

(26) Evening at Mount Vernon

David Goldstein woke up in the dark with a splitting headache and a strong sensation of dizziness. Where was he? What was going on? How long had he been asleep? He was strapped onto a hard metal bed. It seemed that he had a memory blackout.

He wiggled his hands and feet. For some reason, he felt strange. But he couldn't understand why.

He heard a voice that he recognized as belonging to the Director of the Democracy Society. "The election results have been tabulated. In 2012, the Great Deal Party won in 37 states with 80% of the vote in those states. Now in 2014, the Great Deal Party won in 38 states with 95% of the vote in those states."

Goldstein was flabbergasted. Could it be true? Could the voters really be so dumb? This result was incredible. Rojo destroyed the American economy between 2012 and 2014. The American people lived in a state of violence, oppression, and privation because of Rojo's policies. Food supplies would be exhausted and mass starvation would begin in a couple months.

And yet Rojo became MORE popular with the voters!

Goldstein had been a strong believer in universal-suffrage democracy throughout his whole life. But at this moment, faced with this evidence, it was impossible for him to justify his belief any longer.

He exclaimed, "Universal suffrage is wrong! The voters are robbing and killing themselves! The people cannot be allowed a choice if their choice is self-torture!"

Goldstein felt the belts releasing and understood he was

not restrained anymore. He sat up. The room changed from dark to light.

He saw that he was sitting on one of two metallic beds in a large room. A cart loaded with electronic instruments was idled between the two beds. The other bed was empty.

The room had rows of unoccupied desks with keyboards and all were facing a large video screen on one wall. The image on the video screen was a human brain. Otherwise, the walls were decorated with a repeating pattern of a striking wild turkey.

Along one wall a mirror was visible. An elevator stood open near the mirror. The Director stood by a control panel near the elevator.

Goldstein swung his legs over the side of the bed. Hmmm. His legs felt very long today for some reason.

He stood up and approached the mirror. He was completely baffled. He raised his arms to feel his face and his hair. What was going on?

The Director spoke. "No need to be alarmed, Mr. President. Everything is under control following the terrorist gas attack at the end of the presidential election debate."

Goldstein still did not understand what was going on. "Why is everything crazy? Why are you addressing me as Mr. President? Why do I see Roberto Rojo looking back at me in the mirror?"

"Sir, I understand you are experiencing a shocking change of circumstances after having been unconscious for approximately 24 hours," replied the Director. "But, please give me a chance to convince you that what has transpired will be a positive thing for you and for the republic. Maria Diaz is waiting for us upstairs." The Director spun around and stepped into the elevator.

Goldstein calmed down. Things were certainly weird today, but he felt better after learning that Maria was nearby. He followed the Director into the elevator.

When the elevator doors opened at the top level, Goldstein saw he was back in the Mount Vernon mansion house. The hidden elevator had opened up behind one of the Prussian-blue walls in the parlor.

There was one person already in the room. It was Maria. She sat alone on an antique chair with tears in her eyes.

Goldstein was relieved to see her. Forgetting his new appearance, he rushed toward her to give her a hug.

Maria stood from the chair and smacked Goldstein across the face. "Roberto, you are disgusting! You are a liar! I don't care how handsome you look and I don't care how many people vote for you. I believe now and I will always believe David Goldstein is a better man!"

Goldstein stood still as the Director approached. The Director put his hand on Maria's shoulder and spoke in a reassuring tone. "Ms. Diaz, please know that everything is not as it appears. A lawful effort has been undertaken to secure the future of the republic. This effort included a high-technology procedure in which the entire contents of the brains of Roberto Rojo and David Goldstein were uploaded into a supercomputer and then switched. The person before you is David Goldstein occupying Roberto Rojo's body.

"If you are angry at Roberto Rojo, then you must find a man who looks like David Goldstein and smack him across the face.

"This brain switch is top secret. Nobody will ever know what happened except the three of us and a small team here at Mount Vernon."

The Director then removed his hand from Maria and spoke to Goldstein. "Mr. President, I strongly urge that after you spend some time with Ms. Diaz, we get back together to discuss an address planned for tomorrow morning at the Capitol where all of the newly elected Great Deal congressmen will be gathered for their initial guidance following this huge election landslide.

240

"You have been given an opportunity to save American democracy and I trust you will take advantage." With that, the Director turned and exited the room.

Goldstein and Maria, now alone together, embraced.

EPILOGUE

Wednesday, November 19, 2014
(27) Afternoon at Mount Vernon

Captain Jack Cannon sat with the Director of the Democracy Society on the back porch of the Mount Vernon mansion house. Jack was wearing a thick and warm hand-woven sweater from Russia and the Director was wearing a long black cashmere coat.

Jack, feeling much relieved, spoke to the Director. "It's great to hear that you were able to convince the Connecticut Air National Guard to expunge the record of my unauthorized flights in the *Flying Yankee*."

"I've done even better than that," explained the Director. "I've negotiated the purchase of the aircraft. And, I convinced King Abyad to make a financial contribution to the Democracy Society so that we can pay the asking price."

"The King has been enthusiastically supportive since our mission resulted in great benefits for him and his country," replied Jack. "I was overjoyed that he gave Valentina and myself week-long vacations to enjoy the scuba diving at the Sea Hotel and Spa and the snowboarding at the Peak Hotel and Casino. Plus, he paid for the fuel for flying the *Flying Yankee* from Russia to Virginia."

Jack looked over the Director's shoulder to see Valentina and her father Doctor Zaicev sitting together at the other end of the porch. Valentina wore a sweater that matched Jack's since both were from the Peak Hotel gift shop. Doctor Zaicev wore a long black coat that Jack suspected was borrowed from the Director. The doctor's white research pants showed below the coat.

The four heroes had the whole hilltop porch to themselves. The leaves had fallen from the trees and therefore the group had an amazing view of the political rally taking place on the Potomac River far below.

Jack lifted his binoculars and focused on the enormous floating barge that held a speaking podium with huge video screens on either side, and bleachers that were filled with a thousand spectators.

President Roberto Rojo himself was visible behind the podium running his hand through his rippling hair. Jack thought he could see, from a kilometer away, the President's dimples and shiny teeth.

Rojo had his arm around his bride-to-be, former GFN commentator Maria Diaz. Young son Augusto stood next to the happy couple with a big smile on his face.

Jack could hear some speaking and applause, but he could not make out the words. He assumed the speech was the same as the others Rojo had made across the country since his historical election victory two weeks ago.

The series of speeches shocked Rojo's hard-core supporters, since he renounced and apologized for all of his policies from his first term. He was explaining to every audience that people do not have a human right to receive things for free but rather people have to do productive work if they want material well-being. With brilliant speech writing and sincere speech delivery, things were going as smoothly as could possibly be expected. Mass starvation and reversion to tyranny were averted because the government had resumed protecting property rights.

"A great success, Captain Cannon," said the Director. "Already in two weeks the Democracy Amendment was repealed, the Great Deal Act was repealed, the Temporary Police State Act was repealed, all dollars with Rojo's portrait were canceled, the clear-cutting of Yosemite was halted, and the entire staffs of the Central Planning Bureau and Fair Price Agency in Tysons Corner were rounded up at gunpoint and loaded onto freight trains bound for Florida where they will be responsible for restoring the Everglades to its natural state.

"Workers are starting to voluntarily re-appear at their old places of employment, which have all been restituted to the original owners. Gradually, the economy will return to its previous level of productivity.

"Of course, repeal of the Bill of Rights is no longer being considered.

"And this was all possible because of the video and audio recordings you and Valentina made from your flight suits, in particular Clark's comments in the Elbrus hot tub and aboard the Red Sea yacht. When I played the recordings for all of the Great Deal congressmen on the morning after the election, they changed their political views instantly in exchange for my promise not to make the recordings public."

Jack felt proud. "Yes, it seems the country is pulling back from the brink. Thanks in no small part also to your efforts here at Mount Vernon. But I am still stumped by one thing. What is your link to all of this? How did you get to be the Director?"

The Director rose from his chair. "Please come with me into the study." The Director walked into the mansion house through the side door.

Jack followed the Director into the study and admired the collection of antique books lining handsome wooden shelving.

The Director sat at the wooden desk and opened a concealed drawer. He withdrew a yellowing hand-written letter encased in a protective plastic cover.

"You will permit me to put on my spectacles," said the Director, "for I have grown almost blind in the service of my country."

244

JOHN CHRISTMAS

The Director put on the pair of spectacles that sat on George Washington's desk. They fit him just perfectly. Then, he reviewed the letter and handed it to Jack.

Jack read in silence. The letter was written by George Washington and addressed to James Madison. It was dated January 27, 1789. It listed the original thirteen members of the Democracy Society, including Jack's ancestor Colonel John Cannon.

And then came the most interesting part of the letter: a personal secret about George Washington and a slave named Linda. They had been expecting a child! Washington was not without descendants, as had always been assumed by historians. There was a secret line of descent. The directorship of the Democracy Society, and therefore also the management of the Mount Vernon estate, had stayed in Washington's family for all of these years.

Jack nodded and handed the letter back. He chose his words carefully, "General Washington planned the Democracy Society well. Please know the secret will remain safe with me."

The Director put the letter back into the secret drawer and put the spectacles on top of the desk. "There are only fourteen people in the world who know the core truth about the Democracy Society. Thirteen are descendants of the original members." The Director pointed at himself. "And one is the descendant of the original director, a man not publically known to have had any descendants."

Jack saluted and said with sincerity, "Your great great great great great great great grandparents George and Linda would be proud of you, sir."

The Director led Jack back outside onto the porch where they joined Valentina and Doctor Zaicev. Jack held Valentina's hand.

"Captain Cannon and Ms. Zaiceva, words cannot express how pleased I am with your performances on this critical

245

mission," announced the Director. "You were last-minute additions to our team and we were not certain of your capabilities. But now we see that you have incredible talent. We had twelve more members plus assorted employees working on different projects to preserve the American republic, but you are the ones who came through for us and defeated the enemies. You will be valuable assets for the Democracy Society for many years to come."

Jack and Valentina paused and looked at each other, still holding hands.

"We were happy to help," said Jack. "But we aren't thinking about the Democracy Society as our focus in the future. I told Valentina that I want to teach her how to run a maple syrup business profitably. She accepted my offer."

Valentina nodded. "Yes, the forests of Connecticut are calling me. Of course I am interested to learn something about syrup production having heard so much about this art from Jack.

"However, I also have a journalism project that will require some peace and quiet and concentration. I want to write a book about the reality of democracy in Russia. Specifically, I want to write a book about the incredible new development in the upcoming special election.

"It is absolutely fascinating to see the political reversal that has occurred in Russia in the two weeks since President Ivanov died in the accidental yacht crash. The world must be educated about this most-recent failure of universal-suffrage democracy."

Valentina continued speaking while using her fingers to signify that certain words were in quotes. "We will see who gets elected to be the new President of Russia. I wonder what 'David Goldstein' can do there. Who could have guessed he would react to his election defeat in the United States by flying to Moscow, applying for Russian citizenship, and registering himself as a candidate in the Russian presidential election? His rhetoric about being 'reborn' as a socialist has made him wildly popular with millions of Russians. And, he only needs four words in Russian language to deliver his speechs. He just stands up there and yells 'justice, rights, equality, liberty.' Polls indicate that he can win the election next month."

The whole group laughed.

The Director spoke to Valentina while resting a hand on the doctor's shoulder. "The Democracy Society has extended its contract with your father. He will be staying in America also."

"I will continue my research of the human brain here at Mount Vernon," said Doctor Zaicev. "Specifically, I will study the socialist thought process using data gathered from Roberto Rojo in an attempt to determine why socialist brains are unable to think rationally. My work could potentially benefit America and Russia and all of the world."

"With hard work we can make our world better," concluded the Director. "We can change society so that people respect each other and transact in peaceful and productive voluntary exchanges instead of violent and destructive involuntary exchanges. If we can do that, then our democratic republic and other democratic republics around the world will be safe forever."

The Director and Doctor Zaicev headed indoors to the study.

As Jack and Valentina stood on the porch looking into each other's eyes, music could be heard coming from the barge on the river. It was 'The Founding Fathers' band playing their new song.

First, there was a catchy drum beat.

Then came the chorus.

Bang bang bangabanga bang bang clang! "Gold-en-Rule!"

About the Author

John Christmas was born and raised in the United States and earned degrees from Dartmouth College and Cornell University. He left several democratic countries because of bad quality government. Most notably, he was ejected from Latvia for blowing the whistle on a bank fraud. The democratic government proceeded to enlarge the fraud by hosting promotions in embassies and eventually destroyed the national economy, requiring an IMF bailout.

Thanks for Reading *Democracy Society* Drafts
Adrian, Alex, Andrea, Artis, Dad, Dorian, Keidi, Kiki, Mom

Made in the USA
Charleston, SC
07 June 2012